A Tale of The Boatmans Rest

By

S M Wade

Preface

My story begins in Victorian Birmingham during a time of great change for working boat people. It follows a group of good friends who find themselves in the middle of a mystery that needs to be solved. Forbidden romance and stubborn resistance are amongst their challenges to unravel the spooky events that give rise to a hidden secret along the Birmingham canal.

As writers, the memories we make and the people we meet are often the beginning of re-creating, re-imagining, and exploration of a wonderful world of creative tales. It is this that has stirred me to author this story. This is my first book, a work of fiction inspired by the many characters that I have met during my lifetime.

I was truly fortunate as a child having wonderful grandparents that are most often only read about in children's books. I was enchanted by their story telling with fairy tale imaginings that had me sitting still and quiet for what felt like an age!

My school holidays and summers were spent aboard our family narrow boats based in Gas Street Basin, Birmingham. The smell of the coal burning fires and the rumble of the boat engines filled me with joy before we had even entered the Basin. It was there that my Aunt and Uncle taught me about the traditional costume, crafts and working life of Victorian boat people. My Aunt often sat quietly on her boat teaching me how to paint water jugs, door panels and many other miscellaneous items in the customary manner. She made her own candles, crocheted, knitted and her artwork was beautiful.

I share the same passion for history that my parents had and in particular, my Father. The social aspect of how people lived their lives fascinates me and my father fed my interest by taking us to many historic places during my childhood.

These are the people that have inspired me, they have given me those special memories that I have been able to re-imagine and give another life to. I am forever grateful to have had them in my life.

I must say a thank you to all my family and friends that took time out of their busy lives to read my story in its early draft stage. Some of whom would never have otherwise read a story of this genre and for that I am truly grateful for their time.

A huge thank you to my partner, my sons, and their wives for their support during the time that I have spent drafting this story. Their words of encouragement were inspirational and often kept me motivated when I needed it. A special thanks goes to my son Joel Wade for his artwork on the book cover. He captured the essence of the story perfectly and is testament to what a beautiful artist he is.

Contents

Chapter 1 The Morning After

It was the winter of 1874, the rise of the industry had brought with it a need for the faster transportation of goods. Rail had progressively taken over the work that had been previously undertaken by boat people along the canal. Although there was still some work via the waterway, it was not as fruitful as it once was and many boat people had taken to dwelling on their boats as a cheaper way of living. It also allowed them to be readily available for any work that did come along.

Molly had woken early and the fire already burned brightly inside the cabin. It was bitterly cold and her toes had taken a while to come back to feeling in any way normal. She placed a kettle over the flame to boil, with enough water for their tea and a warm wash. As she watched the orange flames twist and turn her mind wandered to the previous evening's merriment. They had drunk so much ale and sang so loudly it was no surprise that her head throbbed so hard. She turned to the bed and smiled as Caleb slept soundly. She felt the warmth from the fire, making the overwhelming smell of the smoke from the damp embers more bearable. The soft glow from the flames cast a warm atmosphere into the small cabin that they were proud to call their home.

She apprehensively, pulled the old cover away from the small window in fear that the canal may be iced over. She breathed a huge sigh of relief that sent her stray curly brown lock of hair reeling back over her head. The ripple of the dark and murky canal water confirmed that all was well. The resident robin already hopped his way along the gunnel with the upmost determination not to drop the twig that he had tightly gripped in his tiny beak. His red breast swollen with pride as he threw open his wings and soared off into the air. Molly had seen this robin every day ever since their arrival into the basin and he had become a symbol to her that all was as it should be in her world! A not so welcome spot for Molly were the rats that scurried through the canal on a hunt for food, she shuddered at the thought and wrapped her shawl a little tighter against her shoulders! Despite living in close proximity of these creatures, she had still never managed to overcome her fear of them.

Molly and Caleb had not been in the canal basin for long. They lived on their boat named Calmolli, which was painted with the traditional décor of castles and flowers on the side and hatch doors. The base colour was a deep blue, trimmed with bright yellow. The full length of the boat was 60ft but the cabin was tiny, having just enough room to accommodate the two of them.

Like other boat folk, they had been forced to look for additional ways to earn their living. Caleb had always worked hard, he was never shy of labour. However difficult, he had taken all the work he could, everyone knew they could rely on him when it came to delivery of their goods. He continued to collect from and deliver to all the places that were more conveniently accessible by canal routes, so he continued to pursue this work wherever he had opportunity. As they now found themselves more stationary than in years earlier, he had begun to help at the canal side public house for extra money and the perks of free ale. The pub called "The Boatman's Rest" was owned by a very fair man named Lucius and the three of them had become good friends.

Molly was an incredibly resourceful, talented and beautiful young woman. Her long, chestnut brown hair cascaded down her back, her big brown eyes and upturned mouth gave the impression of a permanent huge smile against her slightly tanned skin. She was fairly short at 5ft 4inches with a slim frame and ample bust. Her presence in a room was always welcomed because she was so endearing to everyone she met, greeting each as if she had known them for years. Her good nature never stopped her making a stand against anyone who might try to wrong them though, she spoke out when life called for it. Mostly, she was just a lovely woman, who wore her heart on her sleeve and would lend a helping hand to all that needed one.

Her crafting skills had been a great advantage and she had been able to use them to add much needed cash or exchanges to their income. She moulded and decorated candles, adding her own scent by using oils, such as the piny smell of rosemary and the sweet, floral smell of lavender.   The jugs, pots and pans she painted were all decorated in the traditional boating manner, beautiful red roses, leaves and castles with cascading waterfalls. She crocheted all manner of items such as shawls, blankets, cushion covers and doilies. She displayed them on the deck of their boat and passers-by or pub veterans purchased them at a very fair price. Quite often, Molly's wares were brought by drunken men as peace offerings to angry wives, who had been waiting at home with dried up dinners and a few mischievous children running around their feet.

One of her favourite pass times was to sing in The Boatman's Rest, she had a wonderful voice and although Caleb could get very jealous at the way some men swooned at her, he also just loved to listen. She earned a lot in tips and Lucius, the pub owner was grateful that unlike some of the locals, she was a pleasure to hear. In the past, he had been pained at some of the cat wailing he had heard in his establishment and had to physically remove more than one patron for their persistence in scaring away his customers.   Molly had inherited her pitch perfect singing voice from her mother, who sang her way along the waterways of the Midlands during their travels. Anyone who happened to walk by along the towpath would stop and listen to her for as long as they were able.

Without looking, Molly instinctively knew that Caleb had started to awaken because his bellowing snore that could be heard across the waters had turned into a soft kitten like purr. She rested the strainer on to the cup, the steam rose steadily as she began to pour their tea, she turned her head to see Caleb's mop of curly black hair rise from the pillow. Caleb, red eyed and pale, looked rather worse for wear, still smiled at the site of his beautiful wife, "Moll, my head, it feels like I've diggers in searching for gold! Get me some lavender love?" Molly laughed at the thought of tiny little men with pickaxes burrowing around inside Caleb's head! She placed his tea on to the fold down table and reached into the cupboard for the lavender oil, she tipped a tiny amount of the liquid from the bottle and rubbed it softly into his temples and her own while she was at it!

She sipped at the hot steamy tea and made declarations of how they were never, ever going to drink so much ale again. The conversation soon turned to the curious events that Lucius had mentioned during the previous evening. "Caleb, Lucius isn't the sort of man who would make up such stories or even be troubled by such goings on?" She knew that Lucius was in no way superstitious or easily scared, yet he had been truly perturbed by recent incidents.

"I know Moll but how do you explain being shoved like that in the yard and there was no one else around? He also said that recently things have often gone missing only to be found where he knew he wouldn't have put em?" Molly listened intently as she began to roll up the mattress to replace the seating on the boat.

"Do you think he's losing his mind Caleb? I know he occasionally entertains ladies but once he shuts those doors, he's alone. Maybe he's lonely and starting to imagine things?" She pondered.

Caleb thought seriously about what Molly had said but he knew that Lucius was a strong man who had many female friends. Lucius was not lonely, he had plenty of company and more than that, he was the most down to earth man Caleb had ever known. He was not prone to imaginings or superstition, if he said it was so, then it was so. "No Moll, you know Lucius well enough to know that's not the case, there's something not quite right going on and I hope he gets to the bottom of it, or it stops, either way we should keep an eye out for him". He concluded. He pushed the wooden boards under the seats and sat down.

Molly nodded, she knew Caleb was right but could not understand how it could have happened.

Being a Pub Landlord had kept Lucius a terribly busy man. As such he was very diligent, he kept a tight ship but recently things had started to go missing. His petty cash tin was always stored in his wardrobe, in his bedroom above the pub. It was counted and recorded each night after closing, every night the same routine, taken out of the wardrobe, counted and returned. Until a week ago, one evening, Lucius had gone to retrieve the tin and it was not there. He searched frantically, he knew he had put it back there just as he did every night. He was beside himself, he wondered what on earth could have happened. He searched everywhere, the bedroom, the living room, the kitchen area. He searched for what seemed like hours, the whole place was turned upside down, in such a mess at his desperate search. Molly and Caleb had heard the commotion from right across the water, Lucius cursed, swore and yelled but they dare not go over. Eventually he ran out of places to look and just had to sleep because he needed to be up so early to get the pub ready for opening.

He had woken the next morning and had decided that although he did not want to believe it, the tin must have been taken by one of his patrons, maybe one of the street walkers that frequented his establishment. His temper rose, he was a big man and fearsome when angry. His eyes glared as he stomped across the floorboards to get dressed, he could feel his heart pound in his chest and the veins throb in his temples at the betrayal of his kinfolk. He would find some answers, whichever way he needed to. He opened the wardrobe door to grab his clothes and there sat on the bottom was the tin, just as though it had never been missing?! He shut the door at once and immediately reopened it, believing he had gone quite mad. No, there was the tin! He hastily opened the hinged box and expected it to be completely empty. It was full to the brim with the money just as he had left it. He counted it several times and the precise amount was in there. How... why?!

It was the third item that had disappeared and reappeared in that last couple of weeks, just a couple of trivial things initially but then the tin. He had become growingly concerned that someone was playing with his mind but he would not fall for it and that was that! He was just going to keep a very watchful eye from now on. Maybe no more sleepovers for his female friends either …. although he would think on that one because he sure liked his breakfast cooked for him.

One thing he knew for certain, was that all this had started when the strange old lady, Lillian appeared on that abandoned boat just last month. Surely, it could not be her though? She was quite obviously touched by madness but her boat was inaccessible and he was certain that she was far too old and frail to row a small boat, not that he had seen one tethered to hers. She had just simply appeared with her scruffy little dog. She spoke to nobody and if an attempt were made to wave or speak, she would scream and shout as if being attacked. She spoke incessantly to herself and that was the only reason they knew her name! Sometimes she shouted, sometimes she mumbled but her rants most always ended in telling someone or something to go away. Her black almost greying dress was in rags, torn and frayed at the bottom, her black bonnet swayed on top of her straw like, silvering grey hair. Both items had obviously fit her at one point in her life but her bony figure now stood, aged and angry with a life that no one knew of. Her accent was polished to the degree that you would expect of a fine lady, however her appearance was more fitting of a poor widow. Some of the locals had suggested that she may have been evicted from the workhouse. Her face looked full of anguish and despair, her deep-set eyes appeared wild with mania.

Caleb rose and filled the wash basin with the remainder of the water from the kettle and placed it on to the roof of the boat. Although accustomed to the cold he still hurried to wash his face as he felt the icy sting of the wind with each splash of water. He was a good-looking man, with jet black hair, sky blue eyes and olive skin that was now quite weathered due to so much time spent outdoors in all climates. He was a few inches taller than Molly and his muscular frame was both a result of and an advantage toward his heavy work. Having been born to a farmer, demanding work had begun for him as a young child, the change from farm work to that on the boats was not difficult for him, he was familiar with long hours and little rest. He was grateful for the shifts at the ale house as it made up for the shortfall in income, that they had experienced. He was a sturdy, dependable man, who like his wife, enjoyed life and no matter how hard things became he was always grateful for what he had and the people around him.

He looked over the side of the boat before he threw the dirty water from the wash basin into the canal, he kissed Molly goodbye and made his way across to the pub, ready for his shift.

The Boatman's Rest had been in Lucius's family for generations, it was an inviting, friendly venue and exceedingly popular amongst the locals and workmen alike. It was by no means luxurious but most certainly a pleasant place to while away the hours. There were two generous sized rooms downstairs that enabled a substantial flow of patrons to be seated rather comfortably. The counters were finished in oak, as were the tables, benches, and chairs. There was a large fireplace in the main room, with a sturdy brown leather armchair at the side, which was always claimed by Old Man Jack as he had come to be affectionately known. Jack was always accompanied by his dog Teddy who sat at his feet beside the fire. The second room was a little smaller, with a tinier fireplace that was not lit quite so often due to its infrequent use. Upstairs was a kitchen area, sitting room and five bedrooms, which were all used for storage other than Lucius's own bedroom. All were of decent size with large windows that looked out on to the water way at the front and into the street at the back. They offered beers, ales and spirits, along with the pubs own ale that was made from local ingredients.

The courtyard out the back had a water pump, toilet and an outbuilding that was used for brewing ale. The front of the pub was lined with tall rectangular windows and a huge oak door, two hanging baskets decorated the exterior walls and a variety of potted plants that were placed neatly on the ground. There was an additional one-story building to the

6

right of the pub, which had previously served as an office. It was generous in size with a fireplace just big enough to keep the place as comfortable as any, being connected to the pub through a doorway off the corridor.

Lucius was in the pub awaiting Caleb's arrival. He had placed the tankards on the shelves ready for the days' patrons, the smell of ale made its way across the water, mingled with the smoke from the many fires being lit across the land. He had woken early as usual, however today he also had a heavy head. He was not feeling his usual self so moved a little slower than normal. He was dressed but had forgotten his work apron, so returned back up the steep steps to fetch it.

On his descent he suddenly began to feel uncomfortable, he was overcome with the eery feeling of being watched. His skin began to tingle, he stopped halfway down the stairs and slowly glanced around him as he listened in to the silence for a sign. It was bitterly cold, he did not wish to hang around on the icy, cold steps so he continued on his way. As he reached the bottom, he could not shake the unnerving sense that someone was behind him and for a moment, he really did not want to see what that was! He stood completely motionless, he once more turned his head and slowly turned his glance back up the dark stairwell to the top, the light from the upstairs window shone through brightly almost blinding him for a brief moment. To his horror, in the glare of the light, appeared the shadow of a large man, standing tall and still in what appeared to be a top hat. Lucius jolted in shock! He grabbed on to the wall quickly to steady himself. He felt the nausea rise up from his stomach and he swallowed hard to quell it. He knew there could not have been anyone else inside, his heart raced. He remained frozen to the spot, for what felt like an age, he stared up at the strange shape in front of him when swiftly the vision disappeared in a flash! He knew the doors were still locked and there was no entrance to the upstairs other than through the pub. He composed himself and instinctively raced back up the stairs with fists clenched in readiness but there was nothing to see! He slowly moved from room to room, cautiously searching beneath the furniture and behind the doors but nothing .... He felt out of sorts yet managed to calm himself, he blamed his wild imagination on the amount of alcohol he had consumed the previous evening. He sat down briefly and waited for his anxiety to subside completely, after which he began his daily tasks. When Caleb arrived, he could see Lucius was troubled, he was clearly out of breath, quieter and paler than usual.

Lucius was a burley, muscular man and extremely tall compared to most. His working days began as the sun rose and never ended much before midnight, he had little time for chit chat and as such he was in the habit of keeping unnecessary conversation to a minimum. Although seemingly aloof he was sincere, he saw things in a straightforward fashion with little time for sentiment, but he would always be there to help a person in need. His ginger hair had flecks of grey and the ginger stubble on his face was tinged with white streaks. With his rugged handsomeness he was very a popular man with the ladies and a lot of the patrons would find their wives eager to tag along to "Lucius's pub".

Caleb approached with caution, he knew Lucius was not much of a talker but with all the peculiarity lately, he wanted to keep a check on him. On this occasion, he could see he was definitely out of sorts. "Is something ailing you, my friend?" Lucius looked mystified, he relayed the morning's story to Caleb. "Maybe it's the ale, as you said? We did have quite a few last night and you couldn't have had much sleep man!?"

Lucius nodded and continued to wipe the rim of the glasses before replacing them back on to the shelves. His expression did not correlate with his words. "Yes, you're probably right Caleb, it's not like me to drink so much, maybe I over did it a little. Your Molly gave us some sweet ballads last night, lovely lass you have my friend!". He was happy to have changed the conversation, he didn't want to think about it any longer and certainly didn't want his friends to believe him to be scared. Lucius slapped his friend's shoulder and turned again toward the shelving.

"She certainly is Lucius, I am a very happy man!". Smiled Caleb.

Both men continued their work as if nothing were different but both felt a disconcerting feeling of being watched and a sense of something unusual and unexplainable in the atmosphere.

Chapter 2 A Welcome Companion

A couple of days had passed since Lucius had seen what they now referred to as the "shadow". There had been much gossip and hilarity from the pub regulars about the whole event. Some locals suggested the pub had its own spooky gentry whilst others implied that Lucius may have lost his mind and was ready for the asylum. In fact, the pub had grown busier with people that hoped to catch a glimpse of this mysterious figure. Customers had made up their own stories of seeing Indian Princes and all manner of Royalty. Lucius welcomed all the rumours, he was simply happy that it brought more business his way!

Lucius had asked Caleb to make a collection of some empty barrels for him from a local farm on Friday. It was only Wednesday but Molly was already excited. She had been born and raised on a boat, travelling up and down the canals all her life. Caleb had grown up on his father's farm, which is where he and Molly had met when her father made regular deliveries to them. She had never forgotten the first time she saw him striding over towards their narrow boat and noticed his piercing blue eyes smiling at her. Every time she visited the farm after that, they had run off together to sit in the field where Molly shared her traveling tales and Caleb his stories of farming life. She loved the sweet smell of fresh grass and would sit sliding her palms over the field dew, while Caleb watched her every movement in fascination. She spent most of her time onboard the boat or on the towpath walking alongside one of her parents or siblings, so being able to sit in nature and experience a little freedom like that had made her face light up with happiness.

The couples' parents had not been happy about their friendship and when they decided to wed, they had to do so alone because both were shunned by their families. It had not been easy for them in the beginning but they were very much in love and life would have been so much harder had they not spent it together. Caleb's dedication to his work on the farm meant that his father had given him a small wage and allowed him to keep his tips. The money he had, afforded him to buy a rather run down but functional narrow boat, which they both worked on to bring up to the habitable standard that they now enjoyed. He also took his beloved shire horse 'Cobbles' that had been given to him by his grandfather. He had not asked his father's permission to take Cobbles but he knew his grandfather would have adored Molly and would want the best for them. Living on the boat meant that they did not incur too much expense. There were no children to feed and clothe either, which although had come as a surprise to them both, they never questioned it, they were happy enough just having each other.

Molly had nothing more than the clothes she stood in when she left her family behind on their boat. There was little room for sentimental belongings in their living conditions. Her parents had not given her their blessing but had wished her well at the very last moment that she had left. "I can see that you're not going to heed our warning Mol and for that I am bitterly disappointed. You two are worlds apart and that can only mean trouble. We can't send you on yer way with our blessing but we do wish you a long and healthy life." Her father had said in a broken voice. Her Mother had been far too emotional to speak at that moment, she merely managed to nod in agreement with her husband and held Molly tight for what she thought may be the last time. They had hoped that their disapproval would make her change her mind but it soon became clear, that she would not. She was the eldest daughter and as such had taken on much of the caring responsibilities for her siblings. It had been a blow to her family in many ways, as a daughter she had been an essential help to them and as a sister her siblings would miss her dearly. She had felt so guilty about leaving them that way but their unacceptance had left her no choice. Although she never spoke of them, she wished with all her heart that they would seek her out one day.

Wednesday morning arrived and Molly was excited! She knew that they would soon be off on their travels, something she always looked forward to. She slipped on her long brown woollen skirt, strapped on her shoes, buttoned her blouse and put on her white pleated bonnet. As she wrapped her shawl around her shoulders, she heard a commotion coming from the field where Cobbles was grazing.

She stepped up on to the coal sack and out on to the deck. As she looked across to the field, she saw that Cobbles was quite obviously spooked. He bolted forwards, then jumped to the side, then bolted again, as she got closer, she heard him snorting loudly and saw that his eyes were bulging wide. As she hurried along the tow path toward the field, a cold chill seared through her body, it was such an icy cold that it sent shivers down her spine.

She reached the fence and Cobbles was suddenly spookily still, the field was completely silent other than his snorting. His eyes were still wide, crazed and bulging. Molly sensing that she was being watched had to disregard it and get to Cobbles to make sure he was safe. She lifted her skirts slightly so that she could climb the fence, as she turned, she saw the mysterious old lady on the deck of her boat, her bony fingers pointed in her direction and although her mouth moved as if she spoke, she was silent. Molly was already shaken, she yelled across to her, "What is it? What did you see?" The old lady just continued to point ahead and stare in her direction still mouthing inaudible words. Molly did not have time for this, she was frightened for her beautiful horse, her heart pounded in her chest and her stomach churned. She turned back to Cobbles who was now curiously, still and calm. She climbed over the fence and walked slowly toward him, she gently placed her hand on his head and slowly stroked down his back, she spoke softly to reassure him. He was calm now, the steam from his breath was steady and slow as it should be but Molly was still anxious, she just could not understand what could have spooked him so. She had never seen Cobbles behave like that before and that crazy old lady had frightened her. Why doesn't she just speak, instead of staring like that?! She would get Cobbles a fresh coat and tell Caleb, she was sure he would know the answer, it was his horse and he knew him well.

With Cobbles now settled, Molly shut the hatches of the boat behind her, she still felt that she was being observed and turned her gaze back towards Lillian. There she was, in her little chair, just sitting and staring in her direction, with no attempt to turn her head away as her gaze met Molly's. Although she was quite a distance away, it still caused Molly to shudder. She did not understand this strange lady, why did she stare? Why did she shout and act so strangely? In fact, how and why was she here? She never seemed to have visitors and never did Molly see her leave the boat, so how did she survive, how did she get food and refreshment? Predominantly, Molly minded her own business and never got caught in the midst of gossip or prying into other peoples' affairs but this lady had certainly caught Molly's curiosity.

Molly turned away and headed toward the little swing bridge that was pulled to the side of the canal to allow boats through. The Basin was a quaint little place. Although open to the public, it remained fairly private, not many people passed through there, unless on a visit to The Boatman's Rest, or traders were looking for boatmen to make deliveries of some sort. There was an incredibly long tunnel to one side, which lead out to vast open space, lined with a few scattered cottages and a couple of grocery/farm stores. The opposing side was the end of the canal and gave plenty of space for the large narrow boats to turn around and go back on their travels. Just on the corner of the bend, a carpenter had set up business and had made great trade over the years, helping to repair boats and getting his supplies delivered for free. The other entrance to the Basin was off the main street from above. A tall, stoned archway led to a cobbled slope that could be walked down either side leading to the towpath. Many a tipsy pub patron had been seen sliding back down that slope due to stumbling on the wet, shiny stone cobbles. Groups of drunken revellers often gathered at the bottom, clapping and cheering as each attempt they got further up, just to come tumbling back down again.

The only other way to the basin was via a huge field that led to Lillian's side of the canal. It would have been a ridiculously long walk from there and nobody had ever seen anyone arrive that way. Knowing this, gave Molly even more reason to question how Lillian had come to be there. The boat that Lillian lived on had arrived only recently. Caleb and Molly had been on one of their delivery trips and it was already there when they returned from their overnight stay. No one had seen it arrive and it was a while still before Lillian appeared.

In deep thought, Molly walked across the bridge, the sound of footsteps caused her to look up and she could not believe her eyes! There, walking down the slope was the familiar face of her much adored friend whom she had not seen in many years! Molly quickened her pace and threw her arms around her best friend Nora! She was Molly's dearest friend and she had missed her so much. "Nora, my dear! How did you find me? Look at you, so beautiful!" Molly had so many questions, she was thrilled and utterly shocked to see her best friend.

Nora Stepped back but held tightly on to Molly's hands, she looked into Molly's eyes with despair.

"I had to find you, so much has happened, and I know you are the one who can help me. I have spoken with nearly every boatman and farmer this side of the canal just to find you! My pa was so sick Mol, he died only recently and you are all I have left in the world!" Nora had tears in her eyes she spoke so fast she could hardly catch her breath.

Nora and Molly had practically grown up together. Both came from boating families and often had stay overs in the same places, the time spent together had seen them become the absolute best of friends. Nora only had her father, her mother had died of sickness when she was a small girl and her father had raised her. He was a wonderful man and a very loving father, she helped him on his boat and even though they experienced some hardship they had a lovely life together. It was not an easy life and with the death of Nora's father, she was not going to give in and settle for the workhouse. Nora was a young pretty woman with fiery red hair that formed ringlets around her face. Her pale skin gave her emerald, green eyes a brightness that would bring a smile to everyone's face. She was as friendly and outgoing as Molly although a little feistier and never shy of sending someone packing if she felt the need.

"Here Nora, let's sit on the bench outside the pub, I'll get us a drink and we can talk." Molly took Nora's arm and lead the way. Lucius had seen them arrive and went outside to greet Molly, a silly grin appeared on his face as he caught site of Nora. He wondered who this beautiful young woman was, with her flaming red hair, gorgeous green eyes, and a teeny waist that he wanted to wrap his arms around. In a bid to hide his obvious enthusiasm, he tried to compose his expression with a look of indifference, which unfortunately resulted in his approach to them with a menacing scowl. Molly looked up in surprise at Lucius's odd expression and before any introduction could be made Nora scorned, "We'd like two ales please barkeep and less of the face, it's us boat folk, men AND women that keep the likes of you in business!" She glared up at him and even in her anger, noticed he was an extremely attractive man. Lucius's face reddened as he struggled for the right words to say without revealing his embarrassment. Thankfully, Molly realised that Nora had misinterpreted the situation and stepped in quickly!

"Nora, this is our good friend Lucius, he is a good sort really, maybe Caleb has been chewing his ear off all morning and that's the face he has left him with. Lucius, this is my good friend Nora, we haven't seen each other for many a year!" She smiled pleasantly at them both in turn.

Lucius felt the blood drain from his face and wiped his large sweaty palms on his apron, "Good to meet you, Nora." he said bashfully and shook her hand vigorously, "I'll fetch the ale, just busy Molly, you know how it is." He continued bashfully, struggling to speak fluently. He was not used to feeling so awkward around women. He strode off and thought how rude she was to make such presumptions about him! He rounded his shoulders and poured the ales, he placed them onto a tray and suddenly wished the place was a little tidier. "Get a grip man." he thought to himself as he approached them with their drinks.

"Thank you, Lucius." Nora smiled.

"You are welcome, Nora, as you say, women are always welcome in my pub, I know good folk when I see em." Lucius reddened again, "Well, all boat folk are welcome, men and women … you know what I mean." His voice diminished in unease.

Molly noticed Nora watch Lucius as he made his way back through the door. "Surprised you associate yourself with such a rude man, Moll, you and Caleb being such decent folk and all." Nora said half-heartedly.

As they sipped their ale, the alcohol began to warm their faces a little. Molly explained what a kind and generous man Lucius was and how much he had helped them, since their arrival to the basin. Besides, Molly was far more concerned with what she could do to help Nora. She had told her that due to her father passing, the hire boat had to be returned. She only had a little money left as she had spent much of it on lodgings for the past couple of weeks and that was not going to last long if she did not find work soon.

The two had sat for quite some time, catching up on life and discussing Nora's situation but it was difficult. Nora was too old to begin work in service and jobs for women of their background were not so easily found. The workhouse was an unbearable thought for both, but they seemed to be going around in circles.

Lucius had already told Caleb that his Mrs was outside with a right mouthy one, "pretty though Caleb, bit o jam, if I may say so!" he cheekily grinned. There was a little time before opening so Caleb and Lucius joined the women outside for a drink before work. With Nora's permission, Molly told them both about her situation. Nora was insistent that she would not be a burden to anyone after Molly had offered for her to sleep in the back of the boat until she found something more suitable. She declined the offer as she did not want to stay without being able to "chip in".

Lucius listened intently. He had pondered over an idea in his mind but did not want to be misunderstood, he was therefore hesitant to speak up. However, true to his selfless character and of no surprise to Caleb and Molly he came up with the perfect solution, "Molly, I could do with a hand, this place has got a lot busier over the last few months and being on my own has meant little time for cooking, cleaning and getting my washing done. I could do with some domestic help and the pub always needs a clean. I couldn't pay a lot and of course it wouldn't be appropriate for Nora to live in my apartment," he blushed again but continued "there's a room downstairs on the far side of the pub that I use for storage but it would make more than a fair-sized living quarter, if you could all pitch in to help me clear it up? Food and lodgings would be free with just a bit of money in Nora's pocket for spending?" He waited warily for their reaction, he did not know what to expect.

Nora suddenly felt very remorseful, she had judged Lucius harshly. She was so grateful for this fabulous opportunity that she very nearly threw her arms around him but used her better judgement and threw them around Molly instead! "Lucius I am so incredibly grateful for your generosity! I will do all that you ask, I am a decent cook and can keep a home as good as any. I'm a fast learner, so I am sure that I can help you with the pub too!" She enthused.

They were all grateful to Lucius, they thanked him so many times, he almost regretted the suggestion. He was not comfortable with being thanked so much, he did not know why, so he jumped up and suggested they get on with the task immediately. There was little time before the pub was due to be opened and if he and Caleb shifted the big stuff, then Nora and Molly could get on with the rest.

Molly ran back and forth to the boat to collect items that she knew would make Nora feel more at home in her little room. Molly knew better than anyone, that Nora would never, ever have known so much space as she had now. Being cramped in the tiny cabins of those narrow boats is all these ladies had ever known, so Nora was at a loss at what she would fill it with! There was an old table and two chairs in there already, so Molly brought over her handmade doilies and some beautiful, scented candles. Having previously being used as an office before storage, there was a small fireplace so Molly gave Nora her spare Kettle. Caleb and Lucius had brought down the bed from Lucius's spare room and laid a rug that had been found amongst the clutter in storage.

The room had begun to take shape and for Nora, it was the most beautiful room she had ever been in. She sat in the chair and tears of relief poured down her cheeks. Molly put her arm around her "Nora, we will always be here for each other, I am so thankful you came to me today, let us agree, no more disappearing for years!" Nora nodded and thanked Molly again for what felt like the hundredth time.

In time, Nora settled happily in to her new home. Her cleaning and cooking were exceptional and Lucius began to wonder how on earth he had managed before she came along. Unless one of his lady friends had stayed over, he had breakfasted on a slice of bread and butter and most often would not then eat until evening at which time he would simply add jam to the bread! Of course, there were occasions when the patrons of his pub would bring him a meal on account of him being alone but other than that, he was just too busy for what he called "Women's work, cooking and all that tiresome stuff.". He was grateful for Nora but it was strictly business between them and whatever he felt about her kind nature, beautiful face and captivating smile, he was never going to let on.

Nora had missed having someone to take care of and cook for. Lucius was good to her too, if she needed anything, he was there. She was grateful for Lucius but it was strictly business between them and whatever she felt about his generous nature, rugged good looks, muscly torso and mischievous smile, she was never going to let on.

Chapter 3 Samuel Tells Tales

Friday had finally arrived! Molly and Caleb were eager to set off to the farm and pick up the barrels for The Boatman's Rest. It had been a while since they had been on such a trip and they were excited to set off. Caleb stepped up to the hatch with Cobbles strapping and it was then that Molly remembered she had not told him of how Cobbles had been so spooked the day that Nora had arrived. Caleb was shocked when he heard the story, he could not recall an occasion when Cobbles had behaved like that before. He agreed that there must have been a reason for it, something had clearly frightened him, especially considering Lillian's reaction too. "She must have seen something Molly, or why would she have been pointing toward him? I don't understand that irrational old lady, I really don't! In fact, it was probably her that spooked him with her waggling finger, scary eyes and that snappy dog barking all day! One day, I will take myself over there and make her speak to us!". Nothing about Lillian made sense to Caleb, she had appeared as if from nowhere and continued to survive despite never leaving her boat.

Molly giggled, Caleb was so silly when he was angry, "Well, he's been fine since Caleb, and I haven't seen her for a few days now, I hope that all is well with her, she seems permanently annoyed".

They both stopped to wave at whoever it was that watched them from the upstairs window of The Boatman's Rest. "Someone's up very early Moll." Remarked Caleb. With that they set off down the canal, with huge grins looking forward to a couple of days travel.

Nora woke and drew back the curtain, she wiped away the condensation from the misted window to peer through and though still dark, saw that her friends' boat had already gone. She had hoped to catch them before they left, she had retired to bed early the evening before so had missed them both. With a heavy shawl around her to help against the cold, she grabbed the keys off the hook, came out of her room and into the narrow passage that ran between her room and the pub. The door into the pub and the further door to Lucius's apartment were unexpectedly still locked, so Nora guessed he was still asleep. She slipped quietly across the rooms and up the stairs into Lucius's kitchen where she cooked breakfast each day. It was silent, other than a gentle snore, she grinned at the sound and made her way around the kitchen table. She came to a sudden halt when she noticed a pair of lady's boots on the floor, as she glanced up, she found a lady's shawl draped over the back of the chair. She did not know what to do! Would she have time to run back down before he came out of the room or would he catch her halfway down the stairs, why oh why had she gotten up so early??! The snoring stopped abruptly and she heard him whisper, "Wake up woman, you need to go now!" Her heart raced, she quickly pulled off her shoes and ran as fast as she could back down the stairs, she silently prayed she would not be seen.

As soon as she arrived back into her room, she realized that she had forgotten to lock the doors behind her. She was adamant that Lucius would never find out that she knew he had a woman in his room, so how was she going to explain the unlocked doors? Who was that woman in Lucius's bedroom? She did not know he had a woman in his life, she suddenly felt distraught. Why was she so angry and upset that he had a woman in his room, she had no right?! Was she pretty, did he love her, were they to be married?! So many irrational thoughts swam around in her head that she was making herself feel quite

15

ill! She poured herself some stewed tea, with shaky hands she sipped slowly, the steam from the cup stinging her eyes. She imagined all manner of scenarios, each ended with her being thrown from her beautiful new room and Lucius walking hand in hand into the sunset with a beautiful woman at his side.

She must have nodded back off to sleep because the knocking at her door woke her. Lucius, looking rather dishevelled, yelled, "Nora, it's Lucius, I thought I would check you were well?" He opened the door and stood just inside the doorway, "I know you left early last night and well, I had rather a lot to drink after you went. It's just that both doors were unlocked and I was certain that I locked them, very strange?" Had Lucius been more truthful, he would have told her, that he had been in absolute panic with worry had anything happened to Nora ....

Nora who was still half asleep, looked askance, she pulled at her hair in a bid to neaten it, she was still upset by what she had seen and immediately snapped, "Well I suggest you be more cautious in the future or we might both have been murdered in our sleep!! Am I to cook you breakfast this morning or are you already satisfied?"

Lucius was quite taken back, she looked incredibly angry, then again, he had left them vulnerable by not locking the doors "My apologies Nora, it will never happen again, you're quite right, it was a foolish thing to do and yes erm, breakfast please. I'm very hungry this morning". He replied gingerly.

"I bet you are!" she mumbled sarcastically, she barged past him, straightening her skirts as she made her way up the stairs and into the kitchen.

She banged and bashed her way around the kitchen that morning, every noise she made thudded around Lucius's head, ten times shriller than it actually was. She yelled so forcefully when she announced breakfast was ready that Lucius's ears rang louder than the church bells. She could not bear to look in his direction as he entered the room. They ate in total silence that morning and Lucius felt guilty in more ways than one. He knew why he felt guilty about not locking the doors, he had put her in unnecessary danger, but he had no idea why he felt so guilty about having one of his regular ladies in his bed. After all, he was a single man, why shouldn't he?

Their entire day was spent in much the same way, each felt their own remorse. Neither one of them dared to look at the other for fear their eyes might meet and urge them to reveal the truth of what they really thought. As bedtime came, Nora began to feel worse about letting Lucius take the blame for the unlocked doors. She could not let him know that she had seen a woman upstairs, it may have led to things being said she might not care to hear. She went to bed and hoped that tomorrow would be a better day.

Molly and Caleb had travelled for most of the day. The only stop they made was for quick refreshments and with the winter night's drawing in so early they wanted to make haste. It was evening before they reached the small farm where they were to collect the barrels. The silvery moon's glow peeked from behind the clouds and the fog began to settle over the land, like a soft misty blanket. Although the smoke from the fires could not be smelt so heavily here, they could still feel it on the back of their throat as they breathed in the icy, foggy air.

Caleb had already jumped off and put the strappings down for the narrow boat to bring it to a slow and steady stop. The barrels were stacked ready at the edge of the field and from a distance he saw two young men walking toward them. They all greeted each other and the younger lad, Alfie, took Cobbles to rest in their stable. Samuel was around the same age as Caleb and they had met on many previous occasions, when Caleb had visited with his father. "I almost didn't recognize you there Samuel! Hope you are all well?" You could see their breath as they chatted in the cold, night air. Caleb introduced Molly and caught up on news of Samuel's family, Caleb told the farmer all about the basin, that they now called home and their work at The Boatman's Rest.

Samuel, with wide eyes looked intrigued and revealed, "How odd Caleb, our father was telling us recently of the extraordinary tales from up that way, when he visited last week. He had only called by on a quick trip but got caught up telling us his stories, you know what he's like once he gets started". He rolled his eyes.

Molly was surprised to hear that news of the pub's hauntings had reached so far. "I'm surprised you heard about that Samuel! Anyway, I don't think its spooks, it's just the landlord, drinking too much ale" she laughed and gave him a reassuring smile.

Samuel now looked even more fascinated, "Well, I wouldn't be surprised if it were some sort of spooky events from what my father told me but it wasn't a story about spooks, he was telling. No, it was far more frightening but sure I shouldn't tell a young lady such a tale. Especially not on a foggy, cold, dark, night such as this. Maybe leave it to the morning, when we're moving the barrels, might be less frightful in the daylight?" he questioned.

Had Molly pulled any harder on his arm as he went to walk away she may have dislocated his shoulder! "There's not the slightest chance you are getting away from here now Mr.! I will be imagining all kinds of horrors and I'm sure Caleb will agree, I'm not easily scared. I'm no fair maiden, I can listen and no mistake". She assured him. She enjoyed company and would not allow him to leave when she knew there was an interesting tale to be told.

Caleb laughed and showed both the lads into the hatchway to the boat cabin. There was no reason to stay out in the cold when the fire burnt bright in the cabin and the kettle was on the boil. "She's right, please both come on in and warm yourselves, nothing like a good horror story on a cold and foggy night". Everyone chuckled and Molly prepared the tea.

Samuel made himself comfortable next to Alfie on one seat, while Molly and Caleb sat opposite on the other. Samuel seated happily began, "It was a short while ago. A boatman had been taking some coal up that way on a long boat. He was heading up toward the basin to make an easy turn around for his return journey. They had reached the Basin tunnel, it was silent other than their own voices that echoed in the cold, dark, damp void. As he and his son were heading through it in the dark, they heard a loud knocking against the boat, the tunnel causing it to echo all around them. It was pitch black and the heat from their fire was causing droplets of water to drip down off the icicles that had formed on the roof of the tunnel. They wondered for a moment if the knocking sound could be icicles landing on the cabin roof but no, there were none to be seen. The bumping noise changed to a dragging sound, then to banging again. Both called out but there was no reply other than hearing their own voices answered as their echo's bounced back to them. Their hands trembled and their legs wobbled, they feared they may fall in and find out for sure what it was. The two men walked up and down from stern to bow, with just the light from the fire and two lanterns, illuminating their own frightened, confused faces. Neither of them could see what was banging against the boat..." Sam briefly paused.

Everyone listened to Sam's sullen tale and were suspended in action, each of them held their cups tight and edged forward on their seats. Completely still as if any movement might make Samuel stop talking and they would not get to hear the end! Suddenly Molly's impatience got the better of her and she bellowed "Samuel, please! What was it?? What was in the tunnel, do tell or I might burst!!" Everyone jumped at the outburst! Alfie's cup was hurled out of his hand across the cabin but thankfully did not break. He looked across at his brother in horror and expected a clip around the ear. Molly apologized for scaring him and he returned an embarrassed smile back at her.

Samuel looked at them soberly and said, "Dear Molly, as my dad said, a good story is all in the way it is told, it cannot be rushed". With eyes narrowed, head bent forward toward them and the shimmering light from the lantern flickering across his face, he resumed his story.

"As I was saying, it was almost pitch black in the cold, wet stinking tunnel. The knocking against the boat continued and despite their searching, it was just too dark and the waters too murky to see anything. After what felt like forever, the boat was finally leaving the tunnel and the knocking stopped. Both men were so badly shaken that they decided to moor up for the night and drank a lot of gin before bed to steady their nerves. They both slept restlessly, waking at every little creak and tiny sound that came from inside and outside of the boat.

That morning they woke to shouting, screaming and splashing coming from the waters nearby. The two of them jumped from their beds, opened the hatch and saw that just outside the tunnel a small crowd had gathered. As they neared the crowd, their attention was drawn toward the edge of the canal, they couldn't quite work out what they were looking at. Was it a sack of some sort? The people in the crowd had hands to their mouths, some shaking their heads and turning away. Getting nearer they saw there, lying in the water, a very forlorn figure of a man, with a lifeless, grey face who had most obviously drowned!"

All three groaned in horror, each wanted to know who it was and why was he there?! Samuel determined to be the perfect storyteller, ignored their questions and continued in the air of mysterious narrator that he had begun with. He cleared his throat and he continued, "There was a boatman, holding a boat pole to keep the body at the side from floating away, another boatman knelt on the towpath with a hand on the gentleman's coat. As they moved nearer, they saw a man reach into the water to retrieve the top hat that floated toward them." Molly and Caleb exchanged a glance when they heard the mention of a top hat. "The four men reached into the water and pulled the lifeless, grey, sopping wet body to dry land. Everyone gasped at the sorrowful sight before them!!"

Samuel stopped talking and searched each of their faces, they looked thoroughly horrified and depressed. He was assured that he had delivered his story well, his father would be proud!

"Do you know who he was and what happened to him Samuel?" Molly asked after what felt like an age of silence.

Samuel was glad she asked, "Well, he was quite obviously a gentleman, he was wearing the clothes of a gent and when the old bill got there and checked his pockets, he still had all his money and his pocket watch. It was later, that news got out that a gentleman from one of the big houses just at the top there," he pointed toward the back of their farm "had gone out that evening and not come home. Turned out to be him. The old bill reckoned he had done himself in, though his wife swore she would never believe that! You see Moll, there is a house of disrepute close by! Well, the word was that he felt guilty about going there, you know him being of good standing. Dad reckons he may have been seen going in or just felt awful and couldn't face his Mrs??! That's not all though, there was a large knock on the back of his head but the old bill put that down to him hitting his head in the water because nothing was stolen and they never could find a motive. His Mrs wasn't having any of that though, she swore he was murdered and would never have gone there for sinful reasons!! She went missing after his funeral, aint been seen since. Apparently, they were very much in love and happy together, not always so for their folk, is it?"

Molly and Caleb were fascinated and saddened all at the same time and poor Alfie was scared out of his wits! Caleb in deep thought wanted to know more, "What was his name Samuel, did your father tell you?" He enquired.

"He didn't Caleb but next time he comes to call I will find out for you. Now I must get back up to the house! My wife will be cursing and I don't want a night in the chicken pen! We will load those barrels in the morning and then you can both come and breakfast with us! Glad to see the back of them barrels, been in my way they have."

Samuel lived a good life, he lived in the farmhouse with his wife and their three small children. He had been fortunate to marry his childhood sweetheart Edith and it was her parents farm that they had inherited. It was a large plot of land for them to maintain and as well as the crops there were animals to take care of including sheep, cows and chickens. His younger brother Alfie had moved in with them to help with the work on the farm.

Caleb unfolded the bed and after much discussion about Samuel's story, they both concluded that it was probably no coincidence that Lucius was seeing the figure of a man in a top hat. Knowing that they were in for some demanding work in the morning, they both settled into bed to get some much-needed sleep. Caleb's familiar snore, started to rumble from deep in his belly, the rasp before that fretful silence that Molly always detested in fear that he had stopped breathing! The wind howled and caused the boat to rock rhythmically in the water, whilst the pull of the rope kept it firmly in place. Molly listened to the clink of pots and pans as they tapped against each other. The freezing, heavy winds blew through the branches of the evergreens causing them to swoosh and bend along with the rustle of the leaves. Such were the common sounds that eventually helped them to nod off to sleep.

She awoke with the vague recollection that Caleb had told her he was going to the farmhouse to fetch the workmen. She was happy to find that he had lit the fire which took the sting out the chilly air, she slipped on her clothes and rolled the mattress away. She jolted suddenly when she heard a loud thud on the cabin roof. She looked toward the hatch and expected Caleb to appear but three more thuds followed so loud that she slumped sharply in the seat as the blood seemed to drain from her body and left her too weak to move! She called out to Caleb but no reply came. "Who's up top?" she shouted! Bang, bang, bang, more thuds from the side of the cabin now. She trembled from head to foot and reached for the broom under the seat, she flung the hatch doors open. With both hands clutched around the broom, ready for battle she almost threw herself up on deck to see what on earth was causing such commotion. She was utterly shocked as she could see nothing or nobody. The whole place was silent, not a soul to be seen. She called out again but still no answer, the field was empty and no one on the towpath. She was petrified, her hair stood up on the back of her neck, her whole body shook and she felt so weak, she could hear her own heartbeat in her chest. She flung herself back down into the cabin, reached her hand up to snatch the broom back and shut the doors tight. She did not know what to do, she sat in the seat, pulled her knees up to her chin and tears fell down her cheeks. The thudding started again, louder and faster and she was sure that either something was about to burst in or the whole cabin would topple in on her. She hugged herself tight and felt like she might be about to die, her mind raced for a solution!

There was nothing for it, she had to run and fetch Caleb. She would rather run out into the open and hope to find help, than stay in there and face her foe alone! Her hands visibly trembled, she quickly grabbed the broom, this time determined, she jumped straight up on deck and down from the boat. As she landed on the tow path, she could not quite believe what she saw as a potato whizzed through the air, straight past her from up above. She turned her head toward the direction it came from and there, seated on the branch of a tree was a young boy with a potato sack in his hand. She looked to the deck of the boat and it was loaded with potatoes! Molly fumed with rage! She marched toward the tree and jabbed at the branch with the broom, she screamed "Get down from there right now Alfie you little beggar, I'm going to give you a thick ear!!"

Poor Alfie was so scared, he slipped on the icy bark and hung there like an old sloth, upside down with all four limbs wrapped desperately around the branch. He clutched onto the potato sack which slowly emptied one potato at a time! He pleaded with Molly, "I'm sorry Mrs, was just a joke after the story last night, please Mrs, I'll clean your boat, anything, just put the broom down!"

Samuel and Caleb ran down the field as they heard the commotion and arrived to see Molly, who looked like a crazy woman, hair strewn wildly, yelling and jabbing the broom as close as she could possibly reach to the branch. Caleb reached Molly and put an arm out to retrieve the broom when a large potato bounced quite sharply straight off the top of his head, which caused his knees to buckle and sent him straight onto his bottom.

Molly rallied after seeing her husband fall to the floor. She bent down to comfort Caleb, as he rubbed his sore head and was completely baffled as to what he had witnessed. Samuel was overcome with laughter yet cringed with embarrassment at the antics of his annoying, younger brother. He had already begun to climb the tree in a bid to get the young scamp down! Alfie had managed to scurry back to sitting on the branch and was refusing to descend "Sam, she's going to kill me, she near knocked me off this branch with that stick! I'm not coming down till she promises no violence!" He protested.

Molly hearing Alfie shouted up to him "You nearly scared me half to death you little beggar!! Get down from there now, or I will CLIMB UP there myself and tan your hide!!"

Samuel, wanted to calm the situation and didn't want Molly to catch him laughing, so he suggested that she walk Caleb up to the house. The couple walked slowly together, Caleb rubbed at what had become a small pea sized lump on the top of his head and Molly cursed relentlessly under her breath. They were greeted at the door by Samuel's wife, Edith when they arrived at the farmhouse. She was a large lady with a very stern face, which twisted uncomfortably when she attempted to smile. The smell of sausage and eggs already filled the air as she invited them to sit down and explain what had happened. Caleb decided to do the talking as he could tell Molly was still furious by the way she pounded at his already sore head with a wet cloth. His head bounced as Molly "nursed" it back to health. He felt grateful for the warmth of the fire and decided to be gracious enough to give Edith a milder version of events.

"Well, if I know my Samuel, he'll sort him out good and proper! Little scamp should be grateful we gave him a roof, larking around when there's work to be done!" She snapped. With a baby on her hip and a toddler who pulled relentlessly on her apron, she still managed with one free hand to skilfully scoop the sizzling bacon and sausages from the pan and onto the plates.

Just as the three of them sat to the table, Samuel came in with Alfie following closely behind him. He had his cap clasped tightly with both hands, head bent down and one bright red ear! His eyes moved up to meet Molly's as he said "I'm real sorry Mrs, I didn't mean to scare ya. Sam said you can keep all of them spuds on yer roof and I'm to sack them up for ya." Molly turned her head in a bid to stifle her chuckle. She turned back toward Alfie and felt unpredictably sympathetic, she patted the seat next to her for him to sit. Alfie blushed and apprehensively took the seat. Everyone chatted as they tucked into their breakfast, the smoky, salty taste of the meat feast before them added a cosy ambience and Molly's mood finally relaxed.

Molly and Caleb thanked Edith for the delicious breakfast she had cooked and bid them farewell.   The eldest of the three children, gave Molly a peck on her cheek and told her she was pretty. He was a cute little boy, she guessed around five or six years old, she scuffled his mop of curly brown hair and gave him a hug as they left. Samuel and Alfie left with them to load the barrels. They all pulled their clothes tight against them and ventured back out into the cold day's air.

Molly went to the stable to fetch Cobbles, he was a beautiful horse, brown and white, with a broad forehead, large eyes, a strong, muscular body and thick neck. He had never let them down and in return they looked after him with great care and affection. She took hold of his reigns and smiled at the clip clop, from his hooves against the cobble on the floor. She walked closely by him to share the warmth on this frosty day.

She heard the men talk further about the drowning as she drew close to the boat. The thought that she would have to return through that same tunnel on the journey back sent a shiver down Molly's spine. Alfie blushed again when he saw her arrive and strapped Cobbles to the boat immediately, "To save Molly the job". He insisted bashfully.

With all the barrels loaded and a welcome sack of potatoes now on board, it was time to say their goodbyes. Samuel mentioned again that he would ask his dad for the name of the gent on his next visit. Caleb suggested Molly walk the first part with Cobbles as it would be much colder as the day wore on. As the two brothers walked away Caleb reached into the potato sack and shouted, "Alfie!" Just as Alfie turned to respond a potato flew like a missile straight into his stomach!

"Just a thank you for my head!" shouted Caleb.

Samuel was beside himself with laughter, particularly at Alfie who mumbled and stammered curses under his breath! Molly laughed hysterically and blew Alfie a kiss and they continued on their way.

21

Chapter 4 When all return

Meanwhile back at the Boatman's Rest, the atmosphere remained so thick you could cut it with a knife! Nora had barely spoken as she worked and Lucius wore a look of confusion for the best part of the day. Both had a restless night and had a very subdued breakfast together the next morning. Nora was eager to see her best friend return, she needed to confide in her all that had happened. She valued Molly's opinion highly and knew she would have something sensible to add that might help her deal with her erratic feelings.

It was extremely busy in the pub and that was exactly what they both needed, leaving little time for awkwardness. Old man Jack sat on a low stool in the corner of the ale house, he sucked on his near empty pipe, his lips pouted around the mouthpiece to get a good pull. The smell of burnt tobacco mingled with the ale and smoke from the fire. He and his little black and white dog Teddy, fidgeted around to get the closest place next to the fire. The pubs regular couple Maud and George were already in their seat by the window, every now and again she would raise her hand and slap it against the back of his head at some rude remark he had just made! He would just smile and look rather pleased with himself and continue to sup his ale, whilst she shook her head in disdain at him. There were quite a few regulars to The Boatman's Rest and they all seemed to be on a visit today. Lucius thought the roaring fire and warming ale, probably drew them in from the bitter cold. The continuous laughter and chatter from the gathered crowd cut through their silence and made the day more tolerable.

Nora wiped down the tables while Lucius noisily prattled with one of his patrons about the local market. Nora turned to dip her cloth into the water bucket and spotted a pretty young woman that she had not seen before entering the pub. The woman was dressed in green striped skirts with a plain green buttoned top that appeared far too tight and pushed her breasts almost under her chin! Her blonde, curly hair was wound up into a bun on top of her head with little ringlets that fell loosely about her neck. There was barely a man present in that room, that did not look in her direction with a fallen mouth and receive a kick under the table, or a clip on the ear from his wife. Nora watched as this young woman strode directly over to Lucius and threw her arm straight over his shoulder, her hand rested on his chest. Nora looked down at her own attire, her brown drab dress hung loosely off her, she had dirt beneath her nails. She caught a glimpse of her face in the mirror above the fire, she saw her red wavy hair stuck to the sweat that had formed on her face. She very nearly ran out of the pub but instead and more out of curiosity than anything else, edged herself and her dirty bucket of water closer to where they stood and continued to work.

"How about a drink and anything else you can muster?" the woman whispered into Lucius's ear as she twisted one of her blond ringlets around her finger. Nora felt her temperature rise and her jaw clench! She wanted to run over and remove her from the premises, let alone from Lucius! She knew she could not, in an act of impulsive, she splashed the cloth aggressively into the bucket in hope that the filthy water would find itself smattered all over the pretty green skirts! To her disappoint, she missed her target but very nearly copped a soaking herself.

"I'm working Clara, we're busy today and we're expecting a delivery in the next hour or so." Lucius protested. He turned to remove Clara's arm from his shoulder and took a sneaky glance at Nora, in hope she had not seen any of it. He had to muffle his hilarity, as he noticed her swish the cloth with such venom that he was surprised they were not all soaked. He took hold of Clara's shoulders and maneuvered her a little further away from the danger zone and offered her a drink.

"Hmmm, guess I could sit a half hour and drown my sorrows at you being too busy for me, my lovely!" Clara sat down on a high stool at the bar, she tidied her skirts and glanced down at Nora. "Yes, an ale will do dear, I've walked all this way, in this freezing wind without my shawl, think I might have dropped it somewhere, maybe you have seen it, Lucius?" Clara had always had good observation skills and she sensed immediately that Nora was showing envy, she gave her a sardonic smile. Clara had no long term designs on Lucius, she enjoyed his company as much as he enjoyed hers but there was nothing more to it than that. She was a tease though and enjoyed seeing Nora in awe of her. She turned her nose up at her and sipped from the drink that Lucius had just placed in her hand.

Nora threw the cloth into the bucket and went through the door that led out into the yard. She felt so angry and humiliated. She liked Lucius, she accepted it but she had not realized how much until she felt how unbearable it was to see another woman's arm around him. The way that she had looked at her too, she thought to herself, turning her nose up like that, who did she think she was! She leant against the wall for a little while before she went out into the yard with the bucket. It was quite dark and there was only one lantern out there.

She disliked going out into the yard alone after dark. There was something creepy about the place and she always had the sense of being closed in with no escape. She unlocked the door and the rusty old hinges creaked loudly as she pushed it open. She could barely see her way across the yard, it was silent, except for the faint chatter that came from inside the pub and the odd scratch of vermin. She felt the icy chill creep up from the stone floor, through her shoes and into her feet. The smell of stagnant, stale water drifted up her nostrils as she breathed sharply in an attempt to calm her temper. She fumbled her way further across the yard toward the far side. A sudden chilling wind whistled loudly, causing the door to bang shut and then open again with a loud thud against the wall! She jumped nervously which caused the water in the bucket to spill out. The cold crept up from her feet and rose through her body all the way up to engulf her face. She tried to keep herself steady but she had been startled by the door and could not shake the sense that someone stood closely behind her. Her heart began to beat faster and she felt weak as she trembled so hard with cold and fear. She turned her head very slowly to look behind her but no one was out there, if she could only move a little quicker, to get out. Suddenly she felt a sharp thud between her shoulders that threw her to the floor. She dropped the bucket with a loud crash that echoed across the yard! She screamed out in the darkness, suddenly in fear for her life! It was too dark to see if anyone was there, she tried to pull herself up from the floor, so that at least she might be able to run. Alone in the darkness, she saw a large figure walk through the door toward her with a lantern in hand. With utter relief, she realised it was Lucius, who had come to see where she had gone!

He rushed to her side and bent down beside her, relief took over and the tears fell down her cheeks. "Nora, what happened?" He put the lantern on the floor and reached both his hands out to her. She looked up at him and for the first time since she had found the lady's clothing upstairs their eyes met. As they rose from the floor together their eyes remained locked, Nora struggled a little to stand, so Lucius put her arms around his shoulders. They both stood, face to face with lips so close they almost touched. Each could feel the pull of the other, how easy it would have been to just move that fraction closer.

"I was pushed Lucius!" Nora said and dipped her head at the last moment. She was not sure why she moved her face from his but she wished immediately that she hadn't.

"Pushed? By whom Nora, who pushed you??! Who did this to you?!" He was enraged and he spoke so fast, his head darted in all directions as he tried to find if anyone else was out there.

"I don't know Lucius, I was out here putting the bucket away, when suddenly I was pushed to the floor, it was so dark, I couldn't see a thing. I nearly hit my head on that brick on the floor when I landed. I cannot say there was anyone or anything else here, no footsteps, no noise. I don't understand, I was definitely pushed, I felt it!!" She rushed.

He was so confused, he recalled his own incident in the yard, "Nora, the exact same thing happened to me in this very spot! It was a few weeks gone now, I told Caleb about it."

Nora snatched her arms from Lucius's neck, "Lucius, why would you not tell me such a thing, when I live and work here. Do you not think that this is something I should know of?" She exploded.

Lucius shocked, retreated a few steps back, "Nora, how could I explain such a thing without you thinking me insane? I already have half the pub folk joking that I should be in an asylum. I couldn't bare that you ... I mean, any of my friends thought the same." He replied in angst.

"Yet I told you straight away Lucius? With no fear of what you would think?" She could really feel the sting of the cold. The water from the bucket had soaked through her dress and it was painful against her skin. She stormed off and banged the door against the wall on her way.

"Nora, Nora!!!" He roared. "Please, just let us talk about it. I always told you not to come out here ... Nora?!" Nora heard him but she was too angry, cold and upset to stay any longer.

Lucius kicked the brick that he and Nora had nearly bashed their heads on into the corner of the yard. He strode back into the pub disparaged and declared that Old Jack, was in charge for an hour because he needed a break. He made his way up to his bedroom ... with Clara.

Nora went straight to her room, changed into dry clothes and warmed herself by the fire. She un tousled her hair and wrapped it up neatly into her bonnet. She was about to return to her duties when she felt her anger resurface, she could not believe he had not shared such a thing with her! How was she to feel safe, when something like this had just happened and what exactly did just happen? Her thoughts then turned to that vile woman in the bar and that just increased her anger further. She couldn't bear the thought .. well no actually, she thought to herself, she is welcome to him! With that, she grabbed the kettle and decided to make herself a tea before she returned to the bar.

She felt more relaxed now and a little warmer, she knew she had to get back to work. She was an employee after all she thought resentfully to herself! As she reached the bottom of the stairs to Lucius's apartment, she came face to face with Clara who had quite obviously just came down them. Clara wrapped her shawl around her shoulders and smiled smugly at Nora, "Mm, knew I had left this somewhere, no doubt he will be down soon, unless he's nodded off!" She winked and marched triumphantly out.

24

Nora's face was crimson, the blatancy of this horrible woman! She didn't know how much longer she could cope with this awkward situation she found herself in but she knew that for now, there was no alternative. As she looked through the misted window of the pub, she was filled with relief as she saw her best friends husband walk along the towpath with Cobbles. They were back! She scrambled to quickly gather the glasses and make sure all the patrons had what they needed, she threw on her shawl and ran out to meet Molly.

The ladies were happy to see each other again. After a hug, they strapped the boat ready to offload and Molly took Cobbles to the stable to rest and warm for a while. Nora fetched them both a drink and placed it on a table close to the fire. The pair looked frozen and Nora knew that Caleb would want to get the barrels straight off the boat so they could settle for the night. "Where's Lucius, Nora? I thought he would be waiting at the door in anticipation?" Caleb laughed.

"Upstairs." Nora replied abruptly, barely parting her lips.

Molly and Caleb exchanged a knowing glance, they knew trouble when they saw it.

"Could you fetch him down please Nora? I'd like to get this done and then we could have a rest?" He asked.

Nora shook her head in refusal, "Best you go up yourself Caleb, I need to keep an eye down here. I'm sure he would be glad to see you."

Caleb gulped down the last of his drink and squeezed Molly's hand as he rose from the table. He tilted his head toward Nora from behind her back to indicate to Molly that she needed to try and find out what was going on.

"I can see there's something wrong dear?" Molly pushed.

Nora was ready to burst with emotion and told Molly everything, she included the truth behind the unlocked doors. Molly was extremely disheartened with the whole situation. She knew all about Lucius's reputation but had hoped he might tone it down with Nora there, she did not want folk to believe that Nora was agreeable to such behaviour. She also recognised that he had been through a lot recently and had not been himself. She listened to Nora's concerns about the incident in the yard and her shock that nobody had told her that it had happened before, after all she did live there and deserved to know!

Molly realised it was time that Nora knew everything that had happened in the pub and the effect that it's had on Lucius, since it began. She told her all, in the hope that she would understand his concern when he found unlocked doors after he believed that he had for sure locked them.

"You have to tell him about the doors Nora, he's probably thinking it's the spook and might not be sleeping, for worry that the doors are being unlocked?" Molly frowned seriously at Nora with her plump red lips pursed together tight. They were both her friends and she had hoped at the very least they would get along, she had not expected all of this.

Nora felt remorse now she knew the whole story. She would never have let Lucius doubt himself about the doors if she had known the truth. "Well, that's not quite all Molly, you see …" her face blushed and she struggled to force the words from her mouth, "You see, I like Lucius, you know." she widened her large green eyes and raised her eyebrows. "I think he likes me too but … I don't know Moll, we just don't seem to get along and if he did then there wouldn't be Clara would there? That's why I didn't want to tell him I knew that woman was up there. In case he can see …. You know … that I was a bit jealous?" She fidgeted on her seat as Molly's expression changed from shock to concern intermittently. "I live here too Moll, so it's not proper for us to court anyway, I'm not like that Clara, people already talk. If he found out how I felt and don't feel the same, then I might be out on the streets!"

She had got herself so worked up that Molly was worried she was about to leave! "Nora, slow down, you're getting too far ahead of yourself. We must think about this sensibly." Both sat quietly whilst Molly thought it through. Suddenly her face lightened, "Right Nora, how about this, you just tell him that you had gone upstairs, seen the lady's clothing and didn't want to tell him to save him embarrassment? He doesn't know that you're not aware he is equally as brazen as that Clara, does he? If you stumble and go crimson, then it just shows you're not comfortable with talking of such things and there's nothing wrong with that Nora! I'm surprised you didn't just do that in the first place?" She smirked.

Nora looked relieved, "I don't know why I didn't Molly. Maybe I was too emotional, to think straight but you're right. It will be awkward, but it can be explained by embarrassment as you say. I am so glad you're back, I knew you could help!"

"Anyway, I wish now that you had come straight down to us before we left Friday morning, we could have sorted it out straight away." Molly smiled.

"You had already left when I woke Moll, you must have been off real early!" Replied Nora.

Molly looked surprised, "We were Nora, someone was up though because we saw them in the window."

"No Molly, I missed you and Lucius was definitely asleep, remember I went upstairs and well … they were asleep in his room?"

"Dear me then Nora, who was in the window? …" Molly quizzed.

The pair looked at each other in confusion.

Lucius was seated at the table with a cup of tea and a slice of bread and butter when Caleb arrived upstairs. He was happy to see his friend and pointed to the cup inviting him to pour himself a brew. Caleb knew Lucius was a man of few words and guessed that his version of events would be far shorter than Nora's. Lucius scratched his nails into his beard, "I suppose you have spoken with Nora already, I imagine she is in a horrid mood." Lucius questioned without waiting for an answer, he continued, "The woman finds me despicable my friend, getting shoved over on her backside like that and me not warning her about the yard! Oh, and how foolish of me, leaving the doors downstairs unlocked over night! We could have been telling quite a different tale right now. I just don't know if I did forget or if it was that spook! It's not like me to forget Caleb, so I cannot be sure but I aint been sleeping properly since then, I know that much. To make matters worse, Clara comes in flaunting herself again and well … you know how it is Caleb." Lucius ranted.

Caleb smirked and shook his head in disagreement, Lucius ignored his judgemental expression and went on, "One day I might get myself a nice woman to settle with but they don't like me, Caleb. Maybe being a pub owner puts em off, I don't know but they don't like me! My Dad said he wished he had taken more from life, he worked so hard and never did have much happiness. When he got sick, he told me that if he had realized just how short life was, he would have made sure he enjoyed every minute of it, whatever he was doing! Anyway, I'm prattling on, let's go move these barrels." He stood up, his heavy frame dragged the small wooden chair and scraped it against the floor.

Caleb was taken aback and totally unprepared for such a personal outpour from Lucius. He was lost for words and a little suspicious that Lucius might have taken more than a fancy to Nora. She was a fine woman, beautiful inside and out but then so was his Molly. Their generous nature behind their drab grey past added testimony to the character of these determined young women. He smiled, "Maybe she was just frightened Lucius and you misread it and even if you did forget to lock up, its one night in all the years you've been here so not so bad. Few more days and it will all be forgotten, you'll see. Your Dads right too, we might have to work hard but we love what we do. Let's go get these barrels before those ladies drink the old ones dry!" He coaxed.

Caleb thought on what Lucius had said about his father. It touched him because Caleb held the same views on life. He did face challenges but he made sure to enjoy them as much as he was able, he paid attention to the reward he would gain from his work and all that he did in his life. Not just his earnings but he mostly worked with Molly at his side and loved being on his boat or in the pub. He enjoyed the company of the customers at The Boatman's Rest and loved being out on their boat. Yes, he did enjoy life, whatever he was doing and he hoped that Lucius would learn to do the same.

Lucius and Caleb ventured off outside into the cold to retrieve the barrels. Nora had returned to her work and stopped to talk now and again with Molly who was still beside the fire. Molly could see through the window that the work was done. She wrapped her shawl tightly and left to return the boat the short distance to their mooring. Lucius called out a couple of his customers to give the boat a sharp pull to speed up the process to get it in to the mooring spot.

Molly was on the deck, she looked over toward Lillian's boat and the field beyond, it had a thick mist forming as often happened with all the smog. As she stared out in to the distance, she was almost certain she could see the figure of a man, wearing a bowler type hat, walking across the field with a large bag in his hand. He looked quite short and walked extremely fast. It was so dark that she could barely see. She shouted out to the others "Who could that be, walking in the field over there?" They placed their hands over their brows as if the sun blinded their eyes, they all looked over in the direction of the field. The youngest of them, a man who had slipped and slid across the towpath as he pulled the rope, replied. "I'm not sure I see anyone Miss, might just be the light through the mist?" Everyone else shook their heads and other than Lucius and Caleb, they returned to the pub.

"It's unlikely anyone would be walking across that Moll, especially this time of night! Maybe this place is sending us all mad!" Lucius said, much to all their amusement. "Come over in the morning and we will sort out payment before work. Maybe Molly could join us lunchtime for a bite? I'm sure Nora wouldn't mind putting food up for us, if it means time with her dear friend?"

"Yes Lucius, I'm sure it's nothing to do with you needing us to ease the mood now, is it?" Molly raised her eyebrows and smiled at Lucius, which made him extremely curious at what Nora had said. He desperately wanted to know but he would not ask, so he returned a grin and they all bid each other good night. It had been a busy couple of days and they knew sleep would come easy.

Chapter 5 When Nora met Jimmy

Morning arrived with a golden glow. The sunlight beamed through the lace in the windows and cast a pretty pattern on to the wall in the cabin. Although still bitterly cold, the sight of the sun had lifted their spirits. The impending arrival of Spring reminded Molly of something she had recently crocheted, she grabbed it and went off to fetch Cobbles to take him to graze in the field for a while.

Caleb waited outside the pub to catch them as he always did when they wandered past. As they appeared from the stable gate, he desperately tried to quell the roar of laughter that built up deep inside his tummy. He could feel the sides of his mouth twitch and suddenly he had no choice, he could no longer contain himself, he shook with laughter! His eyes teared and his tummy ached from the relentless hysterics that he could no longer suppress. Lucius ran out of the pub to see what was so entertaining and that was it, he was off too! Their laughter echoed around the basin! Cobbles in all his glory, a huge, strong beautiful shire horse stepped toward them with little white lace caps that covered his ears, each with tassels swinging as he swayed from side to side! Molly walked proudly next to him and scowled at Caleb, she was not impressed by his actions and he knew he was in serious trouble when he saw her glare. Lucius laughed even harder at seeing Caleb turn crimson and almost choke from the struggled attempt to stem the laughter. Both hung onto the table in an effort to stay upright, as the laughter took over them. Caleb took three stumbled and stuttered tries to inform Lucius that "If Cobbles could talk right now, he would be begging me to remove those ridiculous things off his head!!" Molly with a bright red angry face, strode swiftly past them with her nose in the air and they watched the tassels on Cobbles little ear caps swing in the wind. Both men were done for, they could barely breath for laughter! For the whole morning, every time they caught glimpse of each other, they giggled like small children and that would start them off again!

Nora had prepared a lunch of bread, eggs, and cheese. She had been noticeably quiet, pondering on how to tell Lucius about her lies and had finally decided to tell him when they were alone. She had heard laughter coming from downstairs all morning and although she was pleased to hear that everyone was in good spirits, she had not felt the need to find out why.

At lunchtime, everyone gathered at the table and thanked Nora for the lovely spread. Lucius winked over at her and she felt a flutter in her tummy as their eyes met. They had barely pulled their chairs under the table before Molly scolded them both for laughing at her beautiful crochet! She reminded them both how important it was to keep the flies from Cobbles ears now Spring approached. How both kept a straight face, they didn't know but somehow, they managed it!

The smell of freshly cooked bread made their tummies grumble. Molly poured the hot steaming tea into the cups that were neatly laid out on the table. Nora sliced and spread the bread with fresh butter and cut into the creamy cheese, she laid chunks onto the plate. The sharp taste of the tangy cheese against the milky butter and doughy bread was a delight. The atmosphere was one of content and appreciation for the food and they chattered together happily.

Molly and Caleb told them about the occurrence Samuel had shared with them. "I remember that morning, I had slept through it and people had gossiped in the pub but non really knew what had truly happened." Said Lucius, after listening intently. "Never heard much detail, just that a man had drown here, with people speculating on who it was, you know me, I don't pay much mind to idle gossip."

Molly frowned and gulped down the mouthful of bread, "I would not consider that to be idle gossip Lucius, a man drowned. I am surprised that you didn't pay more attention!" She remarked bemused.

Lucius ignored her remark and took the loaf of bread to cut himself another slice.

Nora anxiously enquired, "Do you think it has anything to do with what's happening here then? It's so sad that lady lost her husband. She doesn't believe it was an accident either, how dreadful for her!"

"It could be Nora, maybe he's haunting this pub!" said Molly excitedly. "Why would he haunt this place though? Maybe something you have done Lucius! Such as ignoring the news!" she pointed at him and giggled.

"Yes, I probably threw him out for his false accusations!" Lucius mocked.

"Maybe we could get one of those spirit people in who can talk to the dead?" Caleb joked.

Everyone laughed and discussed whether this might be possible, or if it were just superstitious nonsense. It was decided that although it could be possible, it would probably cost a fortune and would therefore not be an option.

Lunch had been finished with gusto and their tummies were full. Lucius and Caleb headed off downstairs to the pub whilst Nora and Molly cleaned away. "Have you told him about the locks yet Nora?" Molly enquired sternly, as she set the white plates back on the shelf.

"Not yet, I will do so this evening, things seem a bit easier today so maybe it will be alright now?" Nora frowned.

Molly shrugged her shoulders, "He still deserves to know the truth, please tell him Nora, I am sure you will feel better for it too." they both went downstairs to join the others.

Molly stood at the front of the bar and feeling happy she began to sing, by the second song, the whole bar had joined in. They banged their hands on the tables and feet on the floor in time with the rhythm. Some clanked their tankards on the bar and others linked arms and twirled each other around to the brink of dizziness. It was a happy scene and one that occurred frequently at the Boatman's Rest.

During the jollies, two young men walked in, they were new to the alehouse and were delighted to find what a fun place it appeared to be. The eldest and first to walk in was Jimmy, whose arm Nora took swiftly and swirled him around before he had chance to get to the bar. Jimmy was not unpleased, in fact he beamed when he saw the nod of approval from his pal Edward. Jimmy was disappointed when the song and dance had stopped, he felt dizzy but quite exhilarated. Nora, panted and puffed after so much exercise and asked what they would like to drink. "Two ales please dear and perhaps you will join us for one?" Jimmy asked bashfully. Nora blushed and went to fetch their drinks.

Nora returned to the table, with her breath fully restored and head less wobbly, she was at once struck by Jimmy's charming, friendly face, and handsome smile. She had noticed straight away that he was easily as tall as Lucius but not quite so wide. He was slim with brown hair in a neat, sharp cut and was clean shaven which gave him quite a youthful appearance. It was evident that he was most definitely not a boatman with his clear complexion, smart jacket, shirt, trousers and polished shoes. Both men stood when she arrived at the table and Jimmy pulled a chair out for her to invite her to sit. She once again coloured, "Well maybe for a few minutes, then I must get back to work." She consented.

"Nice place to have on our doorstep and I think we will be coming here often now." Edward enquired of Jimmy, who had not taken his eyes off Nora.

Jimmy as if being taken out of a trance replied, "Oh yes, indeed we will Edward."

"So, you are locals then, where are you living?" asked Nora, she sipped her drink, the dance and sing a long had made her throat dry.

"We're footmen, just moved from a big house on the outskirts, it's our night off, so we're having a look around the place." Jimmy announced proudly.

"Oh, that's nice, I don't think I have met a footman before. I bet you see a lot in those big house's, all those rich folk in their fancy gear! "How long have you been in these parts?" She enquired.

"Well, we weren't far away before, just briefly at the Ellsworth Manor with our previous Lady. The Manor has closed for a while with just a few staff looking after it. We've been up at a big house just a few minutes away for about two weeks now." He explained. "My names Jimmy by the way and this is Edward and what is yours?" His casual demeanour hid his eagerness well.

"My name is Nora, how fascinating to work in a big house! You must come again and tell me all the gossip of how the gentry live. You will like it in here, we are a friendly bunch but now you must excuse me, I should get back to my work." She got up from her seat and they rose as she left. She felt embarrassed that they rose for her but quite impressed at the same time. What gentlemen, with lovely manners, she liked them and Jimmy was very pleasing to the eye!

Edward laughed quietly at the look of disappointment as Nora left so quickly, "Right then let's get back up to house, before they send out a search party for us." Jimmy followed behind Edward, he glanced back once more at Nora and managed to catch her eye.

Lucius had sat beside Molly and Caleb watching Nora like a hawk! She had only rested there for a matter of minutes but twice Lucius had stopped himself wandering over with the excuse that she should be at work. In truth, he did not like to see her sit and enjoy the company of other men, especially when one of them was quite obviously keen. He was relieved to see them part company and even more relieved when they said farewell and left the pub. He surmised and hoped that they were just passers-by, who were never to be seen again.

Molly had watched every grimace and twist on Lucius's face and was hopeful that one day they might both realise they were perfectly matched, she knew how stubborn they both were and very much stuck in their ways. She knew that Lucius had always been on his own, just choosing to have occasional friends rather than settle down and marry. He was content to have only himself and the alehouse to worry about but since Nora's arrival, Molly had seen a tremendous change in him. He had become far more approachable and upbeat, he took better care of himself and even looked well groomed. Nora, who she had known most of her life, was always a fiercely independent person. She had from an early age, taken on the responsibility of an adult in her work and personal life. She had always been feisty and had never held back but Molly had seen her change too. She knew Nora loved to have someone to take care of. She liked to cook and make a home for those who appreciated it just as her father did. In fact, Molly wanted to bang their heads together and tell them both to sort things out but she knew when not to interfere.

Nora joined their table, in a seat next to Molly. Old Jack huffed as she briefly added a barrier between him and the heat that bellowed out from the fire, his little dog let out a half-hearted whine as if in agreement with his master before he curled up even tighter. "We have new customers then Nora, I see you chatted with them, are they local?" asked Molly with a wry smile.

Nora ignored Molly's attempts to glean more information and replied "Yes, they are footmen at the big house, just moved here from some place called Ellsworth Manor, as it's closed for the time being." Lucius listened intently when Old Jack, suddenly joined in with the conversation.

He continued to puff on his pipe and uttered in his usual gruff manner, "Ellsworth Manor you say girl, God rest good old Lord Ellsworth, was him that drown here a while back, ya know? Good man, they say he was. Never met him me self but everyone had only good to say for him. Helped the farmers he did!" He turned back around and continued to sup his drink. All four turned toward him, each with mouths aghast and equally shocked that all this time and no one had mentioned the man's name before now!

Suddenly, the candles in the corner where they were seated, flickered almost fading out the light to darkness before they sprang back to full brightness again. Old Jack, turned his weathered and wrinkled face back toward them and pointed to the candles with his smouldering pipe, "There you see, he knows we're talking about him." He took the rope that functioned as lead for his dog and untied it from the bar. Giving it a gentle rock against the dog's collar, he raised his cap and bid them goodnight.

"Well, well!" declared Lucius, "We finally have a name to our mysterious man! Perhaps we can find out a bit more now?" He rubbed his fingers into his facial stubble as he always did when deep in thought.

"It would definitely be easier now we have a name Lucius but where would we start?" Nora puzzled.

"With you Nora." smirked Molly. "You could speak to those new customers they worked there! I bet they know all there is to know about it! We could go from there?" Her eyes were wide with enthusiasm.

Lucius was not happy at all! "Hold on Moll, it's not fair to ask Nora to get friendly with men she barely knows. No, no, I think there should be another way to do this, besides, we probably won't be seeing them again, will we?" He hoped.

"It's fine Lucius, they seemed jolly enough and looked eager to talk about their work, proud even! I think they would be happy to talk with me. They were both keen to return too, they liked the place!" Nora smiled.

"Yes, I'm sure they would!" Lucius answered bitterly, he gave a look of resentment toward Molly who shrugged it off in her usual manner. Molly hoped this would be the very thing that would ironically draw Lucius and Nora together.

"Well, we'll see, maybe something more will come up in the meanwhile or maybe they won't even come in here again. That will save Nora the trouble! Right Moll, time for our bed, we will see you both tomorrow." Announced Caleb.

With the pub emptied and closed for the night, Nora knew it was time she was honest with Lucius so she asked him to stay for a while before she retired for the night. He followed behind into her living area. He randomly picked up the candles from the mantle, his large hands almost hiding them from sight, sniffing each with an agreeable nod. Nora caught him as she turned from placing the kettle to hang over the fire. "Ah, you like the candles that Molly makes?"

He returned it to its resting place and mumbled, "Not my kind of thing Nora, still clever work for Mol though." He shrugged.

Nora looked seriously toward Lucius and her tummy flipped as she apprehensively announced, "Lucius, I have to tell you something and I don't want you to be angry with me." She felt her face burn as the blood rushed to her cheeks. She sat down in the chair for fear her legs might buckle.

"You're scaring me Nora, I'm most certain that nothing you tell me could possibly make me angry with you?" All manner of thoughts ran through his mind but he could not think of a single thing that she might be about to say! He felt it best to sit down too.

"Well, you might think differently in the next few moments." She started nervously and brushed down at her skirts, then quickly realised what she was doing and clasped her hands tightly into her lap, she reminded herself of what Molly had told her. "You recall the night that the doors down here were left unlocked?"

"I do Nora and I really am truly...."

Nora abruptly interrupted him, "Please let me speak".

He stood up and anxiously paced the room, he was concerned at what she may have seen and worried that she might be about to give her leave!

"Please sit Lucius" she forced a smile. "You see, I have to tell you that the doors were locked, I opened them when I woke earlier that morning and came upstairs ..." Her voice began to falter and she tilted her head to the floor. "I came across a woman's shawl and shoes and heard voices from your room, so I hurried back down the stairs. I wanted to save us all the embarrassment you, see?" She couldn't look at him. She was relieved that she had finally told the truth but held her breath waiting for his reaction.

Lucius's face had turned quite pale, he felt queasy and was almost certain she was about to tell him she was moving on. "Nora, I ..."

She halted him again, "Please Lucius, though I am shocked and feel more than awkward about this .... this thing, I must still apologise for being dishonest with you. It was very wrong and deceitful of me to allow you to go on believing that you had left the doors unlocked. I believed it to be for the best so that we could avoid the embarrassment. I didn't know that you had already been through some unexplained experiences, which of course didn't help?" She was quite out of breath, in a bid to get everything said, she had forgotten to breath!

The room fell silent. Lucius looked down at Nora, her head still bowed to the floor. She was relieved to have finally told the truth but could not dare look up. Lucius was speechless, he really did not know what to say. He was angry at her deceit but far more concerned that she knew he had Clara in his bedroom. Clara was just a bit of fun, she knew that and that is all she wanted from him, it had always been their agreement but Nora was different, he really liked her and he was upset that he had embarrassed her. He then began to wonder if she was just embarrassed or if she too had finally begun to realise that there was something between them.

Nora's discomfort increased with each second that passed. She could no longer bare the silence and had to say something ... anything to break it! "So, whilst it's up to you what you do with the likes of women such as Clara, it would be nice if you slipped me a note or put something to warn me outside your door. Not that I care, and of course it's your place

32

not mine, it's just that I'm not that kind of woman myself and don't wish to be witness to it. Once again though, I am terribly sorry and if you wish for me to leave then just say so." She suddenly wanted to take back every word of all she had said and kick herself extremely hard! If only she could be less impulsive and pause for thought before she spoke, she thought to herself.

Lucius was visibly perplexed, he felt like he had experienced every emotion known to man in the short he had gotten to know this complicated woman. She lifted her head and looked up at him boldly, which frustrated him even more because he thought this was supposed to be an apology, yet she looked so vexed. His head throbbed and prevented him from simple articulation, so instead he simply replied, "Thank you for your apology and I must apologise too for putting such a virtuous woman in such an embarrassing position." She detected a hint of sarcasm in his reply but allowed him to continue. "I will be far more discreet in my future liaisons and of course I do not wish you to leave. After all, you have a customer to befriend, just to help in our endeavour and of course with no benefit to yourself!" With that, Nora flung open the door and Lucius marched out and slammed it behind him.

Chapter 6 The Figure in the Mist

The days passed by and The Boatman's Rest was as busy as always with the regulars and passers-by looking for a friendly place to rest. Molly was tucked inside her cabin, an array of paints, brushes, oils and fabrics were all stored away neatly into a small trunk that she had removed from under their seating area and placed on to the seat. She was busy painting jugs and bowls, so Caleb had been happy to escape the chaos to go and help at the ale house. Lucius and Nora continued to be at odds with one and another and communicated through sarcastic jibes throughout the entire day. The customers had found them hilarious and humorously referred Nora to Lucius as, 'The Mrs.' which of course would set her off on a rant.

There had been no sight of Lillian for some time and Molly had become genuinely concerned. She knew she was there because she had witnessed lit lanterns inside Lillian's cabin each night and the hatches had been opened and closed for the snappy dog to go in and out of. It was strange not to see her out on deck and although she never exchanged a word with her, she had become accustomed to spotting her in her chair. Molly was aware of Lillian's obvious fragility and wondered if there was anything, she could do to check on her welfare.

It was late one evening when Caleb and Molly returned from the pub that Caleb thought he saw a figure wander across the field from Lillian's boat. "Moll, do you see that? Looks like a man wandering across the field there!" He stopped and pointed into the distance. It was early spring and there was not so much mist around, Caleb craned his neck to try and get a better view.

Molly strained her eyes to try and see far into the distance in the direction that Caleb pointed, "Yes Caleb, I see! It looks like the very same man that I saw before, same hat and he has the bag! Where do you suppose he's going and why would he walk this way?" She paused in thought, "You know Caleb, I'm sure Timmy would lend us a rowboat just to go over and check on Lillian, who knows that man might be calling on her and goodness knows why?" Timmy was the carpenter on the corner of the basin, he liked Molly and loved to go to the pub to hear her sing. She knew he would agree.

Caleb's expression was puzzled as he looked at his wife, "Moll, she would probably set that crazy dog on you even if you dared go near! What are you thinking of woman?!"

Molly chuckled, "She is a frail old lady Caleb, she's got no one looking out for her, I know she's a strange one but I would like to help if I can."

"I know what you're like Molly once you've made up your mind there's no changing it. If we don't see her soon, then we will both go. You must not go alone Molly do you understand?" He looked at her sternly and he searched her eyes for honesty.

Molly nodded and smiled. With the man now out of sight they headed back into the warmth and comfort of their boat.

During the following evening, Molly was telling Nora about her plans to go and check on Lillian, when Jimmy and Edward walked in unexpectedly. Molly gave Nora a firm push and almost threw her into their path and whispered, "At last, here's your chance." Nora looked back at her with a comically scornful grin.

"Nora, we thought we would call in again, we had so much fun last time. Can you sit with us for a while?" Requested Jimmy with a cheerful smile.

Nora glanced at Lucius, who stood behind the bar, he shrugged his shoulders and threw up his hands as if to admit defeat and turned his back on them.

"Your boss not keen on you taking a break Nora? Would it be polite if I were to ask him?" Suggested Edward.

"No, it's fine, he doesn't mind at all. He's good to me really but don't tell him I said so!" She smirked and took a seat with them. She thought that Jimmy was every bit as handsome as she had remembered him to be. He was quite charming too, he barely took his eyes off her and she enjoyed this attention.

"Are you both still enjoying your new position, I bet it's a beautiful house to work in?" She thought she would start subtle and work her way up.

"Yes, it's very grand! A huge house that belongs to an influential family, they own lots of land. They visit London frequently in their carriages as well! The butler says that some of the staff go with them on occasion." Jimmy talked with such pride, he loved his work. "I hope to be Butler one day, I watch them at work and I know that I could do it." Edward nodded avidly in agreement with Jimmy.

Molly had already caught Edwards eye during the evening that they had arrived. He spotted her again, wandering around close by, "Who is that lady Nora?" He asked.

"Oh, she is my best friend, that's Molly and the man over there by the lantern is her husband, Caleb." She smiled apologetically at Edward, who looked sullen. She continued, "So you might go to London then, what an adventure!"

"Well, yes, if we get chosen Nora." enthused Jimmy, "Of course just a few months a time but imagine! It's much busier than the old place in Shrewsbury. We travelled up from Shrewsbury with Mrs Haughton and had a short stay at Ellsworth Manor. Mrs Haughton is the sister of the owner's wife, Lady Ellsworth. We stayed there briefly but she's had to shut the place up for a while because of complications. I bet her husband needs her back as well Nora!" He paused for a drink and to ensure Nora had not become bored of his conversation. To his delight, she looked intrigued.

Edward feeling a little like a third wheel joined in, "It was a funny situation there Nora, not that we are at liberty to tell of course but very odd indeed." Edward widened his eyes and raised his eyebrows, he took a sip of his drink and hoped that Nora would push for more.

"Oh dear, now I shall always wander what Jimmy and Edward found at Ellsworth Manor! I guess it must be top secret and no one must know. Of course, I wouldn't tell a soul if I knew myself." She hoped that would put them at ease, she gave a reassuring nod and pressed her forefinger to her lips to help reassure them.

"Not all of it is secret." said Jimmy, he looked questioningly at his friend for reassurance. Edward nodded his approval and Jimmy continued. "Well, Ellsworth Manor was owned by Lord Ellsworth, you know the man that drown here in the canal?" Nora nodded. "Well shortly before he left the house that day, one of the housemaids just handed in her leave with no explanation. She had been on course to a far better position in the house but just left suddenly. She spoke only to the housekeeper before leaving and that was it, gone just like that! Nobody has seen her since. Then after the body of Lord Ellsworth was found, Lady Ellsworth was committed to an asylum, the Doctor said the shock of it all sent her quite mad! That was a while ago now though of course, so Gawd only knows where the housemaid got to! That's not all!" His voice raised slightly, as his head tilted questioningly "Lady Ellsworth disappeared from the asylum and that's why her sister has closed the house! No one knows what happens in these circumstances you see, they had no children either, so there were no young'uns to take care of? How can a Lady just go missing like that Nora, on her own as well?"

Nora could not hide her fascination, she was also drawn in by Jimmy. He was so animated when he told his story and his facial expressions gave momentum to every word. He spoke about the family as though they were lifelong friends and she found it so endearing. She was genuinely intrigued by the tale and the man who told it. "Do you know the housemaids name Jimmy? It would be interesting to know if we have ever crossed paths?" She enquired.

Both men shook their heads, Edward turned toward Jimmy, "Maybe the housekeeper, Mrs Tranter would know her name? She was the one that the maid spoke to before she left. We didn't stay there long and didn't really like to ask too many questions about that time. Everyone was still so upset by it all, it didn't seem right to enquire further." Edward revealed.

"You're right Edward." agreed Jimmy. "She might know but I don't know if she would tell it. She's still at the mansion Nora. They left staff there to keep the mansion aired and clean but let the rest go. It was sad to see them all leave, they were given good references but none of them wanted to go. Mrs Haughton told them that she would send out word at once if the house were re-opened and they could return to their positions. Of course, they are also in the hope that Lady Ellsworth might return. Edward and I really like it up this way, so we found new positions, instead of going back to Shrewsbury with Lady Haughton, she was disappointed but she understood."

Jimmy looked down at Nora's pretty face, her bright green eyes glowing with curiosity. He really wanted to ask her to take a walk with him but was taking a while to muster up the courage. He was by far the more confident of the two young footmen but he had never met a woman like Nora before, he had been used to more ... timid women. "Do you have a day off from here Nora?" There was a sudden loud clash that came from behind the bar. Lucius had heard Jimmy's question and it threw him off guard, causing him to drop a full tankard, despite the desperate juggle to save it, it landed hard at his feet! Molly and Caleb also close by could not help but chuckle as Lucius fumbled and tried to look composed when the whole pub turned to see where the noise had come from.

"I do indeed Jimmy, though I usually stay here with friends and pass my time with them. If I were to do anything different, I must be back to prepare the evening meal." She quickly glanced back at Lucius who had his back to them and pretended not to listen to their conversation. She did not want to give Lucius any reason to feel bad but he had made it clear, he intended to continue his dalliance with Clara and besides all that, she had warmed to Jimmy. Most importantly, she was also on a mission to solve a mystery and this could only help!

Jimmy, told himself to be forthright and plucked up the courage and asked "Well then Nora I wonder if you might join me in a walk around the park? There would be lots of people around so we wouldn't be alone for a single moment and the cook is a kind lady who thinks a lot of me. I am sure she would pop a few things in a basket for us to have a picnic?"

Edward smiled, he was incredibly impressed with his friend's achievement. If he had a pencil in his pocket, he would have taken notes for when he came across such a situation. He waited with as much anticipation as Jimmy for Nora's reply.

She was so overwhelmed with the invite, he had even respected her enough to make sure they were not alone. "That would be nice of you Jimmy, give me notice and I am sure I can sort out a day off with permission from Lucius. I have never had a picnic or a walk in the park."

Suddenly Lucius loomed behind her seat, he smiled like a friendly giant with his huge frame that blocked the light from the window. She did not need to turn her head, she instinctively knew it was him.

"Can I get you gents another drink?" He asked dryly. "Did I hear mention of my name Nora?" he continued with a wry smile.

"I can get their drinks thanks Lucius and I'm surprised you heard a thing with all that banging over there." she smiled sarcastically back at him. She raised her eyebrows and nodded her head backwards in a bid to tell him to go away.

He saw it but ignored her, "Well, it's difficult Nora, as you can see it's a full house and we're very busy!" He retorted.

She looked up at him with a scowl on her face. Molly watched closely, she nudged Caleb to get his attention and poor Jimmy and Edward did not know which way to turn!

"Well then Lucius, we mustn't keep you here with idle chit chat, then, must we?!" Nora snapped loudly. "I am simply taking my break Lucius, I will be back to work in one moment!"

"No Nora, you will be back to work now!" His eyes were wide, lips taught and he frowned in frustration.

Jimmy stood up from his chair and everyone but Lucius looked nervous at what might be about to unfold. "Sorry Mr, it seems we are keeping Nora from her work, come on Edward it's time we were getting back anyway" Edward stood up relieved, he hadn't rated either of their chances against this beast, "We will call again soon Nora and make arrangements." He tipped his cap and they both left.

Nora grabbed at her seat and scraped it back hard against the stone floor. She marched across to the bar, snatched a towel and scrubbed so hard that Molly thought she might make a hole through the wood. Lucius fumed with resentment at the way she had spoken to him in front of all their patrons and followed behind her, "A word in private Nora." She threw the cloth onto the bar and strode off into the hallway in front of him. Everyone in the bar gathered in pockets of whispers about what they thought was going on. Molly thought it best to get a sing a long going, so she kept them busy and quickly drew their attention away from gossip with her beautiful voice.

Out in the hallway Lucius raged, "You must never, ever speak to me in that manner again in front of the patrons Nora. This is my establishment and while we are in there, you are my employee!" He stabbed his finger toward the bar.

She looked up at him with a steely glare, "Very well Lucius, as your employee I will be on my best behaviour from now on! As a worker at your pub, then I request my day off which is my right and I will give you due notice of. As we are talking of it, then what exactly am I, when I am not in there?!" She stabbed her finger toward the bar.

Disheartened, he slowly walked away and murmured, "My tenant and housekeeper Nora and of course you can take a day off."

Nora watched him walk away, shaking her head in frustration. She dusted at her skirts before re-entering the bar and acted as though nothing had happened.

As night time fell and each of them went to their own rooms, they both felt overwhelmed by sadness. Neither of them wanted to argue or fight but both were exasperated. If only they could be honest about how they felt, they were sure it would turn things around. The strange thing was that they both had the same thoughts and both expected the other to come forward first.

Chapter 7 Maud gets Creative

Lucius woke the next morning with a determination to fix things with Nora. Even if there couldn't be more, then they should at least be friends. He loathed the thought of her going out on a fancy picnic with that young man but he wouldn't attempt to thwart any hope of happiness that she may have. She was a lovely girl, gutsy and strong, with had a good, kind heart. She was all that he admired in a woman, maybe one day he would reveal his true feelings but, in the meantime, he just wanted for them to be back on good terms.

He splashed his face with cold water, dressed and headed toward the mirror. He lifted the comb from the mantelpiece, but it slipped from his grip, and fell to the floor. He Bent down and picked it up but was overwhelmed by the sense that he was not alone. "Is that you Nora?" he called out into the empty room as he stood back up. He received no response and walked precariously toward the kitchen, he glanced around the room, which was empty and silent. He went back to the living area but as he walked through the door, in the corner of his eye, he caught a flash of darkness speed past him accompanied by an abrupt freezing breeze that encompassed him momentarily and chilled him to the core! Determined to ignore it he headed straight back to the mirror. With apprehension, he lifted his head and immediately yelled out in fear, as right behind his shoulder he saw the palest grey, enraged face of a man stood tall over him in a top hat. He dropped the comb and clenched his fists, he turned ready to strike whoever this was behind him but there was no one there! He gripped the mantlepiece tight with both hands in a bid to steady himself and stared back into his own terrified face.

Nora heard the yell and ran up the stairs, she arrived to see Lucius clearly pale and shaken. She went straight across to him and put her hand gently on his shoulder "What happened Lucius? You look distraught?". She asked softly.

Lucius eventually sat down and attempted to explain himself, as he spoke, he was aware of how crazy the whole thing must sound to somebody else. Nora took his hand and gave it a squeeze, "Lucius, I know we don't always see eye to eye but maybe if we all come together on this, we can find a solution? This situation is not going to get any better by doing nothing, I think it's time you let us help you." Nora said calmly. She kept her true feelings well hidden behind a smile of confidence and empathy. In truth she wanted them both to flee the room! She was scared that the ghost or whatever this was might come back and she did not want to catch sight of it.

Lucius sighed loudly, "I know Nora and I am sorry for how we bicker." he grinned toward her, "Perhaps we can all sit down and try to find an answer, I don't want to live like this, there must be something we can do!" He entrusted.

Nora rose and stood with enthusiasm, "Then that's what we shall do! We will get together and make plans to sort this out once and for all."

Lucius felt a little relieved, he was glad that they had spoken and reassured that the situation was being taken seriously. Nora made her way into the kitchen, to make breakfast. He shook his head in a bid to remove the vision he had seen before him in the mirror. He knew she was right, he did need his friends and although he never liked to depend on others, he was grateful for them.

As discussed, later that day the four of them gathered to talk. With all the weird and unexplainable issues, their curiosity had heightened and become a need to know. Maude and George were seated at a table next to them and were within hearing distance of everything that was said. The pair had been regulars to the ale house for many years and had always been well known for their nosiness and idle gossip. Maud, sensing an opportunity, aggressively elbowed George in his ribs and thrust her head toward the groups table. She tugged on her ear violently instructing him to listen. She ploughed her elbow into George's arm again. "Here" she whispered to him, "Just play along George, or you'll be singing for your supper tonight!" George frowned with worry as he often did when he knew that his wife was scheming. His grey eyebrows almost met in the middle and his deep wrinkles bent with despair at what she may have in mind now.

"Excuse me?" she quietly murmured over at the group, her hand hovered at the side of her mouth in an attempt to indicate secrecy. Her dirty grey fingerless mittens revealed almost blue fingers, with dirt engrained nails from years of arduous work and lack of hygiene. "I'm experienced in these matters ... some might say an expert!" She declared triumphantly. "Not that I'm sitting here listening to yer conversation, just couldn't help over hearing." They all turned to look at her in confusion. George who thought he had seen his wife turn every trick in the book to earn a quick penny, realised she may be going a little too far with this one and hung his head with his hand over his brow.

"No of course you weren't listening to us Maud." Lucius replied sarcastically. Maud feigned offence but listened for more.

"So, you're an expert then Maud, what can you tell us? I presume you heard most of it, even though you weren't listening?" Caleb mocked and waited curiously for her reply.

"Well," said Maud, who had risen to her feet and leant right over their table, her odour cast a stench that caught the back of their throats and smarted their eyes. Like a green mist that transcended right up through the nose, down the back of the throat and into the stomach that caused them to wretch! They moved their heads as far back as they possibly could to maintain hearing range without the offensive odour and listened. "I could tune in to em, you know talk to em, find out what they want and such! It wouldn't be easy mind you! Of course, would have to charge a few bob, it takes all my energy, it does, don't it George?!"

George looked over, completely puzzled, and wondered why she drew him into a conversation, he had no idea of where it was to head.

"Yes dear, all your energy." he mumbled half-heartedly.

Molly perked up, she had heard about these spirit mediums! There had been a lot of talk about ladies in America that could talk to the dead and they would respond by making noises and such. She very much doubted Maud was credible but who knew, maybe she was and it might be worth a try?

"Maybe we should give Maud a chance Lucius? If nothing else, it could prove to be entertaining?" Molly spurted. She looked over at Nora who glared back at the group in disbelief.

"Very well then why not!" Lucius declared with zeal. "What do you need Maud and when shall we do it?"

Maud was thrilled and rubbed her grubby hands together as she said, "No time like the present Mr Lucius! I just need you to cross my palm, so to speak. We better off going upstairs, don't want no one thinking I'm a bit weird." George rolled his eyes at her comment as she continued, "Candle and a table is all I need after that."

It was decided, Old Jack would look after the pub and the six of them would go upstairs and hold a séance. Maud went up first, her huge frame spread from one side of the wall to the other as she huffed her way up. She had always been curious to see the upstairs of the pub and now was her chance along with the opportunity to fleece a shilling off Lucius into the bargain. She was an incredibly happy woman! George followed behind and in complete opposite comparison, he was a very slight man, with a tiny slim frame. Both had to be at least in their late fifties, their grey shabby hair, unkempt clothing and deep lines on their faces aged them beyond their years. The couple had worked in their younger lives but alcohol consumption had disrupted their employability and caused them to find other ways to make a quick shilling. A deprived and unhealthy life had become their only way.

The others followed up the stairs closely behind, each of them held their hands over their noses!

Nora opened the window, "To let some air in." much to the relief of Molly and Caleb. Two candles were lit and placed on the table and all were seated around in a circle. Maud had insisted that George sat directly opposite her.

Maud spotted her favourite, sitting high up on a shelf, she put the back of her palm to her forehead and with a forlorn look declared, "I see you have a bottle of the old gin there Lucius, maybe just a drop to settle me nerves before I begin?"

Lucius shook his head in mild disgust, he walked across to the sideboard and retrieved the bottle and a glass for Maud. He put the glass on the table and poured a short measure of gin. He went to walk away but felt Maud's grip on his arm, "Probably best, leave it there ya know, just in case." She stuck out both her hands in a trembling motion, her long fingernails encrusted with black grime. Lucius knew her tremble was fake but he slammed the bottle down on to the table regardless. Maud smiled up at him and revealed the few remaining teeth that she had left, "Good on ya Lucius."

Caleb struggled not to laugh and questioned, "Can we get on now Maud?"

"You can't rush these things young man!" she retorted and shuffled in her chair. "Light the candle on the table George and snuff the rest." she ordered. "Right before I start," she commanded, enjoying the prospect of being in charge for once. "I will need you all to keep yer mouths shut unless I say different! Absolute silence or I can't be responsible for what happens, do you all understand?" She had a formidable look on her face, as she scoured the group one by one to ensure their compliance. Everyone nodded in agreement and George began to believe that his wife could in fact speak to the dead.

The dim light and slight breeze from the open window cast a flicker of candlelight across their faces, adding to an already eerie atmosphere. Molly and Nora were quite relieved at the next request, "Everyone needs to hold the hand of the person next to them, do not let go unless I say different, the circle must not be broken, do you all understand?" Again, the scary scour for approval as Maud met the eyes of each one of them, they once again nodded in agreement.

George sat in the middle of Nora and Molly, he was more than happy to hold their hands and his big smile certainly showed it. Maud was seated in between Caleb and Lucius and happily took their hands in hers. Molly reached over for Caleb's hand and Lucius to Nora's, the circle was complete. "I'm about to start!" declared Maud, "You might see and hear strange things from me but you must not break the circle at any time, till I say so! Do not disturb me either, I might be in a trance!" George was impressed with his wife, she never failed, well rarely anyway...

41

Maud closed her eyes and dramatically thrust her head back, "ooh, ooooh, ooh!" she cried, like an owl with an added high-pitched screech for maximum effect. She thrashed her head from side to side as her face twisted and contorted as if she was in torture, "ooooo, is anyone there? Is anyone there?!" She hissed through the gaps in her missing front teeth. Everyone looked at her half amused and half petrified at what they witnessed. "If anyone is there, knock once..." She opened her eyes and looked around. She closed them again and shouted with more gusto, "If anyone is there, knock once..." She opened one red hazy eye and scowled over at George, giving him a swift, sharp kick into his bony shin under the table and shouted louder this time. "If anyone is there, knock once!" George tried his hardest not to scream out in pain and wondered how on earth he was to knock, when she had made them all hold hands. Maud, with her one angry red eye still fixed on George had become increasingly impatient and tried her hardest to eye under the table to him. He finally understood her gestures and tapped his foot on the floor. Everyone turned, looking at one another in astonishment and nodding to acknowledge that they had heard it. Maud was pleased, they had seemed to believe it, she went on, "Can you knock once more to show us you are there?" George tapped the floor again and was rather happy with himself.

The four of them felt unnerved but still unsure. Maud continued, she threw her head up and rolled her eyes back, so that only the whites were shown. The girls gasped in horror and Nora very nearly fled but Lucius grasped her hand as he felt her grip loosen.

"Who is here with us?" Maud asked as there were another two loud knocks. Then suddenly, in a voice that sounded like she was in an audition for amateur drama class, she boomed back, "I am a ghost, I am him, what drowned in the canal."

Lucius began to fidget in his seat, he wondered to himself what kind of gent would use such expression. He could feel his irritation rising but he did not want to be hasty and settled back into the chair.

Maud continued, "Tell us your name, who are you ghost?" Her eyes returned to normal positioning again before she thrust them back, once again she boomed, "Mind yer own business, I am him what drowned!"

Lucius had gone beyond irritated and nearly threw the table over in rage, whilst Maud still sat in her fake trance like state. George's head bobbed around like a budgie on his perch and the others laughed hysterically.

"Him what drowned in the canal Maud!" Lucius fumed, "Do us a favour! You expect us to believe that?! He would say his name or something, not I am him what drowned in the canal, he was a gentleman, not a bloody peasant. You're lucky I gave you that shilling before you started or you would have nothing now, go on clear off back downstairs!!"

Maud looked seriously insulted, she quickly grabbed the glass and gulped back the remainder of the gin. "I'm offended I am!" She sulked. "Maybe it's another man what drowned in the canal ey? Who knows?! I don't know, do a man a favour and this is the thanks I get! Don't be asking me for my professional help again Lucius, you won't be getting any!" Suddenly with a pensive look her manner changed. "We aint barred are we, just for a misunderstanding?" she grimaced at him, her tongue slightly protruding through the gap in her teeth.

"No, you aint barred... YET! Clear off downstairs before I change my mind, the pair of ya!" George had already headed for the doorway.

Maud mumbled about how unfairly she had been treated and set off down the stairs closely behind George. "Your bloody fault!" She hissed at George. "I didn't signal for you to make those last two knocks, you went too far!"

George shook his head in disbelief, he could never be bothered to argue with her, it was always futile and it was always his fault! "I would agree dear, but it was not me that time, I thought it were you that knocked the floor! Maybe there were a ghost?" Maud knew George was telling the truth, his left cheek and eye twitched rapidly when he told a lie! With that, they both fled as quick as they could, almost tripping over each other to get back to the safety of their seats!

Lucius picked up the bottle of gin and with a roar of laughter, gladly poured them all a glass. "What on earth were we thinking?" They all laughed and glugged down their drinks, despite being duped by Maud, it had helped to break the ice between Lucius and Nora and had given them some fun entertainment.

Nora and Molly stayed upstairs whilst the others went down to look after the pub. Molly was curious to know what Nora had thought of Jimmy, "So Nora, you are going out walking with Jimmy then?" she enquired with her cheeky grin that informed Nora she wanted to know more!

"I am, he's sweet aint he Moll! He is so charming and was being so lovely, telling me all about the big posh houses. Besides, he can help us get more information?" She said excitedly.

Molly chuckled at her, "It will be good for you to get out of here and take a nice walk Nora, you deserve some happiness! I do have an idea though." She scanned the room to make sure no one could hear, she wanted Nora's thoughts on her suggestion first, "What if we were to go to Ellsworth Manor?" Nora frowned in confusion but Molly went on, "We pretend we are looking for work and ask to see the housekeeper ... that Mrs Tranter, who Jimmy mentioned? You could ask him on your walk what he thinks, just tell him that I want employment Nora. What do you think?" Molly was quite excited at the thought of it all.

Nora thought for a while, "Wait Moll, we couldn't go dressed like this? We need some proper clothes and Moll, I really could do with something to walk out with Jimmy. He might feel like he's walking with a sack of potatoes if I turn out like this!"

Molly's bright eyes widened with excitement, "Then we go to the market just as they open in the morning, there's that stall with all the clothes that nobody wants anymore. We both have a bit saved by Nora and they won't cost us much at all!" Molly sprung from foot to foot with joy at the thought she may be able to own a real dress for the first time ever. "I reckon we could talk him into selling us each one for a couple of bob! I can make the alterations Nora, no problem!"

Nora beamed at the thought and they talked of colours and styles and how they would fashion their hair until it dawned on them that they really should have been back downstairs quite some time ago! As soon as they reached the bar, they realised that they had no need of worry because the sight before them made them weep with laughter. Caleb had wrapped on Molly's shawl and mimicked Maud's performance from upstairs, whilst Lucius swirled around behind him with a bar towel over his head and pretended to be a ghost. Maud shouted profanities and threw small lumps of coal at them both, whilst George clung to his belly as he laughed so hard! It proved to be one of the most fun days that they had in a long while and in a strange way, it was all down to Maud's cunning ways, though no one was about to let her know that.

Lucius looked around his bar that evening with pride and began to realise just what a lucky man he was. He did not have riches beyond dreams, but he had his kin folk and his friends. He had a reliable income and a little savings put by for whenever he would need it. He had always believed that this would be a life for a single man, but as he surveyed the room full of happy faces, he thought that actually it would be appreciated even more if he were to share it. Sure, he had his female friends in the past, including Clara but they were women who just wanted some occasional fun which had once been all he wanted too. He thought differently now, he was a fortunate man and ready to share some of that with someone he cared for. Maybe even a stroll in the park was not such a bad idea, after all that fresh air must be nice, especially if you're walking with your sweetheart.

At the end of the night everyone cheered George on his numerous attempts to get to the top of the slope, he had drank so much that his legs no longer felt like they belonged to him. He had found every endeavour to step on the wet cobbles so humorous that he collapsed in giggles each time his alien foot hit the ground. He slid back down on those cobbles more times than anyone could count and even Maud was beside herself with laughter.

The smog and the mist lifted from the night air, as fires and lights were extinguished all around the town. The night fell silent and everyone slept soundly after an enjoyable evening of kinship and fun.

Chapter 8 The Market Place

There was still a chill in the air but the icy sting that bit into fingers and toes had now gone. The dark grey skies were replaced with the sun peeking over the clouds during the misty mornings. Over the past couple of weeks Molly had convinced Caleb that her idea of going to Ellsworth Manor had been a good one. She had even managed to sell the idea of getting a pretty frock to him and that was no easy feat to accomplish! Lucius and Nora had come to a much-needed truce and apart from a little bicker here and there they had become far more tolerant of each other. Of course, she was yet to go on the impending trip to the park with Jimmy this Sunday and hoped this would not affect their progress. Random items had continued to disappear from around the ale house, only to return in a different place a few days or sometimes hours later. It had become such a part of their everyday lives that they just accepted it and barely took much notice anymore.

Lillian had still not been seen as much as she had been when she first arrived. She rarely appeared on deck and when she did it was for barely a minute or so to watch her dog jump off and then immediately retreat inside. Molly had become increasingly concerned for her welfare and was still determined to row across one day and check on her.

At 6am Molly and Nora were ready to leave for the market, both were beside themselves with excitement. The sun shone bright over the basin when the ladies greeted each other noisily, neither of them seemed to have a care for anyone that may still be asleep!

Huddled together arm in arm, they headed off up the cobbled slope and out into the dusty street. Wet clothes were already hung out on string outside the homes of the cramped smoky streets. Children ran barefoot calling to each other, barely dressed enough for a summer day, let alone early spring. It made Molly shudder to think how cold they must be but their giggles and hollers made her smile. The tall, dank buildings shaded much of the sun and Nora jumped to a halt as she manoeuvred around a middle-aged lady who bashed at a tiny bit of rug with a large stick. Clouds of brown dust burst from the fabric and settled on to the floor, intermingled with the rest of the dirt and muck from the surrounding factories.

The women strolled on, these dark, murky streets had a life in them that could never be explained. The people in this neighbourhood did not have a lot but they had homes and neighbours they knew all the names of. The children knew each other and ran errands together, worked in the factories together and with little time they had to play, they did so together. It was a community united by the understanding of tough labour, each person knew and felt the hardship but were grateful for the work and a home to rest their heads in.

As they approached closer to the market, the atmosphere changed, the welcome familiar smells and sounds carried down the street in prelude to the hustle and bustle of the busy stalls. Fires bins lined the streets and traders warmed themselves with hands hovered over the smoky yellow embers. Mothers with their babies wrapped in shawls called out their wares alongside the men with their differentiated deep, loud almost melodic tones. Nora breathed in deeply as they passed the fruit and vegetables stand, her mouth watered at the thought of biting into a juicy red apple. "We'll get some on our way back, if we have change!" Molly chuckled when she saw the desire in Nora's face.

Nora agreed and smiled widely when she spotted the clothing stall, she nudged Molly, "There it is Molly! Oh, I am so excited Moll but what if we can't find anything that fits!" She quizzed.

"We'll make it fit Nora, we find something we like and make it fit!" Molly was already rifling through the clothing and pulled out some dresses that she thought might be suitable quickly replacing them as they looked too worn.

It proved to be quite a difficult task, much of the clothing was as drab as the clothes they had on, they were both a little disheartened. The trader made his way over to them and Nora nudged Molly, "He's on his way over Mol, remember we need to soften him up, he does look a bit hard faced though!".

He was an exceptionally large man who looked like he had seen a brawl or two in his day, his thick wide moustache and bushy beard barely hid a deep scar down his cheek. "What can I help you fine young ladies with this morning? A beautiful bonnet to compliment those sparkling eyes perhaps. A pair of silk gloves to keep those delicate fingers covered on these coldest of days?" He pulled out the items and placed them in front of the ladies as he delivered his well-practiced sales pitch.

Nora and Molly giggled and smiled at him, their aim was to make him feel like he was the only human being present in their company. They knew these stall holders would say anything to sell their wares and they were about to play him at his own game. They lent against the makeshift table that was the man's market stall and paid him their undivided attention. Their fake laughter resounded loudly at every quip he made and they told him what an outstanding choice of clothes he had, they had drawn quite a lot of attention to his stall. "My kind sir," Molly beamed, "me and my friend here must get work, or we might find ourselves landed in the workhouse or even worse if you understand? Well, we certainly won't get a look in with these old rags we have on now, will we?!" She lowered her head and feigned sadness, Nora complied. Mutters of pity came from the group that had gathered around the stall. "Go on love, help em out, pretty young things deserve your help!" came a woman's voice from the group, Nora turned to the lady and acknowledged her with a solemn smile.

"Right, you are ladies, you chose the right man here. I do presume you intend to pay of course, I mean I can help but I'm no charity!" He quipped. He heard an "Argh!" come from the crowd, "I'm sure I can do you a deal though, now the rest of you lot, be off with ya, let a man do his trade!" The last thing he wanted was everyone to see him being soft. He knew if they saw him cut too much of a deal, they would send all manner of folk to his stall in expectation of trade for practically nothing, no he needed to do this out of ear shot!

He ushered them toward an alleyway, just behind his stall where there were two wooden boxes covered over with large sheets. "Take a look in there, ladies I save these for me best customers when I do me trip up to London. Now they aint cheap but as you got me quite a gathering of folk today at me stall, I'm willing to compromise with ya. Mind you, it's got to be kept between us, you don't go breathing a word to those scallies out there! Are we agreed?" Molly and Nora nodded eagerly. "Right, I'll leave you to look and there's nowt in there worth less than a shilling and that's at a bargain price! I know exactly what's in there so no pilfering!" Molly gave him a look of shock at such a suggestion and both women dug in the box before he had time to get back to his customers.

The ladies chose three beautiful outfits, Molly had insisted Nora had two, one for her outing with Jimmy and the other for their visit to Ellsworth. Despite Nora's protests, Molly was adamant that Nora took both but now to convince Will the trader to take a shilling for all three! Nora stuck her head around the alleyway entrance to gain Will's attention, with a finger bent beckoning him over, Molly paraded up and down with the dress held in front of her. "Sir, doesn't that look grand? How did you happen upon such beautiful items, you must have a great eye for clothing!" She continued quickly, "Can you imagine my friend and I parading around in these fine garments for all to see and we can tell them to go and see Will the Trader, he has the finest clothing on offer!" Will hid the smile that would have told them that he knew exactly what they were up to, he was far too amused by their shenanigans. He would easily have knocked any man into the middle of next week had he tried to pull the wool over his eyes!

Will leant against the wall and chuckled to himself, he secretly thanked the Lord, he never had a daughter himself. "Right ladies, so that's three outfits chosen, at my reckoning, that's three shilling" He smiled and opened out his hand to them, squeezing his fingers back and forth over his palm.

"Well sir." began Molly, "You see, we don't have three shillings but we adore these outfits, so maybe we could be your advocates, you know. Tell everyone where to go for such fine items." Will frowned and shook his head from side to side, he returned his hand back toward Molly without comment.

Molly looked at Nora in desperation. "Yes sir, we will most definitely and we do have two shillings, surely two shillings is better than having them stuck in that box and stinking away till you go to London?" enthused Nora. Molly frowned in confusion at her, she believed that they had agreed on one shilling. Nora shrugged her shoulders, she knew a tradesman from these parts wouldn't go that far.

Molly gazed right into his eyes, she clutched onto one of the outfits, "Yes, two shillings' sir and we will ask our landlord to wait this week's rent money because I'm certain, showing up in these outfits will get us just the work we need."

Will looked back at his stall and saw a crowd still gathered, he felt a mix of anger and happiness at his own generosity and suddenly said, "Right, one shilling for the three and I expect to hear my name all around town! Not a word to anyone about prices, do you hear!" Both ladies jumped for joy and gave Will a big hug! He wrapped their clothing in paper and tied it with string. As they made their way from the stall Will shouted, "I expect you to come back and tell me where you are working, that's the best three shilling you spent!" Molly turned and winked at him and Nora blew him a kiss.

The smell of hot cocoa and coffee filled their nostrils making their mouths water as they wandered around the market. The pair just couldn't resist the smell of freshly cooked hot meat pies. The idea of juicy red apples that they had vowed to buy earlier was abandoned and they joined the queue for a hot meat pie and a cup of cocoa instead. It was time out of their regular day to day existence and not only was the market a busy, vibrant place to be, they were also exceptionally excited about their purchases! They bit into their savoury delights tasting the delicious, warm, meaty gravy bursting into their mouths. With exclamations of approval, they both devoured their pies within minutes. The pies were washed down with a hot, cup of cocoa sipped slowly to relish every sweet, chocolatey drop.

Feeling full and warmed, they passed by the jellied eel stall, the distinct scent of the fish sauce lingered thick in the air. Another vendor shouted, "Come and get yer hot pea soup! ½ penny!". As they ventured past, they both agreed that they wished they could have stayed the entire day to sample all the tasty treats that were there on display before them.

At the end of the market, they stopped to chat with the lady on a flower stall. She had a baby at her breast, covered with an old blanket and a small child who sat on a blanket on the floor. She was a cheery soul, her little boy on the floor looked up at them with a big smile and widened his large brown eyes. She recognised Molly from The Boatman's Rest and had brought some doyleys from her. "You should get yerself a stall up here love! Sell all those lovely things you make! I reckon you would make yerself a fair few shilling!" She boomed loudly. After a little discussion about the marketplace, Molly decided to give the idea some thought and thanked the flower seller for the suggestion. She had dreamed of having a proper place to sell her wares one day and this might be a possibility for her in the future.

Nora and Molly chatted excitedly all the way back to the basin, on arrival they ran into Nora's apartment to try on their new garments. None of the outfits needed much alteration, just a little tuck here and there and Molly planned to add a little lace around the collars of their blouses. They were more than happy with their choices and both were keen to wear them as soon as possible.

Chapter 9 A Good day for a Picnic

Nora was excited about her imminent walk with Jimmy, however her mind was focused on Lucius, she was concerned about how he might react as they had got along so well recently. She did not want to jeopardize their newly found truce. Molly arrived early to help her get ready and they were excited! Lucius prepared his own breakfast, he knew that Nora would be away for the day. He had tried not to think about where she was going but images of Nora and Jimmy at the park, arm in arm had haunted him since he had woken. He felt that there was nothing he could do, the thought of her going off to get married and leaving him alone made him feel so terribly sad.

Downstairs Molly was aghast at just how beautiful Nora looked in her new clothing. Her hair was loosely tousled up on the back of her head with red ringlets draped strategically to frame her pretty face. She had an elegantly fashioned blouse in striped purple and white, that hugged her bosom, fastened with cute pearl shaped buttons. Molly had sewn a lace trim around the edge of the breast seam, which gave the whole look a rich lift. Her skirt was purple velvet and slightly bustled at the back, it flowed to the floor and swished as she paraded up and down the room in absolute glee. "Nora, you can look in the mirror now" Molly exclaimed!

Nora's eyes welled when she looked into the mirror and saw her reflection. She could barely recognise this fine young lady in the reflection ahead. Molly gave her a huge hug. "Oh, my goodness!" Nora managed to exclaim, "Molly, I look so different! I look ready to go to a fine ball, let alone a walk in the park!" She pinched at her cheeks to give them a rosy glow.

"Nora, you already have rosy, red cheeks, you don't need to bruise yourself." Molly scoffed. Molly was even more eager to wear her fine garments now she had seen Nora in hers. For now, though, she was thrilled to see her friend look so happy, confident, and extremely beautiful. It meant a lot to both women, as young girls they had not been exempted from the mockery of their reputation as boat people, their status had always been predominantly identified by their clothing. Their new purchases would give them an anonymity that they had never known before.

Molly knew Caleb had arrived when she heard him shout up the stairs to Lucius, she shook her head and grinned at his loudness. She popped the kettle to boil over the fire and told Nora to sit still, so as not to spoil her hair or clothes, Nora in agreement complied. Both women had been so eager to see Nora in her finery, that she was ready an hour early for Jimmy. They sipped at their tea and used the time to speculate on how fantastic the walk and the picnic would be.

With ten minutes to spare, Molly rose and suggested they head across into the pub to be there before Jimmy. Nora stood and with one final look into the mirror, smiled, gave her cheeks one last pinch, smoothed down her skirts and followed behind Molly into the bar.

Molly opened the door and ushered Nora in, as if she were presenting her at a fancy ball Lucius stood in awe at the sight of her, he was speechless as he watched her swish across the floor, his expression shifted in and out of smile as he tried to take control. "Who is this Lady of The Manor you have brought into our fine establishment?" Caleb joked to Molly, he took Nora's hand and twirled her round. Molly chuckled at his silliness and Nora's face was crimson at all the attention. Lucius managed to take control of his emotions and came out from behind the bar. He walked slowly toward Nora and as their eyes met, he again found that he struggled to find the right words. She smiled at him and he just wanted to kiss her plump red lips and hold her tight in his arms. "Nora, you look … grand! I mean you look beautiful Nora." She stared up at him with her big green eyes and wished he would kiss her. Molly and Caleb could both feel the connection and fidgeted uncomfortably, as they felt like they should not be there.

Suddenly, the door was opened by Jimmy who walked in with a large basket in his hand. Nora felt immediate disappointment at the sound and it took her a moment to remove her glance from Lucius. She could see the grimace on his face and just knew why he looked so discontented. He wanted to take her by the hands and beg her not to go with him and if only he knew that if he had, she would have gladly stayed. In a bid to save both their feelings, Nora strode straight over to Jimmy and shouted a quick farewell before she almost pushed him back out the door.

Lucius felt uneasy the entire day and just wanted her back home. It was this thought that convinced him Nora was the one for him and he became determined to do whatever it took to make her see it too. He had suddenly realised that this place, the pub, the apartment upstairs and the basin had suddenly felt so much more homely, since her arrival. He looked forward to returning home, whenever he had been out. He looked forward to mealtimes with the conversation and laughter they shared. She had added to his enjoyment of everyday life and given him even more to look forward to than he had ever imagined before. He would always get by and be fine on his own but with Nora by his side, life had become so much more gratifying.

Jimmy held out his arm and Nora promptly placed her hand through it as they walked through the dusty streets toward the park. He felt as proud as punch with such a fine lady at his side, he tipped his hat toward passers-by, with a huge grin on his face. "Nora, you look very fine indeed, that's a pretty dress." Nora blushed slightly as Jimmy continued. "We have ham sandwiches, with the finest butter. A bottle of freshly squeezed lemonade, apples and some delicious home-made fruit cake!" Nora desperately tried to get the image of Lucius's forlorn face from her mind and did so with a reminder to herself that Jimmy was a lovely young man and this was just a picnic in the park, not a promise of marriage.

As they reached the park her spirit lifted. The grass glistened with tiny droplets of morning dew, the trees stood tall, their branches stretched out across the winding pathways with tiny sparrows perched on them calling to each other. The lake spread out as far as they could see with little ducks nestled on an island in the middle. The chilly air did not seem to bother them at all as they slid in and out of the water and shook out their feathers before plunging back in again. The pigeons bobbed their heads as they waddled along the pathway and pecked at the left-over food that people had dropped. It felt like a whole different world in the park and reminded her of her travels through the countryside with her father. The sights, the sounds were all familiar but here she was in her finery, with a charming young man by her side. Jimmy had been right, there were couples all around, some were chaperoned by elder parents or grandparents and some alone, like herself and Jimmy. She liked it here, she felt a sense of peace and tranquillity that could never be felt in The Boatman's Rest.

Jimmy steered her over toward a picnic table and carefully took out the cloth that the cook had put in for him. He threw it over the table, and smiled at Nora, who smiled back in approval. He took out another woollen blanket and handed it to Nora, "Here you go dear, put this round you, so as you don't get a chill." The Housekeeper had advised him to do this as she packed the basket and he had thought it an excellent idea!

Nora was so impressed by Jimmy, "Thank you Jimmy, that is so kind but please let me help you lay out the food."

After they had unpacked the food and carefully laid it out on the table, Nora and Jimmy discussed their backgrounds. Even though both had been raised in quite poor situations, their circumstances were vastly different. "My parents still live in the mining area of Shrewsbury, I visit as often as I am able". He told Nora. "Edward and I moved into service as soon as we were able. Our parents were terrified of the horrific accidents that happened so frequently in the mines, and they didn't want that for us. We were fortunate that our fathers held good status within the mining community and were in good standing with their governors". He explained, "I am the youngest and my elder brothers are all mine workers, I remember we all had nights of little sleep because the family were kept awake by ceaseless coughing because of the dust that filled my brothers' lungs." He smiled at Nora as she gently squeezed his hand, "I was glad that I did not have to go into the mines but I wish so much that my siblings did not have to mine either".

Nora poured some lemonade for them both, "I am also glad you don't have to Jimmy! I am sure your brothers understand and are proud that you have managed to get away. It is after all, the same thing that you wish for them." She reassured him. "And are you glad you stayed here Jimmy, instead of going back with Lady Haughton?" She asked.

Jimmy felt his cheeks quite flush at this question, in a bid to stall and think before he replied, he took a sip of his lemonade. As he gulped from the cup, the shockingly sharp, tangy taste caught the back of his throat causing him to splutter and giggle with embarrassment. He coughed to clear his throat and desperately tried to get back to grips with himself. He finally responded, "Well yes Nora, being here has been better than I ever thought it would. An excellent job and look at me here with a fine lady and a feast fit for the Queen herself!" He raised his cup and clinked it with Nora's, although he decided not to try another sip just yet, he did not want to take the risk.

Conversation between the two flowed easily and the food was delicious. Nora took a bite from the wedge of fruit cake, she could taste each different fruit as it burst into flavour. The intensely sweet cherries, the slightly less sweet raisins were mixed with the earthy taste of walnuts, the cake melted in her mouth with each tasty bite.

Nora realised that she had almost forgotten one of the reasons for why she was there. She knew she had to broach the subject of Ellsworth Manor but did not want anything to spoil this wonderful day! She waited until they were ready to pack away the picnic and casually asked, "I wonder Jimmy, if there would be any work available at Ellsworth? Molly was thinking of looking for something different you see".

Jimmy appeared to be surprised by her question but couldn't hide the smirk that quickly followed. He helped Nora to fold the blanket and replied, "You know they don't really take married folk in service Nora, on account that they generally live in. I don't think that they would have anything for Molly". He placed the blanket inside the basket.

Nora narrowed her eyes curiously and wondered what that smirk meant, "Oh I see, I hadn't realised Jimmy, then perhaps you're right, Molly would be wasting her time". She lowered her face and tried to think of another excuse that could mean an introduction to Mrs Tranter.

Jimmy saw her struggle and decided to put her out of her misery, "You know Nora, if you really are that curious about the story of the maid and the Lord and Lady of Ellsworth, it may be easier to just visit as trades people?" He had a little chuckle as he closed the lid on the basket.

Nora was embarrassed but relieved that he knew the real intention behind the visit. She just hoped that he didn't think that this was the only reason she agreed to walk with him, "I'm sorry Jimmy, you must think me such an awful person, wanting to know such business that is of no concern of mine! It's just an intriguing story and to be truthful, there are two women missing and it would be good to know more, don't you agree?"

Jimmy's smile widened as he saw the excitement emanate from her emerald, green eyes, "Nora, it strikes me that agree or not, you are quite determined to meet Mrs Tranter and even though I only know you a little, I can be certain you will make sure that it will be sooner, rather than later. You will not need my introduction by the way, I am sure she is so isolated and bored with the limited company she has right now that she will drag you into the house. Just go through the gates, round to the side, and ring the bell on the Tradesmen door." He instructed.

Nora saw her chance to explain, "Jimmy, you know I have really enjoyed my walk today and this was not to have you introduce me to Mrs Tranter, I wanted to come to the park and have this picnic with you."

Jimmy was incredibly happy to hear her say this, his face said it all! The thought had crossed his mind but he had hoped to charm her anyway, whatever the reason she had agreed to meet with him. He hooked her arm into his and they began the slow walk back to the Basin. Nora told Jimmy all about her life growing up on the boats and working alongside her dad on trips along the canals. She told him of the relentless taunting that she had experienced as a boating child and how her father taught her to be proud of who she was and to stand up for herself. He was hugely impressed at the woman she was, having grown up without her mother and working in such harsh conditions. Everything she said just endeared her to him even more. However, the nagging reminder of work in service and the expectation to remain single just would not leave him alone. He hoped and prayed that Nora had not yet realised the same applied to men in service as it did to women. He wanted more time with her, to dream and imagine a normal life with a beautiful woman. He had for an awfully long time wanted to become a Butler and this was a dream he would hold on to for the time being.

The entrance to the Basin came far too soon for them both as they ducked and dived the little rascals between their feet in the streets. Jimmy took Nora's hand and gently kissed it. "Thank you for walking with me Nora, I would like to come and call on you again, if you would agree? You could let me know how it goes with Mrs Tranter as well?" He gave her a cheeky grin.

Nora giggled, "Thank you too Jimmy and please tell cook that the food was delicious! I would love for you to call again and I will be sure to tell Mrs Tranter that you sent me!" She grinned.

Molly was already outside the pub in wait for Nora's return. She wanted to know everything and did not want Caleb and Lucius to overhear. Nora walked toward Molly with a big smile and Molly could see that she had obviously had a grand day.

"Look at you Nora, you look like the cat that got the cream!" Molly enthused!

Nora smiled and knew she was not about to escape Molly's inquisition. "I had a very pleasant day Moll, Jimmy was quite the gentleman." She acknowledged Molly's smile of approval before she continued. "The food was delightful, tiny sandwiches, fruit cake and fresh lemonade! He even brought a tablecloth to place it all out nice." Her happy grin lit up her face and as pleased as Molly was, she still wanted to know the answers to the other situation in hand.

Molly stood up and slowly walked to the opposite end of the table, her fingers twisted at the lace on her skirts, she turned her head toward Nora and spotted Lucius watching them through the window. She knew he would be anxious for news. "Nora, I am so happy for you, you must have felt so grand walking arm in arm through the park like that!" She could wait no longer, she was as intrigued by the Ellsworth story as Nora was and needed to know, "So, were you able to find more information on Mrs Tranter, or was that not spoken of my dear?"

Nora chuckled, she had wondered how long it would take her to ask that question! She explained all that Jimmy had told her and Molly gave Nora a pained expression when she mentioned the requirement to be single for work in service. "No Moll, its fine because I could have said that I was looking for work but like I say we could take some of your wares and just go as trades people. She may be used to seeing boat folk selling their craft?"

Molly looked at Nora for a short while, she needed to decide whether she should say what she was about to say, "Nora, Jimmy works in service ... Do you understand?"

Molly could see the sudden insight as Nora's face turned from blissfully happy to one of concern. She felt awful to have to say this to her friend but felt she needed to understand now before seeing more of Jimmy. She had clearly become quite fond of him.

"Oh Moll, I do not know why I never thought of it …. I know Jimmy has plans to become a butler but maybe he hopes to find an alternative if his life takes a different turn?" Nora's expression turned to one of stubbornness as she always did when she felt vulnerable. "Besides Moll, it was just a day in the park, with a picnic. I dare say it will never happen again. I must go in and change, I don't want to ruin my pretty clothes. We will plan Ellsworth Manor visit later this evening if you like?" She said abruptly.

Molly knew she was upset, she felt dreadful now "Nora, you are probably right, maybe the family he works for are different?" Nora had continued to walk away and Molly hoped that she had heard her.

As Nora entered the Pub, Lucius tried his hardest to act casual. He had the silly grin that always appeared whenever he tried to be anything but natural. "Oh, you're back Nora, I didn't see you come in." he fibbed, "I trust you enjoyed the park?" really, he wanted to say, I hope you had a dreadful time and will never see Jimmy or any of his like again but he refrained. He stood with his elbow on the bar, leg bent with one large foot crossed over the other and waited a reply. Suddenly, out of nowhere, Teddy raced toward him, his tail wagged furiously and tongue hung loosely from the side of his mouth! He hit the wet surface and completely lost control of his legs, as if skating on ice, he glided straight through the middle of Lucius's legs hurling him backwards toward the ground! Lucius's huge arms flayed in the air as he tried to grasp on to something …anything, to stop his fall.

His bottom hit the floor hard! "Teddy, you little bastard, wait till I get up, you'll be on tomorrows menu!!" He screeched. Teddy was far too excited to see Old Jack returned from the yard and gave Lucius not the slightest bit of notice. Nora placed her hands over her mouth to stifle the laughter, the rest of the patrons were not so kind and shouted all manner of taunts. "Lucius, we knew you would fall for Nora!" "Lucius, that dog would taste better than the usual slop you serve in here!" and finally Maud, "See, Teddy was probably spooked! Should have let me finish my Seance properly!"

Lucius, rose from the floor like an angry Viking about to go into battle! He scorned, "Shurrup the bloody lot of ya, or you'll all be finding somewhere else to drink and believe me, it won't be as good as you got it here!" Jack in his usual, indifferent manner, gathered up Teddy and took him back to his seat right next to the fire, he picked up his glass like nothing had happened. Lucius looked over at Teddy and shook his head in despair, he was sure that if dogs could, Teddy would be laughing at him right now! He stomped off out the back and up the stairs to change.

Chapter 10 The Journey Begins

Nora and Lucius had managed to go a whole couple of weeks without a single argument, thankfully neither Jimmy nor Clara had been seen.

The trip to Ellsworth Manor had been planned meticulously and they were eager to go on an adventure. The only decision that had not yet been made was whether Lucius and Caleb were going to tag along. Both men were concerned that the ladies should not travel alone, especially with Molly's trade wares on board. Between them all they had finally decided and almost at the final hour, that they would take the boat along the Grand Union to the nearest section of canal to Ellsworth. Lucius would then walk with the ladies to the Manor. Molly was quite relieved, she didn't mind operating the locks but it was always easier with more hands to help.

As always there was excitement in the air at the thought of taking a trip on the boat. There was a lot to prepare, Molly's craft ware was wrapped nicely inside two pretty wicker baskets, Caleb had Cobbles strapped to the boat securely and Lucius fussed around like he was about to leave a small infant instead of his pub! It felt like a day's holiday for him, it was painfully rare that he ever took time away from the place.

Old Jack and Jack's son Tommy were to oversee the pub while they were away. They had on occasion looked after the place before, so Lucius knew they could be relied upon. Jack had always been dependable, he had almost been a part of the furniture since before Lucius's arrival. There was truly little known about Jack but he was a man that demonstrated he could be trusted on many occasions. As arranged, Tommy arrived first, he was a large, bald man, he wore a flat grey cap, and toyed with his neckerchief as he listened intently to Lucius's instructions. "Mind you don't be over generous with that gin Tommy!" Lucius bellowed as he opened the door to leave, "I'll settle up with you and your Pa on my return and don't go letting that mutt in my yard, without cleaning up after him!" He shut the door behind him and made his way outside to meet with Nora.

Molly and Nora came out of the room together. The ladies had dressed suitably for a visit to the Manor and wore the dresses that they had brought from the market. Lucius was quite taken back when he saw them appear from the door, "Well, well, I was not expecting to happen on such fine ladies this morning." he quipped in his best mock of an upper-class accent. "Are we ready for the Manor Ball my ladies, shall I fetch the carriage?" He held both arms out for them to hook theirs into and they both joined in the façade as they laughed along the way toward the swing bridge.

Nora looked elegant in a pale green blouse, with cloth buttons that came up to the neck, which was finished with a tiny ruffle. Her skirt was dark green with a small bustle at the back. She had a dark green cloak that clipped at the breast with side openings for her arms. Her hair was finished in a neat bun, with green ribbons and loose curls that fell at the back. Lucius was of course delighted to see her!

Molly had a beautiful peach ruched skirt, with a lower tier of dark peach. Her fitted jacket matched the skirt, with the darker colour added at the collar, the sleeves and the lower section of the jacket. She wore matching hard bonnet with a ribboned bow on the side.

Caleb tethered Cobbles to the boat and caught site of them, "Nora, I thought you was bringing my beautiful wife along with you, who is this fine lady you are escorting?" The party chuckled and Molly gave Caleb a shove as they approached. "Ladies you look ready to dine at a fine table with the Lords and Ladies, are you sure we should be using the trade entrance?" He joked.

The basket that contained the doilies and scented candles for the big house was placed neatly at the front of the deck along with a second basket filled with finely painted jugs. With Cobbles now tethered, the four were ready to set off.

The friends chatted happily and discussion led to what might be the best approach to the subject of the maid. It was agreed that it would be safest to see how Mrs Tranter took to them before they decided on what to say, "She might be one of those loose lipped Housekeeps you hear of, always gossiping and chatting with the workers." Lucius speculated.

"We can certainly hope so, it would make things a lot easier!" replied Caleb. The men jumped off the boat and walked along the towpath with Cobbles, whilst Molly and Nora remained on board. Spring was now well and truly established but the ground was still very wet. The grass had begun to spring high and fresh leaves were bursting forward the hedges. The smell of new growth was all around them, tiny buds ready to burst into flower poked through the hedges. Although it was not yet warm, the temperature was much more forgiving than their last trip.

All around them, they could see the stark differences of the changing times. In the distance the steam rose from a train that made its way steadily across the land, a machine that had made such profound changes to the lives of many of the people they knew. The smoke climbed high from the factories that had increased in number at an alarmingly fast pace. Of course, the factories and the railways had created work for the people. The hours were long and the work was hard but there was food on the table and roofs over people's heads. Yet still, there were the farmers who worked their land and had been there for generations and would continue to be for many more. There was so much to see from this small strip of water in such a vastly changing society.

"It's nice to be back Moll." grinned Nora. Molly squeezed her arm and nodded in agreement. Nora turned her head and looked into the distance, she felt the tears well in her eyes as memories of times on the water with her dear father flooded back. She was soon distracted by a shout from Lucius that they would get the lock gates open. With a man on each gate, they were opened quickly. The boat was guided in to place and the men closed the gates. Nora and Molly watched as the waters gushed in to lift them up to ground height. They moored just off to the side of the lock to stop for a bite to eat.

"Your first experience of working a lock, Lucius. You did a grand job!" Caleb confirmed to his friend.

Lucius looked pleased with himself, "Thank you! I hear folk complain all the time that the locks are cumbersome. I must say I found that fun I don't know what all the fuss is about!" He proclaimed.

During lunch, Lucius looked out toward the farmer ploughing his land with his son at his side, "That reminds me of my younger years, I was that child standing next to his Pa watching every move and trying to help, making a right mess of it mind! Still though I was young." his shoulders shook with laughter.

All three looked at each other in amazement at this unexpected revelation from Lucius. He was such a private man, he had never mentioned anything of his past and as ridiculous as it sounded, before this, none of them had ever thought of him as having parents. He

56

was just always there, mysterious Lucius that no one knew anything about, other than the man that stood before them!

"You were a farmer's boy?" Said Molly astounded, she never knew this and as her husband came from a farming family, she wondered why Lucius had never spoken of it before. "You never spoke of being raised on a farm Lucius." quizzed Molly.

Lucius looked directly at Nora as he answered, "I am a private man Molly but sometimes a man has to change a little." Nora felt her cheeks flush, why did he look at her like that she wondered? He continued, "I realised that my good friends know truly little about me and travelling this canal has brought back some cherished memories. My younger years aren't so different from Nora's, so it happens." Everyone listened intently, it was strange to hear Lucius talk of his past but they were also quite intrigued. "Although not raised with boat people, my mother also passed during my birth, I was raised on a farm, not too far from Ellsworth with my Father and Grandmother." He took a bite from his buttered bread and drank a little from his tea, then wiped his mouth with the back of his hand.

"Do you have sisters and brothers Lucius? It's not so bad with a good father is it, I bet your grandmother adored you?" Nora was getting her questions in quickly before Lucius realised!

"No, I have no siblings, I was a first and only child, my Pa died before my grandma then she went shortly after him, I was sent to live with her brother, my Uncle Earnest who had The Boatman's Rest." He smiled happily. Nora searched for a sadness in his face that was not there.

"You were not old enough to keep the farm for yourself Lucius? There was no guardian that could have come and helped you to look after it?" asked Molly.

"No Molly, I never knew of any other family. Any profits from the farm were trusted to me and transferred to the pub, a lot being spent on making the apartment liveable. My Uncle Earnest had used it as storage, along with all the other upstairs rooms, he slept on the floor in the sitting room. Earnest lived quite simply and the pub building has been in the family for generations, he was never really interested in the living area, so long as the pub itself was looked after he was happy. I never really knew much of the transactions but when my uncle died everything was handed over to me and although I am not a rich man, I have certainly felt that I am. I had good people around me, my Pa took me out into the fields and showed me how to farm. We sat round the table with Grandma who would tell stories that sometimes felt like they lasted for days." He chuckled at the thought, "My uncle taught me everything he knew about the public house and brewing industry. He was a tough task master who would soon put me right if I made a mistake. He was loud and sharp but he had a good heart and wanted me to do well. Anyway, enough idle chat, it's time to move!" He jumped down from the roof of the cabin, his long leg stretched across to the towpath easily from the side of the boat, causing it to sway heavily as the water lapped against the side.

Nora and Molly were keen to know more about Lucius's past and were both quite disappointed that the tale had ended so abruptly. They decided between them that they would pursue the matter further as soon as the opportunity arose! The pair continued to chat about the past and filled in the gaps of the time that they had spent apart.

"I have missed my family dearly." Molly said sadly. "I have become accustomed to the separation now but being shunned by my family has been the hardest thing. I know they felt that they had no choice in the matter and I am certain that they miss me too.

Especially my siblings!" Molly was the eldest of five, she had two younger brothers and sisters, each were no more than eighteen months apart in age. She knew in her heart that one day she would see at least one of her siblings again, if not all of them! In the meantime, she cherished the memories of their years together and the adventures they enjoyed as a family. She knew her parents' stubbornness would never allow them to relent but perhaps they would happen upon each other one day. She just did not know how she might react if they should shun her again.

"I am sorry that happened to you Molly, if only your parents truly knew Caleb, they would see what a wonderful man he is." Nora comforted her friend. "I miss my Pa too Mol, I barely had time to think about him after he died. I had to act so fast to get work and a place to live!" She spoke solemnly.

Nora was still clearly in grief for her father but survival had not given her time to dwell. She had no other choice but to move on and find a place to lay her head and put food in her stomach. Such was life for people of their upbringing, despite life's knocks and challenges they had to keep moving and pressing on, taking opportunities as they arose. She was grateful that he had not had to endure prolonged suffering. His illness had arrived so quickly and unexpectedly, followed by his fast demise that she was caught up in shock before her grief could begin.

"Thank goodness we found each other again." Molly declared with a squeeze of Nora's hand.

"Here we are!" shouted Caleb, pointing into the distance, he pulled on to Cobbles reigns to make him halt. "You need to walk through the lane there, it starts to wind into the trees but follow it up and you will come to the huge manor gates."

"Now there's a site if ever I saw one." confirmed Nora. The huge manor was now visible far into the distance, the building was surrounded by a high brick wall, they could just about see the sides protruding above it and the space where the courtyard would be.

"Well, we are about to go inside and take a good look." Lucius said with a big grin on his face.

"Lucius, you will not be coming inside, you are just to walk with us, we will go in alone." Molly insisted.

"Moll, I am not coming all this way to stand outside that building like a little boy waiting for his mother, I will be coming inside with you. I am sure they would think it gallant of me to accompany two young ladies, so that they are not travelling alone." Lucius had already begun to wipe down his shirt and trousers in a bid to make himself appear more presentable. He would not let this opportunity pass him by, Molly could protest as much as she liked, he would go into that Manor whether she wanted him to or not.

"You will not be able to change his mind ladies, you know once he has decided on something, there's no going back." Caleb laughed as he spoke. He had already agreed with Lucius that he should be with them when they enter the house. It was settled that he would find a reason to excuse himself and see if there was a chatty footman about.

Molly picked up the wicker basket that she had lined with some fancy lace. She pulled back the linen cloth that had been placed over the top and the scent of the candles filled the air. She breathed in deeply with a huge smile as Lucius shook his head mockingly, "Please, let's move I would like to be back before dark." He winked at Caleb.

Caleb bent to Kiss Molly's forehead, telling her to be safe and to stay close by the others. He wanted to go with them but had to remain behind to take care of their boat and

Cobbles. Besides, he felt that it may have been a bit too overwhelming if all four of them had arrived at the door, along with a horse! They may well have just turned them away.

Chapter 11 Ellsworth Manor

The three set off, the sun shone brightly and for a Spring Day it was pleasantly warm. The calm breeze set the trees rustling above them and the birds were singing a variety of song. Bluebells sprawled across the grounds, their violet blue, bell like droplets added a splendour of colour and aroma to the rugged forest floor.

Lucius walked a little way ahead with a large branch in his hand that he used as though it were a walking cane, much to the lady's amusement. Every now and again, he kicked a random stone as far as he could, like a child on an outing with his parents. The path was certainly very winding and at times it felt that they were headed in the opposite direction to the Manor rather than toward it. After what felt like an age, they arrived at the gates.

The trio paused in the courtyard to marvel at the remarkable building, of course Lucius had seen it before but never this close. The creamy white building had enormous windows that seemed to go on forever and gave evidence of the numerous rooms the manor had, you could easily get lost in this grand home. The turret like structures strategically placed on the roof gave the building the appearance of a castle or cathedral. The wisteria flanked the front walls beyond the height of the door, the flowers cascaded with their purple blooms added a dramatic burst of colour against their creamy background. The huge lawns stretched as far as the eye could see, flanked by trees surrounding the grounds and perfectly crafted statues standing tall.

Nora pondered what the rooms might look like behind those windows, she envisioned them to be luxurious with huge chandeliers and plush leather seats that cuddled you when you sat down. She wondered what conversations took place, did they chat about the market or what chores they might get done before bed. She bet they did not, she imagined their conversations were very business-like and formal with little laughter. Such was her brief experience with rich folk.

After they took in the grandiosity of it all, Molly was the first to move on and they headed toward the Trade entrance. The pebbled pathway was loud under their feet and for some reason made them giggle. They approached the large oak door, Lucius nodded to Molly to ring the bell. She reached up tall on her tip toes and gave it a pull, the loud clang could be heard quite clearly. Taking a step back and all with heads bowed they waited in anticipation for the door to be answered.

After a few moments, a smartly dressed, yet nervous looking young man with blonde hair swept neatly back came and opened the door. He looked at them quizzically, and abruptly announced, "I am sorry, we are not accepting any trade, due to there being no Lord or Lady in residence." before they could utter a word, he shut the door. The three looked at each other in dismay, they had come all this way and could not give up now.

Nora spotted an elderly lady peering through the window, behind the lace curtain. She rang the bell again with a determined glance toward the others, Lucius looked at her curiously, "We cannot give up Lucius." She snapped.

The young man once again came to the door, he looked even more nervous than previously, "Mrs Tranter, I mean the Housekeeper would like to know what your business is?"

Nora twisted her hair in her fingers and replied, "We have some fine wares for sale sir, your Housekeeper herself may like to see them. We have travelled quite some way to get here today, maybe you could tell her that Jimmy told us to call".

His eyes lit up when he heard the name Jimmy and they could tell he was desperate to chat more but could feel the eyes of Mrs Tranter on him. "Please wait here, while I go and explain." He shut the door again.

They looked hopefully at each other and stared at the door willing it to open with good news. They didn't have to wait long before it was re-opened, "Housekeep said you may step inside." The young man looked delighted, he had not had company in such a while he was happy to welcome fresh faces!

The group walked in behind him, he directed them through a long passageway that felt like it would never end! The bottom of the passageway led into a large and well-lit kitchen. There was all manner of pots, pans and utensils hanging neatly from the walls and ceilings on iron rods. A large oven and stove stood over on the far wall and to the left of them a fireplace, that crackled loudly as the flames twisted high. The huge sink had a giant bar of soap attached to a rope and potted herbs including mint, parsley and thyme all in early growth lined the windowsill. The table almost stretched from one end of the room to the other with a variety of stools and chairs tucked neatly underneath.

They stood at the kitchens edge scanning the room with interest when Mrs Tranter arrived. Her presence was most certainly felt, her rosy, red cheeks puffed out with a stiff, yet friendly smile and her blue eyes were glazed with an age of wisdom, "Good morning to you, I'm Mrs Tranter, Albert tells me you know our Jimmy! You must tell me all his news but first let's take care of the business of your visit. Let us go through to my office." She boomed. She was a plump elderly lady with a thick head of hair, which was predominantly grey with a hint of brown showing the colour it once was. She stood with her hands folded at her belly, over her apron.

Lucius tried to take his chance quickly, "If you wouldn't mind excusing me Mrs Tranter, I could stay here with Albert and take a drink? I have quite a thirst since walking along the dirt track and I am only here to escort the ladies with the merchandise."

Mrs Tranter suddenly turned around to face Lucius as if seeing him for the first time. She stared for so long that he began to feel uncomfortable! Her face became quite transfixed for a few seconds before she visibly had to take control of her senses, shaking her head and body as if trying to wake herself. "Oh, err, yes sorry, I have not had visitors in a while please do excuse me! Albert, see to it that you get this man a drink while we go and talk in my office." She turned to Lucius and looked a little less flustered and more curious, "I am sorry, I did not catch your name." She inquired.

Lucius was used to people being a little suspicious, he was a large and somewhat intimidating man, he guessed she probably felt a little uncertain of him. "I am Lucius Mam, Lucius Turner".

Mrs Tranter softened her gaze a little, she could see he was polite and sincere, "Are you a local lad Lucius, born in these parts, your accent suggests that you were?"

"Yes Mam." said Lucius with a big grin, "I was raised on the Turners farm, not far from here, until my father and Grandma passed".

Mrs Tranter stared again, everyone else stood silently, listening to the conversation. She suddenly walked toward the exit of the kitchen, "Do excuse me for a moment, I fear I may have left my spectacles in the other room."

Everybody stood in the kitchen and considered the Housekeeper's odd behaviour, Mrs Tranter went into the servant's parlour. She sat alone for a moment or two to think quietly. She could not be certain, but she thought she may know who this man was. Why was he here with these women and what does he know? She would mention nothing and gather herself together and see what, was what!

She made quite an entrance as she swished back into the room and caused them all to turn with a start! She looked much brighter, a pair of round rimmed spectacles rested on the tip of her petite nose, she ushered Molly and Nora through an oak door. It was a medium sized, square room, comfortably furnished with the fireplace low lit to keep out the chill. The large writing desk was full of documentation placed into various neat piles tied with ribbons to keep them bundled together. A quill, ink and stamp pad were to the left of them and there, on the wall behind Mrs Tranter hung the painting of a very impressive, handsome looking couple. Mrs Tranter noticed them both gazing at the painting, "That's the Lord and Lady of the Manor, never a kinder pair of human beings you could ever wish to meet." She smiled widely but the sadness behind her eyes was clear to see, she went on, "Neither are here with us, the good Lord has met his end and we have not seen her Ladyship in quite a while." She hesitated, looking up at the painting, she had obviously drifted away into a distant memory. Before either of them could speak, she showed them to a chair and asked to see their wares.

Molly proudly took out the candles and doilies from her basket handling them carefully, she placed them on the desk in front of her. The scent of lavender filled the room and the ladies gave each other a nod of approval. "I make them all myself." Molly beamed. "I fragrance the candles with my own oil and crochet the doilies with the finest fabric, I learnt it all from my Ma." Despite her friendliness the Housekeeper made both women feel nervous, she gave the impression of being a formidable woman that you would be sorry if you ever tried to cross!

"Well, my dear," She chirped happily at Molly, as she picked up the items and inspected them before she replaced them carefully, "I can see this is exceptionally fine work indeed." She held a candle under her nose and sniffed deeply. She then removed a jug from the basket, she twirled it round to look at it from all angles. "These water jugs are beautiful quality, did you paint those yourself sweetheart?" she asked Nora.

Nora replied in an unusually quiet voice, "Yes I did Mrs Tranter, like my friend here I learnt from my family, from my father."

"Well, well, you ladies have fine talent! As you are a friend of our Jimmy's then I know you are to be trusted, we can settle payment terms and have some jam and scones before you head off." She scraped her chair back and headed for the door, where she paused and enquired, "Do excuse me, I haven't asked your names? Please call me Mrs T, everyone else here does."

"My name is Nora and this is my good friend, Molly, Mrs Molly Green" Nora blushed at having been so formal.

Mrs T confirmed, "Mrs Nora Turner and Mrs Molly Green! I can call you Nora and Molly? I do hope you can bring me more candles some time, the good Lord knows some of the staff here could do with a few in their rooms!" She laughed, her belly shook with her and her cheeks shone redder. She wiped at her nose with an embroidered handkerchief, that she had just retrieved from her sleeve.

Nora's face was crimson when she heard herself being referred to as Mrs Turner, "Oh no, Mrs T!" She proclaimed waving her hands in the air frantically. "I am not married to Lucius, he is a very good friend of Molly's husband and agreed to escort us on our journey." Molly chuckled at her friend's unnecessary animated distress. Nora continued,

"Well he is a friend of us all but mainly of course Caleb." She pointed at Molly, "Molly's husband …" her voice ebbed as she looked at them both and realised, she had been far too dramatic. "My name is Nora Baker." she chuckled at herself.

On their arrival back into the kitchen, Albert was seated opposite Lucius and they were busy chatting. He instantly stood to attention when Mrs T entered the room. "I was just telling Lucius what a great footman our Jimmy were, Mrs T, how he was bound for great things! Had it all planned out like." Albert rushed to try and rescue himself from being caught idle. Lucius averted his gaze from Nora in case she showed too much interest at Jimmy's name.

Mrs Tranters attention was at once bent again toward Lucius, she tried to look away but she found herself drawn to him in search for clues. Lucius was oblivious and too caught up in his own thoughts to even notice her persistent glare. She turned her notice back to the group and gave instruction to Albert, "Fetch me the cups down from the shelf over there Albert, we will get a brew on and plate up the last of those scones. It's been a while since we had company, probably will be again! Best we make the most of it!" She chirped.

Albert jumped up like a puppy who had been let off his leash! It was not often that he got to sit at the table with Mrs Tranter, let alone have different people to speak to, he was also eager to get his teeth into one of those delightful scones!

"So please do tell me of our Jimmy, I know he left the employ of Lady Haughton. He never did want to stay in Shrewsbury, he was happy to come here to us, even if briefly." Mrs T beamed at the thought of him, he had been like a son to her during his brief time with them. Just like Albert was, although he did not seem to know it, Albert had helped Mrs T to get through this most tough time.

Nora lowered her head and swept away at non-existent dust from her skirt. Lucius watched her in amusement, he had become familiar with all her mannerisms, he had begun to know them so well, he found himself in anticipation of them. He had noted that she brushed at her skirts when she felt a little anxious or embarrassed and hopped from foot to foot when she was excited. She often raised her voice as a result of anger with herself rather than others and in fact, he found them all endearing.

Molly thought it best to take the lead on this conversation, "He is well, he is working in a large house as Footman with his friend Edward, whom you may also know. The family often take trips to London, so he is hopeful to go with them when they do." As Molly spoke, she was aware that Mrs T glanced between Nora and Lucius with a look of awareness, the latter never able to hide a facial expression and smiled widely at the thought of Jimmy tucked far away in London.

Mrs T turned to Molly and smiled, "Well that is good news indeed! Please should you see him again, send him my dearest wishes, now I must help Albert to prepare this tea, or we shall be here all day. Albert, tea needs to steep now stew!" She yelled.

When their host left the table, Lucius took the opportunity to quietly ask if they had managed to get any information. "Not yet," Molly whispered, "but there is a portrait in that room of the Lord and Lady, I thought she was going to tell us more when we asked about that."

Nora joined in, "She just changed the subject quickly though Lucius, right after saying they were no longer here, how about you, any luck with Albert?" She inquired.

63

Lucius, once again avoided eye contact with Nora, "No Nora, he was too busy asking about someone else." He rolled his eyes in exasperation. Nora knew Lucius was talking about Jimmy so let the subject drop.

Mrs T and Albert clattered around with plates, cups, and utensils, they were far too busy to notice the three huddled together in deep conversation. "I have an idea!" Lucius narrowed his eyes as he mulled over a thought. The ladies looked at him curiously, to prompt him to divulge more. He wagged his finger at them "just go along with what I say, they're coming back now." Nora's stern expression warned Lucius to be careful.

"Mrs T, before we begin feasting on those delicious scones. might I trouble you for something first?" He said with a charmed smile. Mrs Tranter crooked her brow and felt a knot of apprehension tighten in her stomach at what he may be about to ask.

"Of course, Mr Turner." she replied unconvincingly, she attempted to twist her face into a smile, "What is it?"

Lucius continued, "Well firstly please call me Lucius, Mr Turner is far too formal for a man such as me, it's just that Nora and Molly here were just telling me of the fine painting you have in your office. I would love to see it, if yourself or Albert would be able to show it to me? As a child I would often ride past here with my Pa and wonder who might live here?"

Mrs Tranter felt slightly calmer but still somewhat unsure. She could not think of any reason to deny him a view of the portrait so decided to show him herself. She happily gestured for him to follow, "Of course it would be my pleasure, Lucius." she had already risen, left the kitchen, and walked along the hallway with Lucius close behind.

She opened the office door and pointed up toward the painting, "Here they are Lucius, the Lord and Lady Ellsworth." As he looked up into the faces of these strangers portrayed so beautifully, he felt the most intense feeling of familiarity that quite shook him to the core. He found himself lost for words, he could not possibly know these people, yet it felt like he had always known the lady in the picture and there was a strange sense of recognition for the gentleman too.

"It's a perfect likeness of them both, it feels like I am looking at them in the flesh as I stand here now." Mrs Tranter could sense something was amiss with Lucius but couldn't fathom what it was. She just wanted to break the awkward silence that had suddenly descended. Lucius glanced briefly toward her and then directly turned his attention back toward the painting without saying a word. He hoped he would feel differently this time but no, he still felt the same, what was it, he wondered!

"Shall we go back through to the kitchen?" she enquired gently as she gestured toward the door. Lucius made his way out the room without speaking a word and sat down again opposite Molly and Nora. The ladies glared at him with eyes wide in anticipation of his great idea to come to fruition, neither of them had expected him to come back looking so perplexed.

Albert, who had never been able to read a room, asked, "What did you think Lucius, fine looking couple weren't they?! Imagine, having your image painted like that ey!" Mrs Tranter nervously scoffed and Lucius finally rallied himself! He looked toward Nora who frowned inquisitively at him, he managed to feign a smile to confirm that all was okay, even though he was still totally baffled!

"Yes, a fine couple indeed Albert! I don't think I would look as grand as that." He quipped. He watched Mrs Tranter skilfully pour the tea from the pot into the cups and place a scone on to everyone's plates. "I understand Mr Ellsworth is no longer with us, God rest his soul. I am sure that his loss has not been easy on you all. I am sorry if I speak with too much familiarity but seeing his likeness makes me feel he will be profoundly missed, he looks like an interesting character." Lucius spoke softly but confidently in the hope that he could get further conversation.

Mrs Tranter took her seat opposite Lucius and passed over a crock bowl filled with fluffy, white clotted cream, followed by a second bowl of bright red, strawberry jam. The sweet smell of strawberries filled their nostrils and made their mouths water, "It has certainly been a sad affair." Mrs Tranter revealed. She stirred her tea and replaced the spoon on the saucer, "We were so shocked when the police knocked the door that night. Mr O'Reilly, our butler gathered us all together in this room to give us the news." She observed the room and every detail of that night came back to her. "We could hear Lady Ellsworth's wails from way back in the mansion, she was so distraught they had to fetch the doctor, he insisted he visited her daily afterwards. All the staff here were heartbroken. His Lordship was such a good man, kind-hearted, you know. He looked after the Farmers on his land with good rents and paid them for produce. Not many gentlemen around like him Lucius, a real treasure he was." Albert nodded solemnly in agreement, Lucius just knew with a little more delicate prodding, Alberts's tongue would loosen and he would tell all.

Molly picked up the teaspoon from her plate and scooped a little cream on to her scone, followed by a huge dollop of jam. "That sounds terribly traumatic for you all, how dreadful it must have been! How is Lady Ellsworth now?" Although, trying to get more information, Molly felt genuine compassion, how would she cope, should her Caleb just suddenly be taken from her like that?! Her mind was with him now, she wished that they had found a way to bring him with them.

Albert, eager to join in the conversation jumped in, "She was sent away to hospital Miss, the Doctor tried to help her but she was in a terrible way. She wasn't eating or sleeping properly, she kept going out in the middle of the night shouting for her husband, didn't she Mrs Tranter?" He turned to face Mrs T and expected to be told to shut up but to his surprise she nodded in agreement. "I don't think her favourite maid leaving helped either, they had become close, she went everywhere with her." He paused to take a bite of his scone and the group glanced at each other, each waited for the other to ask the question but Albert went on, "Poor Daisy, she was about to go up to Personal Maid officially, for the Lady herself." Lucius at once cast a telling nod at Molly.

Mrs T picked up her cup and put it to her lips, she removed it again to reveal, "The Lady has been missing from the hospital a while now. Lord knows where that poor woman is, she is such a wonderful person, to think of her out there all on her own somewhere just breaks my heart, it really does, still grieving her husband too." Her eyes watered but she collected herself and continued to sip her tea. "She will come back soon, I just know she will." she declared with conviction.

"When she does, she will see that you have taken loving care of her beautiful home and be happy to see familiar faces here waiting for her." Nora reassured her. Mrs Tranter squeezed her hand in gratitude.

Lucius was pensive, he suddenly recollected a distant childhood memory, "I knew a young woman by the name of Daisy, when I was on the farm. She must have been a couple of years older than me Albert, Daisy Jameson, I believe was her name. I doubt it would be your Daisy?" He questioned.

"Yes, that's the one Lucius, lovely girl, she just left, spoke to our Mrs T and the Lord and was gone the same day. Not a reason for leaving or a goodbye for anyone, very strange." Albert sulked. "How odd that you should know her too! The Police wanted to speak with us all after Lord Ellsworth …. Well … you know drowned." He turned to check Mrs T was okay before he continued, "Daisy has not been found though. Have you seen her Lucius, in the last couple of months or so?"

Mrs Tranter now shuffled a little uncomfortably in her seat and started to collect the empty plates. "Oh Albert, what a silly question." She retorted with the fakest chuckle. "Anyway, I am sure we have kept these lovely people for far longer than they intended. I am sure they have heard enough of our sad woes! Tell me before I see you out Lucius, do you live locally? I mean do you have far to travel back?"

"Oh, not at all Mrs Tranter, we have all had a great morning and those scones were delicious! No not far in the least, just a couple of hours further along the canal. I have my own Ale House called The Boatman's Rest in the Basin." His smile widened. "You and Albert would be most welcome to come by and visit anytime." Albert was overjoyed at the thought and truly hoped that Mrs T would take that offer up one day.

Mrs Tranter took both Lucius's hands in hers, she looked up at him and spoke earnestly, "Thank you Lucius, it has been lovely to meet you all, please come by if you are ever in these parts again."

The group moved towards the door, Albert was sorry to see them leave. He had enjoyed having the house come alive again. The clatter of pots and pans, the chatter and laughter from around the table had all been a welcome revisit to better times.

"Wait one moment." Mrs Tranter waved her arms and made her way back into the kitchen. "Please take the rest of these scones with you, don't want them going to waste do we, I just can't seem to get used to cooking smaller portions! You will also want payment for those beautiful items I have bought." She addressed Albert, "Don't you fret, there will still be enough scones for the rest of us later." Alberts solemn face lifted back into a grin. She passed Molly the scones wrapped in a brown paper package and reached into her apron pocket to retrieve a small coin bag. Molly thanked her profusely and placed it into her basket. They bid their farewells and the group made their way back to the giant Iron gates that led out to the wooded area.

There was little conversation on their return walk other than acknowledgment of how odd Mrs Tranter's behaviour had been around Lucius. The walk back seemed to take forever, they were all tired. As they reached the boat, Molly met Caleb with a tight hug, the story from the Manor had really unsettled her and she was relieved to see him.

They sat down together on the grass beside the towpath and told Caleb all about their visit. Caleb had to raise his hand in a bid to stop them all from talking at once, his head twisted and turned from one to the other as he tried to keep up with the conversation, "Wait please, I can't keep up! So, you know Daisy, then Lucius? This is the girl Jimmy spoke of?" Caleb moved his head from Lucius to Nora, in an invite for one of them to reply.

"Yes." Lucius gazed upward as he tried to recall a memory, with a look of realisation, he announced, "She was a lovely girl, very timid as I remember her …. Of course… Arthur is her older brother! They lived in a tiny cottage about a 20-minute walk away from the arm."

"When did you last see her?" enquired Molly.

Lucius recalled, "I left the farm when I was 13 years old, so it must have been at least 13 years since Mol!" Everyone's eyes were on Lucius again as he retreated back in to thought. The last few weeks had seen them learn more about this mysterious man than they had in all the months that they had known him. "Arthur Jameson! I see him on occasion but could not remember his surname!" he yelled! "I remember her clearly now, they always walked together everywhere, he was very protective of his little sister. Large lad he was, still is! She was very tall and both had blonde hair, almost white!" Lucius was impressed with himself having remembered such details from so long ago.

Nora was hopeful that they would find Daisy, "Do you think she would be back at the cottage Lucius? Would you recognise her, should you see her now?"

"I've seen Arthur at the market on the few occasions I have been there Nora. Never Daisy though and he always talked of his sister being in service, my memory is not so good, he talked of his sister often but in my ignorance, I never remembered her and just went along with it." He paused to think, "Of course, that would have been while she was at Ellsworth! He's married now, living in rooms on the far side of the market. Right rough place it is, I left him by his door on a walk back from the market one day. He might know where she is now though?"

Caleb was drawing random shapes into the soil with a tiny little twig that he had found on the ground as he listened intently. He threw the twig to the floor and stood tall to add poignancy to his statement, "Then that is what we shall do next Lucius! You and I will go and speak with Arthur and find out where Daisy is!"

"Great idea," agreed Molly "but what reason would you give? He might not be too happy to have two men enquiring after his little sister! I do not think he will inform you of her whereabouts."

Everyone agreed, they would need to think of a good reason to give to Arthur. Until then, much to Caleb's delight they finished off the rest of the scones and began their journey back home.

It was dark when the group returned, as they emerged from the tunnel, they heard the chatter and bustle from the pub. They were all tired and after they had checked all was well, they retired to bed early.

Chapter 12 Daisy

Daisy had fled the Manor that day in a terrified hurry. Her mind was in a hundred moments all at once and she struggled to make sense of anything. She was a timid young woman, the very thought of so much as a cross word struck fear into her, this situation had been a terrible shock and she struggled to cope. Thankfully, the independence from working in service had helped her to strengthen her resolve and she was in a better position to cope than she once might have been.

She had managed to gather a few of her belongings before she left the house, she went straight to her bed in the attic room and had spoken with nobody else after she had conversed with the Lord and Mrs T. She did not take a lot, she left behind all that had been given to her whilst she was there. She had however picked up her cherished embroidered handkerchief that Mrs Tranter had made for her. She had sewn a tiny little yellow and white daisy into the two opposing corners. Daisy had nearly cried when Mrs T gave it to her, it was for her Birthday and she had also made her some little cupcakes decorated with icing. The memory of that day had almost made her weep but she did not have time for sentiment, she needs to leave quickly. She tucked it securely in to her sleeve to ensure it was not lost.

Daisy had raced through the courtyard, pausing only at the gates to take one last brief look back at the manor that she had called home for the best part of her adult life. She took the handkerchief from her sleeve and wiped away the tears that flowed down her cheeks. It was a bitterly chilly day and the tears had stung her cheeks as the brash wind had blown against her face. She had marched on, her tall figure strode across the country fields. The soil beneath her feet had sunk with every step and she felt the mud squeeze over the top of her shoes. The rustle from the tree branches became louder with each gust of wind as she hurried on in fear. She had first thought of going back to her parents at the cottage which would have been much closer and easier to reach on foot. She knew she could not do that, she would not have been able to face the dreadful look of disappointment when she told them she had left the Manor. No, she would go to Arthurs, she had told herself and that would give her time to find a story to tell as to why she had left. What could she say...?

She had thought of various stories to tell them as her reason for leaving but non that sounded plausible. Her head spun with the weight of it all. She would miss the Lady dearly, they had become such good friends, as good as friends that a maid and her Lady could ever be. Then there were her companions who had felt like family to her, dear Mrs T, Albert and his incessant chatter, Lucy who barely left her side. She had loved her job, it was all she wanted and she had been so lucky to get such a lovely place. The stories that she had heard from others in service had been so unsavoury that she knew she would never seek a place anywhere else.

With her skirts sodden and dirty, she had finally spotted the park through the clearing. Not far now, she had told herself. The air had become thicker with the smoke from the houses and the factories. The smell changed from the sweet scent of rain dampened grass to the heaviness of embers and metals. Her thoughts had reverted back to the house as she entered the park. Her biggest hope was that they would look after Mrs Ellsworth, she was so vulnerable now and she had never seen her like that. She was an elegant lady, who always looked pristine, her mannerism and character exuded purpose and aim. She had been a shadow of her former self when Daisy had looked in to that room. Daisy suddenly wanted to kick herself for being discovered behind that door, if only she had been more discreet, she might still be there now and in a position to help!

She looked back over her shoulders and mustered the determination, despite exhaustion, to march across the park. The sun was almost set and she so desperately wanted to be safe indoors. Arthur had always looked out for her and made her feel safe, she needed to see his face and then she would know all would be well. Her heart raced as she turned the corner in to the dusty streets. It was not the place for a woman to walk alone, she ignored the taunts from the two women that stood outside the pub and had to pull her arm away from a man who wandered out of the alley way into her path.

She kept her eyes straight ahead and gathered pace as she could see her brothers' door in the near distance. Just as she was about to knock, she realised that she still had no valid excuse for her unexpected arrival. She could not possibly tell the truth, it would be far too damaging. She could not give an overly far-fetched story either because she knew her brother so well and he would pursue his anger! Nor could she say naught because he would go there to seek out answers. She paused to slow her breath and quieten her thoughts in a bid to concentrate. She knocked the door with two firm loud bangs.

Arthur's frame almost filled the doorway, his blonde hair brushed against the top. His face lit up when he had seen his little sister on his doorstep. He stepped down and lifted her up from the waist and swung her round. "Daisy what are you doing here?" He smiled and frowned simultaneously in confusion. "Surely, you haven't walked all this way, did you have a day off, where have you been?" He was so confused, he was delighted to see her but it was so late, there must be a reason for her arrival at this time.

Daisy stepped back and took his hands in hers, "I am sorry Arthur, I have left the house, I really don't feel like talking about it now, I need somewhere to stay tonight. Can I come in?" She gave him a smile of reassurance and squeezed his hands.

"Of course, Daisy come in now, let me get your bag." Arthur picked up her bag from the floor and showed her inside. "Ruth" he called out to his wife, "Our Daisy's here, she's going to be staying for a while." He closed the door behind him and placed the bag at the foot of the stairs.

Ruth came into the front room from the kitchen and smiled warmly at Daisy, she gave her a tight hug. Ruth's hair was half in a bun at the back of her head, the rest tousled down her face. Daisy loved Ruth's hugs, it was like being wrapped in all your favourite things all at once. Daisy felt instantly calmed and accepted the offer of hot chocolate to warm herself. "Daisy, you must tell us how you come to be here so late. We are happy to see you, of course you know that without question but we will worry if you do not tell us what has happened. You look exhausted and upset." She brushed Daisy's hair from her brow and patted the chair next to her. Arthur took the seat opposite them both.

Daisy held back her tears, she loathed lying to them both but knew she absolutely could not tell the truth. "I just couldn't keep up with the work Ruth." The lies came so naturally in that moment it scared her. "A lot of the maids had left to work in the city and there was too much work to be done all the time." She searched their faces for a reaction and was relieved to see that they both looked at her with concern and sympathy. "I have been given a good reference and I will begin looking for something else first thing in the morning. I left the house incredibly early but I hadn't realised it would be such a long walk." She spoke without pause to avoid allowing them time to ask questions that she may not be able to answer. "They were lovely folk, all of them but I was exhausted and sometimes falling asleep at my duties, I thought it was best to leave before it got worse. I have a little money put aside though, so can pay my way until I find something else, then I can get out of your way." She rushed.

Arthur and Ruth nodded in agreement and Arthur reassured Daisy, "You are welcome to stay Daisy, you can bunk in with Hettie, I am sure she will be excited to see you in the morning." He smiled at them both, "We can talk again tomorrow but I will be up for work soon, so I must get off to bed. He squeezed her shoulder, "Don't you go fretting now Daisy, everything will be clearer in the morning." Daisy smiled at the memory of that being their mother's favourite phrase, she could hear her repeat it vividly as though she were there in the room with them! "Everything will be clearer in the morning." Of course, it was always true, mornings were a far better time to think things through.

Daisy entered the bedroom as quietly as a mouse. The last thing she wanted was to wake Hettie. She felt safe here, she was with her family and her big brother had always been on her side.

When Daisy woke the next morning for the first few seconds she had wondered where she was. The usual sound of bird song from outside the window had been replaced by chitter, chatter of people out in the street. She could hear the clanging of machinery that came from the various factories in the distance. As her current circumstance slowly began to dawn on her, she began to flicker open her eyes. She was startled by large brown eyes and flaming red hair looming over her, it was Hettie. "Hettie!" she shrieked, "You are such a darling but you startled me, come here and give me a cuddle." Hettie giggled and jumped on to the bed next to her favourite Auntie. Daisy could not believe how much Hettie her little niece had grown since the last time she had seen her. She was six years old now and Daisy adored her, she had not seen her nearly as much as she would have liked to. They both ventured downstairs and found Ruth who had already prepared breakfast in the kitchen.

After she had helped to clean away the breakfast dishes, Daisy dressed ready to go and look for work, she wore her best dress and hat with rim, trimmed with a purple bow. Being in service had meant that she had the advantage of being able to sew, spending time repairing various garments for the household and her stitching was impeccable. She had also spent time with Mrs T helping with the house keepers accounts, she had not enjoyed that quite so much but Mrs T had told her she was particularly good with calculation. She hoped she might find something in a window for a store or a tailor that may need someone who could sew, it was a long shot but worth a try. Either way, she would not come back until she had a job or her feet were too sore to continue to look. She said her goodbyes and gave Hettie a soothing hug. She promised to return with a toffee apple, to stem her wails and cries because she could not accompany her.

Daisy knew the town well, therefore she knew the best places to look for work. There had been some stir recently about women finding it easier to get work than men, some had said that women were being prioritised when it came to certain jobs. Of course, the truth was that women were being paid less and this meant cheaper labour for the owners. Lots of men had shown their support in giving women higher wages for this very reason. While this had been good for Daisy to know, she did not have time to concern herself with it. She needed to help with the bills and food and wanted no more conflict in her life.

Chapter 13 The Crown

As always, Caleb arrived early morning to The Boatman's Rest, the sun's rays glimmered across the water. Lucius had already opened the door and was seated at the table by the fire, it looked as if he had already prepared the pub for business. Caleb wondered how long he had been awake, or if he indeed had even been to bed!

Lucius, looked chirpy, he waved Caleb over and tapped the seat next to him enthusiastically.

"Morning Lucius, you look like you have been sitting here all night! Have you even seen your bed?" He mocked.

Lucius chuckled, he could understand why Caleb might think that. He responded heartily, "You know me well Caleb but I have slept a little." He indicated how little with a small gap between his index finger and thumb. I have been mulling things over in my mind all night! It suddenly dawned on me that each time I saw Arthur at the market, it was on a Tuesday. As you know, I usually go on Wednesdays but if I can't go that day then I go earlier on Tuesday to avoid missing the delivery." Lucius looked up at Caleb, who mocked him as he pretended to yawn. He ignored his folly and shook his head at him, "So if I were to take a walk to the market today, I might see him and we won't have to knock his door to inquire after Daisy?" He smiled, "It would require less explanation for why we want to find her and just be a casual encounter?"

Caleb felt a little disappointed, he had looked forward to taking some time out to do something different. Even if only a small trip, he enjoyed getting out of the basin, he had found the whole situation intriguing too, like they were all detectives piecing together clues. It was a puzzle that they had all agreed to piece together and he wanted to play his part in it. He had missed out on going to Ellsworth Manor, so had been eager for this. He picked up the poker from the side of the fireplace and solemnly poked at the coals, "Sounds like a clever idea Lucius, of course I am happy to look after the pub today while you're gone."

Lucius looked over at him in surprise, "Well, I had hoped you may join me, Caleb? I was going to ask after Molly's commitments today to see if she might be able to look after this place with Nora. Of course, Old Jack will be in early doors so he can help too."

In his mind, Caleb was already in the market, dipping into a bowl of eels and hoping to catch glimpse of a tram, he never tired of seeing the trams, he thought them a stroke of genius! The way the horses pulled those huge vehicles with such ease was certainly a sight to be seen. In his enthusiasm, he had already headed to the door and announced, "I'll go and fetch Mol now Lucius, she will be happy to help, I know she will!" He raced across the bridge, unaware of being watched from the upstairs kitchen window by a broad shadowy figure of a man. The silhouette of a tall gentleman in his top hat who stared across the water, who watched and waited, then disappeared as quickly as he had emerged...

Molly and Caleb returned together in good spirits, both looked forward to their day.

Lucius and Caleb set off immediately after Nora had joined Molly in the pub. The market was extremely busy when they arrived, the familiar shout from the traders on the stalls rose and fell in a rhythmic flow as they wandered past. Lucius stopped to look at the flat caps that had caught his eye, they were the darkest grey in colour and looked to be cut from sturdy cloth. His current cap had become quite shabby and he had thought to replace it on multiple occasions but never actually got round to it. "It looks like you've been playing fetch with Old Jack's dog, Teddy with this one" Caleb teased as he held Lucius's cap for him, while he tried on another. Lucius gave Caleb a playful elbow and paid the trader for the cap and placed it on his head.

Much to Lucius's dismay, Caleb insisted on buying himself a bowl of eels and began tucking into them as they walked along. Lucius tried to avert his eyes, the pungent fishy smell had already begun to sting his nose. He had never understood how anybody could enjoy them, the smell and appearance made him feel instantly nauseous! As he looked over to the bowl filled with green jelly, he felt his tummy roll, the back of his throat smarted and his cheeks involuntarily puffed out. He gave Caleb a look of revulsion as he desperately tried to hold back the retching, "For goodness' sake man!" Lucius struggled to say, "Why do you have to eat those things, while you're with me? You know I don't have the stomach for it!" He walked a little ahead to avoid the view and the smell.

Caleb had always been amused by Lucius's disgust of eels, he would buy them even if he wasn't hungry just to tease and watch his friend squirm, it made him chuckle. He made a show of chewing with delight when he caught Lucius glimpse back at him. Lucius stormed off even further ahead, he held his hand over his mouth as Caleb chuckled like a naughty schoolboy and finished off the last of the eels.

Caleb caught up to Lucius, they turned the corner from the market and out on to the main street where the stores lined both sides of the street. They were both distracted by the clip clop of horse's hooves and the loud clank of the tram as it headed along the lines travelling directly past them. "We couldn't have timed this better Lucius!" declared Caleb happily. The huge crimson and cream carriage had both decks full of passengers, all headed to their various destinations, those on the top deck peered down to the street below. Caleb watched in awe and vowed to himself that one day he would jump aboard a tram with Molly.

Lucius stopped suddenly and grabbed Caleb's arm to get his attention, "There Caleb, there is Arthur! I can see him through the crowd up ahead, let's take a short cut through the gully we will bump into him on the other side." Lucius guided Caleb to the right as they both gathered in pace to reach the end of the narrow gully before Arthur would get to the street ahead. Arthur had been at work all night and fortunately did not move as fast as they did. At the exit, the men stood outside a vegetable store and behaved as casual as they were able whilst they visibly scoured the street looking for Arthur. "He's not here Caleb, maybe he's gone a different way." Lucius looked frantically in every direction and certainly did not appear at all casual!

Caleb laughed, "Lucius, even if he were running, he wouldn't have reached here yet! Have a little patience you look like a scared rabbit with your head bobbing like that!!"

Lucius pulled at the front of his cap and chuckled, pretending to be interested in the vegetables, he squeezed and inspected them for firmness and colour.

"Good day!" came a deep and bellowing voice from right behind them. Caleb turned round to see an exceptionally large man and instantly noticed the strikingly blonde hair sticking out from below his cap and knew this had to be Arthur.

"Hello again Arthur." Lucius replied, feigning surprise at seeing him. "I haven't seen you for a while! How are you keeping? Oh, and your family of course?" He felt that he had added family in quite casually and smiled inwardly at his own cleverness.

"I am well Lucius, just heading for one in the Crown." He lifted his cap and the dust from the factory fell about his shoulders, the smell of metal blew in the wind.

"My friend Caleb and I could join you for one if that suits you? It's been a while since I have seen the inside of a pub!" he laughed loudly at his own joke and thankfully they both chuckled with him. He raised his eyebrow to Caleb in question to see if he agreed. Caleb nodded eagerly!

"That would be grand!" enthused Arthur, "Far better to share a drink with a friend than alone, shall we go in?"

The group walked the few short feet to the entrance of The Crown, Arthur complained about the mess in the streets left behind by the horses and questioned who was responsible for clearing it. They walked through the workmen's entrance into a lively atmosphere, the bar was crowded with groups of workers gathered together in loud discussion. Arthur appeared to know everybody in there as he was greeted by so many people, Lucius and Caleb began to worry that all hope of conversation with him might be lost. It felt odd to Lucius to be in a different pub, his was busy but never on a scale such as this. He knew that being situated on the main drag was an ideal place for this sort of establishment but his pub had its benefits too and he was happy with his location. He found himself surveying the place, inspecting the small round tables, the glasses, the worn wood on the bar and he really looked forward to tasting the drink, secretly hoping it would be inferior to his own.

As he scanned the room, he recognised the lady seated in the window. Although she her back to them, he knew instantly who this was. He let Caleb know that he would not be a moment and wondered over to say hello. As he approached, he could see an overwhelming look of awkwardness on her face. She greeted him with a crooked smile and spoke uncomfortably appearing to look beyond him, "Good afternoon, Mr Turner." she shook his hand, he furrowed his brow at her strange formality. Immediately she directed his attention to the gentleman who stood behind him. "Mr Turner this is my husband, Thomas Barton." She revealed quietly.

Lucius was stuck for words and struggled to hide the emotion that rose from the pit of his stomach. He was utterly shocked by this revelation and wanted the ground to swallow him up! Keeping things as simple as possible to avoid giving anything away he mumbled, "Good afternoon, Mr Barton, nice to see you again Mrs Barton, please excuse my rudeness, I must get back to my table we are here on business." He quickly shook both their hands and took his leave swiftly.

Mr Barton took the seat next to his wife and watched Lucius walk back to his seat with curiosity.

Lucky to have grabbed a table so quickly, Caleb had observed the whole encounter. He could see the anguish in Lucius's expression as he returned to the table, "Lucius was that who I thought it was?" he questioned.

Lucius continued to frown as he took a seat, "Well she certainly isn't who I thought she was Caleb but that is a conversation for later in private." He shook his head in disbelief and took one more glance over at Clara who met his eyes with an apologetic expression.

Caleb called across to Arthur and let him know that they had ordered drinks. Arthur sat down to join them, they clinked their glasses together in cheers. "Lots of workers come in here on their way home, thirsty work it is in those factories! I don't like to get home too late though, our Hettie's growing fast and getting a bit gobby with her ma." he chuckled a he raised the glass to his mouth.

The others joined him in laughter, Lucius had already sipped his drink and thought it was a little sour compared to his. There was no sweetness to it, quite bitter he had thought smugly!

"You have a daughter Arthur? Just the one I take it?" Caleb inquired.

"Yes Caleb, surrounded by women at home I am, our Daisy's back as well, so the three of them are all there when I get home." He smiled at them, he was an incredibly happy man, he loved his family and would not have it any other way.

Lucius avoided Caleb's eyes as if somehow Arthur would be able to read their minds. "The last time we spoke, your Daisy was in service up at that big house we used to stare at as kids?" Lucius enquired casually.

"She was for a long time Lucius but it took its toll and she's here with us now. She's just taken on work in a factory but she's finding it difficult. It would have been better had she stayed where she was but she's having none of it, too proud to go back, I think? I can't understand why she would leave a place like that to go and work in a factory, doesn't make sense does it? I think there's more to the story than she lets on. Like you said we used to admire it as kids, she finally got inside and chooses to leave!" He puzzled.

Lucius in deep thought suggested, "The truth will out eventually Arthur! I'm looking for help in the bar if you think she might be interested?"

Caleb looked at Lucius with a deep bewildered frown, he wondered what on earth he was up to.

Lucius continued, "It's not too far to walk from yours and I pay a fair wage, better conditions than a factory and I have Nora there too, so she would have female company."

"Very grateful for the offer Lucius but I don't want my sister working in a pub, I'm sure it's a fine establishment and all but not for my sister to work in. I will pass on that you made the offer though, I am sure she will be thankful that you remember her." He smiled at them as he took his last sip, "Are you heading back my way?"

"Yes" Caleb jumped in, "shall we head out?"

Lucius determined to push further, "Are you sure Arthur, I would guess that Daisy is working the same hours as you, it's such a long day, I would ask for less? I know it's not really place for a single woman but Nora has been accepted very well and Caleb's wife Molly helps us out too. There would be no gossip, I can assure you of that!" He supped his drink and placed his glass back on to the table. Clara watched as he walked out behind them but Lucius avoided her.

As they walked along the road, Arthur added, "Daisy works during the day Lucius, so not so bad for her as it could be, she doesn't have to work so many hours. I do appreciate your kind offer my friend but no sister of mine is going to work in a pub. My Daisy is a timid girl, she would never cope if rumour took off."

Lucius was satisfied, he had only pushed to find out when he might be able to bump into her. He was happy to know what time he might catch Daisy on her route home, so he let the matter rest. The men shared stories on their way back and got to know each other a little better. It seemed all three had experience of farm work and all had completely changed paths in adulthood through no choice of their own.

Lucius hoped it may be her day off and that he might catch Daisy as they walked to Arthur's home. They loitered to talk for a while at Arthur's door but Daisy did not appear.

The pair headed back to the basin, they were both more hopeful that they would be able to speak with Daisy soon. It was agreed between them that they would leave it for a few days before heading back into Town to try and catch her. Lucius beamed as he walked back into his pub, he loved his establishment and all the people he had come to think of as family. It was not just his workplace but his home too and everything within was just how he had created it. It had certainly become a far brighter place since Nora's arrival and as he looked fondly toward her, he found she was sharing the same glance back at him.

The group sat together to chat, Molly relayed how sternly Old Jack had informed her that he was in charge for the day and had taken his role very seriously. He had issued their orders in his usual grumpy manner and had Molly and Nora working harder all day than ever before. He insisted that they swept and scrubbed at floors that were already clean, Molly chuckled as she conveyed the tale to them. Nora had not found it so funny and still sulked with her arms folded tightly across her chest in protest. However, Nora's mood lifted at Molly's fabulous impersonation of Jack, "Lucius relies on me to keep order when he's not here wench, so you do as I say or I'll be reporting back!" She mocked and shook her fist at them all to add emphasis.

"He's a good man!" Chuckled Lucius. "I should have him in charge more often, I have never seen this place look so clean." He teased.

His teasing earnt him a slap across the shoulder from Molly.

Chapter 14 A Proposal?

A few days passed by with nothing out of the ordinary at The Boatman's Rest until one evening when a familiar face appeared through the door. "Edward!" Nora shouted, "How good to see you!" She reached up on tip toes to try and see beyond him, she asked, "Are you alone?" She had expected to see Jimmy following behind but did not want to be too direct. Lucius, who stood next to Nora listened closely hoping to hear that Jimmy had left for somewhere far, far away…

"I am alone." Edward replied seriously. Lucius discreetly inched closer, he needed to hear all. Edward went on, "I am here on an errand for Jimmy, he has asked me to come and speak with you as he couldn't get away himself. He would like to know if you could meet with him in the park tomorrow. He knows it's not always easy for you to get away but he said to tell you it's particularly important he speak with you directly." He paused for breath and took a sneaky glance in Lucius's direction before he quickly turned back to Nora. "He said he would like to meet at 10am, the same park as the first time if that would be possible or you can tell me now, if there is another convenient time for you?" He looked relieved to have finished, like he had written a speech and had forgotten to bring it with him! His eyes darted from Lucius to Nora the whole time. He could tell Lucius was listening to every word and he did not want to annoy him further.

"Oh, I see…" Said Nora surprised, she did not know what to say, she glanced at Lucius for some sort of approval or input. He ignored her, with his back turned and pretended to be busy. "Can you give us a few minutes Edward? I will pour you a beer and you can take that table there, while I check if it will be convenient for me to go." Edward happily took the drink and sat down at the table. He was happy for the stroll and the opportunity to help his friend, though he had hoped that Lucius would not be around when he arrived. He sat and enjoyed his beer while he waited for Nora's return.

"I know you heard all that Lucius, I saw you skulking close by!" Nora snapped as soon as Edward was out of ear shot. She was angry at the situation really and not at Lucius. She had hoped deep down that Jimmy would be gone from her life so that she would not have the confusion of imagining a life with him. She quickly changed her tone, "I'm sorry, do you think I might be able to go tomorrow, Lucius, I will make sure I am not gone for long, let us say I will be back by one, how does that sound?" As she looked up, she was relieved to see Molly walk in through the door.

Lucius felt angry and sad all at the same time. He too, hoped that this young man had gone from their lives, or at least that Nora would want nothing more to do with him. "Why Nora, why would you go? You have no need of any more information from him, so what would be your reason?" He hissed quietly through his teeth. Molly who was happily heading toward the bar to greet them, noticed the tension and wisely retreated to sit with Edward.

Nora knew he would be angry, she had long accepted that he did like her more than he let on but for some reason neither of them could admit to it. She thought that maybe he did not want to share his establishment or let go of the freedom that he had been used to for so long. It was not fair to her though, she could not keep waiting until he made up his mind. She had watched Molly and Caleb these past few weeks, seeing them so happy together had made her long for that for herself. She wanted marriage and a man to share her life with, someone to cuddle up with on cold nights and complain to when things were not going so well, walk arm in arm along the street. It was not for her to pursue him, she would not do it, however much it pained her not to, she was not going to chase him!

"I know he has no more information for me Lucius, he was good to me though, the park and the picnic!" she looked up at him with her back to the rest of the pub. Lucius's face was taut with resentment. Nora glanced round to ensure Edward was not privy to all the fuss, she was relieved when she saw that Molly and Caleb were seated with him. "So, you see Lucius, it would only be right for me to go, it would be rude not to, it sounds important and it's a couple of hours, it will be quiet in here!" She appealed.

"It's not because of the pub Nora and you know it's not!" His lips were stiff as he whispered angrily, struggling not to yell for the whole pub to hear.

"Well then Lucius, you need to tell me what the real reason is because if you do not, I shall go?" She desperately wanted him to just tell her the truth, it was all she needed to hear and she would not go but give Edward a note instead.

"Go then and lock up tonight, I'm turning in!" he finally yelled, causing all the people in the bar to turn and stare, he threw the towel on to the counter and marched out up the stairs like a petulant child and said no more.

Nora was crimson, everyone looked at her in expectation of an explanation. She shrugged her shoulders at them and took the seat between Molly and Edward. "Sorry about that Edward, you know what he's like about time off with short notice" she said with a grin. "Edward, do you know what Jimmy wants to talk about? I will go anyway but would rather be prepared."

"We have already tried to get it out of him Nora." Chuckled Molly. "He's telling us nothing, sworn to secrecy he is!"

Edward smiled, "It's not my place to tell, he just asked me to stress that it is particularly important he speak with you. He couldn't leave this evening and made me promise to come instead." Edward was proud that he had been able to keep his friends secret, he had found Molly's inquisition quite difficult, she was not easily put off he had thought to himself.

"Well Edward" Nora said, as she gave his arm a squeeze "You tell Jimmy I will be there at 10 tomorrow morning."

"He will be so pleased Nora, I know he will, sorry if it's caused you any bother." Edward said his goodbyes and left. He had achieved all that he had gone there for and had left unscathed!

Molly looked at Nora with concern, "Lucius seemed angry Nora, you realise he doesn't want you to go? Do you think Jimmy is going to propose?" She asked with a frown. She had asked Edward if that was Jimmy's intention but he had denied having any knowledge surrounding the reasons for a meeting and refused to comment further. He had lowered his head, only further convincing Molly that this was Jimmy's intention.

"Oh, my word Molly, why would you say that! I was already anxious of going and now I'm terrified!" Nora was visibly shaken, she had not thought of that but now she did, it made sense. He had said it was particularly important that he speak with her directly. She had no idea how she felt about that, in one way she was excited, he was a lovely man, caring and kind. Then there is Lucius, stubborn and mysterious but for some reason, she could not bear to think of not being by his side. One thing she did know was that she was not going to sleep tonight!

Caleb frowned curiously, "What would you say Nora, if he did ask you, do you know the answer?"

Nora thought deeply before she answered, "I do not know Caleb, I have to say I do not know!" She jumped up from her seat, "One thing I know for sure though, these good folks need their glasses filled so I can't sit here chatting all night now can I."

Molly felt sad for Lucius, she knew his true feelings and she also knew he could never find it easy to express them. She had never seen him walk out with anyone. Both guardians in his formative years were single males, first his widowed father and then his uncle, although his grandmother had been around for his early years. She realised that he hadn't really been around couples, only herself and Caleb. She left Caleb to his work and went to speak with Lucius.

She walked up the stairs and thought it best to knock on the kitchen door before entering, "It's Mol Lucius, can I enter?"

"Yes." He replied and opened the door for her. As she walked in, she saw the table laid for two, with teacups, plates, and utensils. He noticed Molly's surprised look and decided to let her in on his secret. "I know why you're here Mol and I appreciate your kindness but me and Nora have to settle this between ourselves." He gave her a reassuring smile as he continued, "You see I know that young man is going to ask for her hand and I realise I can't bear it!" Molly tried to interrupt but Lucius went on, "No Mol, it's fine, I've decided if there is anyone, I want to share my life with its Nora, I won't allow this young fella to take her away ... Well, not if she will have me anyway." He paused to glean Molly's reaction.

Molly jumped for joy! "Lucius, this is just the best news! I am sure she would be so happy! I mean I presume you are going to ask her to marry you. Please say that you are! Shall I go and fetch her right now?" Molly already had her hand on the door latch.

Lucius laughed, "It reassures me that you think she will be happy." he chirped! "But no, not now, you know how we are when we have had a dispute, we both tend to be stubborn... I have set the table for the morning and I will do it before she leaves for the park." He looked at Molly in earnest, "You must NOT tell her, I know what you are both like but you have to promise me that not a word of this will pass your lips to Nora!" He ordered. He knew it was a little risky to tell Molly but he also knew that if anyone had insight to how Nora may feel about him, it would be her. Hearing her confirmation purred him on and he placed his hand in his pocket to make certain that his grandmothers gold ring was still snugly placed inside.

Molly was far too excited with the prospect that her two best friends might wed to even think of doing anything that might jeopardise the chance. It did not however prevent the most ridiculously silly grin that appeared every time Nora looked at her for the rest of the evening. Nora just presumed it was the prospect of Jimmy's proposal and ignored her friend's silly teasing.

The next morning Nora woke early after barely sleeping, her mind was so fretful about the chance of an impending proposal from Jimmy. She had decided, she would not be able to face Lucius that morning and was out so early the birds had just begun their morning song.

She took her place in the que with all the workers on their way for their morning shift and grabbed herself a coffee and a thin. She then planned to wander around the market and on to the main street for a peek in the store windows. By that time, she would be close to the park just at the right time to meet Jimmy.

Meanwhile, back at the pub, Lucius was in a ghastly mood. He had risen early, washed, shaved and put on his best shirt and trousers. He had made tea and sliced the bread. He had waited and waited, walked up and down the stairs to see if she was on her way so many times that he had lost count. His Grandmother's ring was safe in his trouser pocket, it might not fit Nora straight away but he intended to fix that. Finally, he had given in and knocked on Nora's door (repeatedly)... When Nora did not answer, he let himself in to realise that she had already left! He was mortified, his first thought had been to go in search of her but then he remembered that she was to meet with Jimmy at ten. He realised that there would be little chance to reach her on time. He lost all sense of calm and went back upstairs, threw the tea down the sink and put everything back where it had come from. He paced the room briefly and then stormed into his bedroom and changed out of his smart clothes. By the time Caleb arrived Lucius was in such a stew he barely spoke a word.

Molly had been busy crafting, she had crocheted intricate lace collars that could easily be stitched on to a dress or blouse. They had proven to be popular and she had sold many recently. In her excitement she had found it difficult to concentrate and decided to put all her sewing equipment away early, she was eager to go and speak with Nora and Lucius! She put on her straw bonnet and wrapped her shawl around her shoulders before she headed over the little draw bridge.

She was met by Caleb as she walked through the door, "I would go back if I were you Mol, he's in a terrible mood this morning, barely said a word! Didn't sit down with me at the table this morning either." Caleb sulked, he enjoyed his morning talks with Lucius, it was his wake-up time and a chance to sit before the busy day ahead.

"What, why?" Molly shrieked, "Where's Nora? She will know what's going on." Her eyes darted around the room.

"I wouldn't ask him that!" Caleb exclaimed, "He nearly bit my head off when I asked him. He just said, he's not her keeper and she's been out since early and not to expect her back till this aft."

It dawned on Molly that Lucius must have missed Nora leaving and that he must feel like he has lost his chance with her. She would be on her way to the park to meet with Jimmy. Lucius could be so stubborn but she must at least try and reason with him. "Oh no Caleb, I am not surprised he's not happy."

"Oooh of course, Nora has gone to meet Jimmy, damn it Mol, I forgot! No wonder he's like this. I wish I had remembered and not asked." Caleb looked worried.

"Don't worry my love, it's not your fault. He will be fine, you'll see! I'll go and speak with him and then get back to my work." She kissed Caleb on the cheek and went out the back to speak to Lucius who was furiously tossing barrels to the far side of the yard.

"Morning Lucius, it looks like you are not in good sorts?" Lucius turned to give her a sarcastic smile and continued his work. Molly persisted, "You know, if you left now, you would reach the park, just as she does."

"You know Moll," Lucius kept his back to her as spoke, "If Nora genuinely wanted my opinion, she would have seen me before she left this morning. It seems quite clear to me that I am the last person she wanted to see and she was so desperate to get to her Jimmy that she left before the birds had even risen." He slammed a barrel on top of another.

"Lucius, I don't believe for one moment that this is true, please go after her, I think you may regret it if you don't. Why does she have to ask your opinion, why did you not just tell her that you did not want her to go?" She spoke softly and tried to appeal to him to go.

He put the barrel down and turned to look at her, "I do not regret Molly, I do what I do and I live with the consequences. I made my decision to speak with her this morning, which did not happen, now I live with the consequence of that." Molly tried to interrupt. "No Molly, I am grateful for your consideration but I will not interrupt her meeting with Jimmy and you must respect my decision. It will not change. I did ask here not to go and she would not accept it. Now if you don't mind, I need to shift these barrels because we will be open soon and I need to be ready." He smiled half-heartedly at her and turned his back once more to continue his work. He did realise that he had asked her not to go but had not been brave enough to reveal why, he regretted that decision but true to his word he was prepared to live with the consequences.

Molly returned to Caleb, "I am sorry, I tried to cheer him but he's not budging, I am sure all will be as it was soon enough. I will get back to my work now." Molly felt so deflated, she had woken excited for them both. She had imagined the whole scenario and how happy they both were. Instead, it had all gone so very wrong and now all she could do was wait for Nora's return.

Nora arrived in the park, she wore her green outfit that Jimmy had not seen before. She felt so conflicted, she so desperately wanted to be happy at the chance of a proposal but deep down she knew it would lead to a life of "What ifs." She approached the entrance with trepidation and saw the familiar happy smile of Jimmy who stood waiting for her.

"Nora, you look as beautiful as always!" he enthused, as he held out his arm for her to take.

Nora felt her stomach flutter as she took his arm and noticed once again, his charm and impeccable manners. However, there in that moment she realised that what she felt paled in comparison to how she felt from a simple wink given by Lucius. Her thoughts were conflicted on whether she could let him down gently should he propose or, accept and agree that her and Lucius will probably never be.

"Jimmy, it's so good to see you again. Edward said it was important that you spoke with me. I do hope everything is well with you?" She spoke fast and was quite unaware that she squeezed his arm quite rigidly in hers.

The smile fell from Jimmy's face and he lowered his head toward the floor. Nora noticed at once that the atmosphere had changed and she was concerned. She wondered if Mrs T had complained about them or was there some other unwelcome news he had to share.

"Nora I ..." he paused and squeezed his lips together as if he didn't want the words to leave his mouth. "Nora, I am sorry, I have news and I am not sure how to tell you. I do not want to sound presumptuous either, but I feel it may be sad news for both of us." He said solemnly.

Nora looked up at him inquisitively, she had an idea of what he may be about to say.

"You see Nora, I have been asked to go to London." he forced a smile and continued. "I have been asked to go and train with the butler and as you know it has always been my dream."

Nora stopped and stood still in front of him. She could sense his nervous awkwardness and did not want this lovely man to suffer as he was right now. She took his hands in hers, "Jimmy, I understand, you have been working for this for an awfully long time and I would not want to come in the way of that. We have spent such a lovely time together and I will be sad to see you go but you may not get this opportunity a second time. Of course, you must go!" She reassured him.

Jimmy looked so upset but he was relieved and overwhelmed by her kindness and understanding. "I want you to know it was not an easy decision for me Nora. I have given it a lot of thought, it was made far harder knowing that I will have to leave you behind. I just want you to know that it was a tough choice, not that I had any presumption that you would want me to stay but …. well, you understand?" He said coyly.

Nora gave his hands a squeeze and took his arm again. "I completely understand Jimmy." she smiled. "Let's go and take a seat on the bench and you can tell me all about the new house and your new position. I am genuinely happy for you and it's not easy for me to say goodbye to you either. You are following your dream and you could not possibly allow this opportunity to pass you by."

The pair took a seat and Jimmy talked about his new place with great enthusiasm. Edward would be joining him as Footman so he was keeping his best friend at his side. He needed to see Nora urgently as they were to leave in two days' time and there was a lot of preparation to be done. It was a huge house in a prominent location within London. It was to be occupied by a young couple who had a small child and were keen to take on extra staff. Nora listened with genuine interest, she liked Jimmy and really wanted him to be happy and do well for himself.

"Nora," Jimmy said with a straight face, "I know I am being a little familiar with you but as this may be the last time we will speak with each other, I would like your permission to be frank?" He waited for her answer.

Nora valued little higher than honesty and forthrightness and she was also very curious, so nearly bit his head off, "Yes please do, out with it!" She enthused.

"I have only seen you on two or three occasions in the company of Lucius." He noticed that she seemed to shift nervously in her seat. "Please allow me to continue Nora, it's merely an observation?" Nora nodded in agreement. "I think there is unfinished business between the two of you. He is a stubborn man, I can see that without having known him. I think that if I had stayed here, you would never have truly been mine anyway. You clearly belong to each other, or at least need to think about it. I will ask you to spare me your thoughts on it but I felt it was something I needed to say to you. I want your happiness too."

Nora closed her eyes for a few seconds to try and hide her true feelings. Jimmy stood up and once again offered Nora his arm, "Let's take a very slow walk around and I will walk you home for the last time."

The couple soaked in the scenery, the tall trees blossoming, the tiny blue bells poking through the grass and the ducks floating across the water to the small island in the middle of the lake where they were nesting. The sun shone brightly and the park was full of people wandering around together happily. Conversations were flowing, children were running and little dogs occasionally barked as passers-by dared not to pay them attention. On the outside it was a normal day but for Nora and Jimmy, walking arm in arm it had been a day of huge change.

They reached the Basin at 11.30 and walked down the cobble slope to the doorway of the pub, where they stopped. "I will not come in with you Nora, I will say my farewell here. Please say goodbye to everyone for me and think on what I have said." Jimmy tried his hardest to smile. He glanced through the window of the pub and saw Lucius, Caleb and Molly watching them, although all quickly turned their heads away when he caught their eyes.

Nora had not noticed them as she threw her arms around Jimmy's shoulders. She gave him a gentle kiss on the cheek and said softly, "Jimmy, my time spent with you has always brightened my day, thank you! Goodbye and good luck my dear friend and if you are ever this way again, please call on us. Now please go before I cry." Her voice was broken with sadness.

He pecked her cheek, "Goodbye my dear and know that you have brightened my days too."

Nora watched Jimmy walk away and quite unexpectedly burst in to tears on her way to her room. She lit her fire, sat down in the chair and wiped her hair away from her face. Her tears were as much from relief as they were of sadness. She had genuinely liked Jimmy but had felt intensely that she could never like him as much as she should, not just because of Lucius but she knew there was something lacking in her feeling toward him. She would still miss him though, he had great humour and though their companionship had been brief, she felt they would have become close friends. It would have been nice to have had more time together. She wasn't ready to face everyone yet, so she made herself a pot of tea and sat alone with her thoughts for a while.

Back in the pub, Lucius who had seen the hug and kiss, had presumed there was going to be wedding bells and threw himself into work as distraction. He swept floors that were not in need of sweeping and scrubbed counters until they were almost scuffed. He gave Nora a short quick smile as she entered the side door and made his way toward the other side of the pub to fake his lack of interest in anything she had to report.

Molly raced over to Nora the moment she spotted her entrance. "You look beautiful Nora." she said with a beam. She could tell that Nora was upset and invited her to sit, "You do not start till one Nora, come and sit with me for a while? Tell me what happened?! You know I have been longing for your news."

The women sat down together, "I will get straight to the point Molly." Nora took a big breath, in truth she felt a little silly after all the fuss when they thought there may be a proposal. "There was no proposal." She announced and watched as Molly's mouth fell open in shock. "No, it is fine Mol, he is to travel to London to train as a butler and I am honestly happy for him."

Molly was stunned! She really did think that Jimmy was about to propose, everything pointed to it. "Are you alright Nora? I was sure there would be a proposal, I hope you are not too disappointed?" Molly squeezed Nora's hand across the table. "I feel so dreadful for putting the idea in your head, I would never have ..."

Nora shaking her head interrupted her, "No I really am very pleased for Jimmy, it is what he has always wanted and from the moment I had thought he might propose, I was quite shaken." With a short giggle, she continued, "That is not evidence of being happy about getting married is it, Molly? Feeling shaken and worried that you might accept? Please do not fret, I am happy. I will miss his friendship, although brief, I did enjoy spending time with him, just not enough to marry him. He was kind enough to meet and speak with me directly, he is a good man and I am happy for him."

Molly reached over and gave her best friend a hug, "Then I am happy for you both Nora!" Just as she had said it, Lucius walked by their table. The words hit him like a punch to his stomach and halted him to a stop. Never one to crumble, he stood over them.

"Hello Nora, you're back!" He faked. "I see congratulations are in order, I am sure you and Jimmy will be happy!" he said with the most fake smile.

Nora looked up at him, "Yes I am sure we will be, thank you." She beamed. Lucius was about to turn and walk away as she continued, "Although, only Jimmy should receive congratulations, not me. He is going to London to be promoted as Butler and unless you have plans to promote me, then I have nothing to be congratulated on." She stood up, "Right, it is a little early but it's getting busy now, I will change and start making myself useful."

Lucius had already turned away from her, so that she would not see the look of happiness spread across his face!

Molly waited for Nora to leave before she approached Lucius with the question she had been burning to ask, "Will you tell her now? Jimmy will not return so you have no need to worry. Please say you will." She pleaded.

Lucius smiled affectionately at his friend, "No Mol, like I told you this morning, if Nora had wanted my opinion on her future plans, then she would have sought me out before leaving for the park this morning. I am pleased she is staying but I won't be expressing my own interest any time soon. Let's leave things as they are for now." He noticed Molly's disapproving expression and stopped her before she could comment further. "You know me better than most Mol, so you know there will be no changing my mind." He patted her hand and walked away, still smiling.

Chapter 15 – Arthur Remembers

It had been a couple of weeks since Arthur had come across Lucius and Caleb in the market. Daisy, Arthur and Ruth were seated at the table, when Arthur suddenly remembered his conversation with Lucius. "Oh Daisy, I forgot to mention! I had a chance meeting with an old friend of ours a couple of weeks back now, Lucius Turner, you must remember him?" Arthur wasn't sure what had prompted this memory but he was glad he remembered.

Daisy stopped chewing on the mouthful of pie that she had just bitten in to and stared at Arthur, she was worried at what may have been said. She gulped the food down quickly, "Yes of course I remember Lucius! Lovely young boy, who of course is a fully grown man now! How was he Arthur? What news did he have?"

"Well as you may already know, he owns his family pub called The Boatman's Rest, just down in the Basin by the canal?" He cut into his pie and watched the hot gravy spill across the plate.

"I didn't know that." Daisy fibbed. "I hope he is well, did he ever marry?"

"He seems happy enough Daisy, never did marry but he seems quite content. He asked after you." Daisy began to feel quite uncomfortable and wanted to leave the table but did not want to give rise to any suspicion. Thankfully, Arthur was so engrossed in the contents of his plate that he barely looked up while he was chatting. "Yes, I told him that you had left service and was working in a factory now." Arthur laughed loudly, "You won't believe this, he said that you would be welcome to go and work for him in the pub." He leaned back in his chair and wiped his mouth with the back of his hand as he finally looked up, "Of course I told him that there would be no chance of you working in a place like that!" He eyed her directly with a look of confirmation that said this was not open for negotiation.

"No of course not Arthur! Whatever was he thinking?!" she forced a nervous giggle. "Is that all he said? It's so nice that you saw him after so long, we must have all changed so much." She sipped at her tea and chased the tiny remains of the pie around her plate with her fork.

"Yes, that's the most of it, of course he made mention of Lord Ellsworth drowning in the canal near by his pub. Strange you have never spoken of that Daisy. It was the gossip around town for quite some time afterwards. I have been waiting for you to make mention of it." He stared directly into her eyes and waited for an answer to a question that he had not directly asked.

Daisy felt the panic rise, it started in her stomach and made its way up into her chest, like a volcano had internally erupted and stuck in her throat, she felt hot and uncomfortable. It had been a while since she had been forced to think about the house in detail. She needed to think before she spoke so she shoved the last morsel of pie into her mouth in an effort to stall a reply.

"It's fine Daisy, I understand. I presume it has been difficult for you." He could see his sister was upset, her eyes were full and her face was red. "You should not feel guilty about leaving, you would have had no idea what was about to happen. You could always take a visit up there and pass on your condolences if you wished. Just say the word if you would like me to come with you." He raised his cup and took a large gulp, he regretted mentioning Lord Ellsworth, he could see she was upset.

Ruth picked up the teapot and refilled Daisy's cup, "Leave her alone Arthur, I am sure she will talk about things when she feels like it. Some things are best left forgotten. She's happy here with her new job, our Hettie is over the moon to have her auntie close. The reason she is here is of little importance when compared with everything else. So, let's not fuss and be glad we are together under one roof." Ruth smiled and winked at Daisy, she knew Arthur could be a little overbearing when it came to his sister. He meant well but he sometimes over stepped.

Daisy took her cup with an appreciative smile, "I am so grateful to have you all, honestly, I am fine and happy to be here. It was the most dreadful news but I cannot change what was already happened. Too much time had passed when I got wind of the sad news so it didn't feel right to turn up at the house. Maybe one day I will go back and visit." Daisy had been sincere in this, she had thought of returning to the Manor but she knew she couldn't.

Ruth brushed Daisy's shoulder warmly, "That's the ticket our Daisy! Onwards and upwards as they say!" She turned to Arthur, "Now sup that tea Arthur before it's stone cold, I won't be brewing another before bed."

Daisy loved Ruth's candid attitude, she was never one to fuss and her no nonsense approach was always reassuring. She was calm and nothing ever phased her, she sought the answers to any challenge with minimal bother. Daisy knew that with her brother's fierce protection and her sister-in-law's affection, she could not be in a better place.

Daisy tossed and turned all night long, despite being desperately tired from a hard day's work. She woke with a sore head and heard Hettie downstairs, complaining that her mom brushed her hair too hard. Hettie had a head of beautiful thick red hair and every morning, it took Ruth an age to tame it.

"Ouch! I shall have no hair left if you brush it so hard!" Hettie yelled with both hands spread across the crown of her head in protest.

"My Goodness Hettie, why do you have to carry on so much!" Ruth returned, snapping Hettie's hands away from her head. "It would save us both torture if you would just sit still and let me brush!"

Daisy took the brush from a very thankful Ruth and continued to brush through Hettie's hair. "Mommy, Daisy is not pulling my hair, you see! She does not hurt!" Hettie yelled.

Ruth shook her head in frustration and Daisy chuckled, "Your mother makes a far better job of it than me though Hettie." Daisy confirmed.

"Pain for pretty hair! I will wear it like yours Daisy and then nobody will care!!" Hettie laughed. Daisy tapped her in jest with the brush for her cheekiness.

Daisy had wondered if Arthur's meeting with Lucius was just by chance or if there might be more to it. Her curiosity had kept her awake. She wondered if he had come to hear anything and if so, what?! It was true that even though her job in the factory was long and difficult, she would never go and work in a public house. She did want to see him however and it was that which had prevented her from getting the rest she desperately needed. Could she just go the pub and walk in alone, she wasn't sure it would be right? She couldn't think of anyone she could ask to go with her without having to answer questions about why she wanted to visit such a place. Arthur would never agree to a visit with her either so she would have to go alone and today was her day off.

Hettie prattled on relentlessly during breakfast, Daisy tried to keep up despite her overwhelming desire to go back to sleep!

"Why is Ma sewing clothes Daisy, all day she sews clothes, why does she do that?" enquired Hettie.

Daisy explained, "Your Ma is paid to sew clothes for other people and that helps to pay for food and other things."

Hettie looked thoughtful and cheekily replied, "I want to sew clothes when I am older Daisy, I don't want to get dirty and grubby like you." She giggled.

Daisy playfully tweaked her nose, "You cheeky monkey!" To which, Hettie responded by sticking out her tongue.

Daisy dressed and headed out to the door, "I am leaving now Ruth, I won't be late back, just paying a visit to Rosie from work." she shouted from the bottom of the stairs. She knew very well where the Basin was, it wouldn't be a long walk and if she went early enough, she should get there before the pub opened. Hopefully Lucius would be about to speak to her. Arthur had been moved back to the day shifts and had left a couple of hours earlier so there would be no fear of him seeing her.

She walked through the dusty streets and bid good morning to the many people she passed on their way to work. It was a warm, pleasant day and the sun already peeked from behind the clouds. The resounding clanks and scrapes from the surrounding industry had begun almost from sunrise. It was a sound that she had quickly become familiar with, despite the thought when she first arrived that she never would. Three small children ran in front her, kicking stones down the street, while their mothers stood on the doorstep chatting to one another.

She turned down the quiet street that led to the cobbled slope down to The Boatman's Rest. She stopped at the top and had dialogue with herself about whether she should continue or just turn back. Her curiosity won and she began the walk down the slope. There was a time when she would never have contemplated doing such a thing as this but she had been forced to become more courageous. Although she had moved on to a certain degree, she knew that her circumstance would catch up with her eventually so the more information she could glean, the quicker she could see an end to it. Some days she felt the disturbing thoughts would never go away and on others they were fleeting but they were present every day. She expected her visit might be awkward and possibly of no help at all but it was worth a try.

She walked to the front door of the pub which of course was locked. She held her hands around the top of her forehead to peer through the window into the dark room. Just as she began to focus, she saw the fleeting shadow of a tall man in a top hat who appeared to glide across the room, he travelled faster than any human could possibly move and hurtled straight toward her! She jumped back in terror, her hands shook violently and her heart thumped in her chest! She was horrified, she felt the strength drain from her legs as she pressed her back against the wall to prop herself up.

She dare not look back in, she did not want to see that again! What on earth could that be, it moved so fast yet floated as if not walking or running! She told herself that she should have known it was a huge mistake to go there. She managed to compose herself and with eyes averted from the window she began to walk away and head back up toward the slope to make a quick escape.

Lucius was seated at the table counting money from his tin when he saw her peering through the window. He had noticed that she was startled and guessed that she had not expected to find anyone in there. He headed behind the counter to get the keys and open the door for her.

"Hello there, do you need help?" She heard a voice call out.

Terrified to turn around, afraid of what she might see, she shouted without even a look to whom she replied to, "No I am fine thank you, sorry, my mistake."

"Daisy, is that you?" A voice muttered. Daisy immediately recognised the voice but couldn't quite recall who it was, she knew it couldn't be Lucius, he had been a boy when they last spoke. She turned around slowly, something didn't feel quite right, the voice sounded almost in her head rather than her ears. She turned to see that there was nobody there, she looked left, right, behind and far into the distance but not a single person! She was close to tears with fright! Just as she was about to run for it, she heard the jangle of keys and the tall figure of Lucius came from behind the door.

"Daisy, is that you? It's me Lucius." He stood with a big smile on his face and a hand out to greet her.

She remained motionless, unable to move a muscle, she tried to make sense of the last few moments. Was she having Deja Vue? Was she in a dream or ill, or some other weird explanation for what was going on right now?

Lucius frowned, he had seen her move from the window with quite a start and now it seemed she was terrified. "Daisy are you quite well? You look as if you have seen a ghost! I have not changed so much over the years, have I?" He coaxed.

She began to regain her senses, "Lucius would you mind if I come inside and take a seat? I have come over quite strange, I will explain." She said warily.

Lucius held out his arm and led her through the door to a chair by the fireside which was lit low enough to keep off the chill. "Sit there and warm yourself a little Daisy, I will get you a drink, you look quite pale." he said concerned.

As he walked to the counter, Daisy asked, "Lucius, were those your first words to me when you walked out the door, or had you already called to me from the window? Are you here alone or is someone else here?" She looked all around the room, in search for a man in a top hat.

"I am here alone and no I did not shout from the window, Daisy are you feeling alright? I saw you startled when you looked through the window. I presume you are here to see me so surely you were not surprised to find me here?" He pressed.

"No Lucius, please forgive me, I wasn't planning on this being how our first meeting would be after so long! You see I looked through the window and saw ..." She paused as she felt too ridiculous to continue. "Well, I saw a shadow of a man, which seemed almost to glide across the floor, please do not think I am mad! Maybe the light from the fire or a reflection but it put fear into me that I am unable to explain."

Lucius had already sat down opposite her and was amazed that finally someone else had seen what he had seen on so many occasions before! "Then Daisy, you and I are both mad because I have seen the very same apparition on numerous occasions in this place!" he lifted his hands in the air in despair. "Daisy as selfish as it sounds, I am so relieved to know that finally someone else has seen it!"

"Then what is it?!" She exclaimed, she lifted the glass to her mouth, and gulped down a third of its contents.

"I have no idea and that is strangely something I was hoping you may be able to help me with..." He muttered.

As the pair talked, they stopped abruptly and looked at each other in horror when they heard the desperate cries and screams of a woman in the distance who seemingly shouted for Daisy. She sounded as though she were in great distress. Suddenly there was a loud splash and a dog barked frantically!

They both instantly jumped-up and raced to the door! "My goodness, it's Lillian, look the dog is on the edge of the boat." Lucius exclaimed in horror.

"Lillian??" Daisy shouted, "Never mind, please help her!"

Lucius had already ripped off his shirt and kicked off his shoes, he was in the water and headed toward Lillian's boat. Caleb who had also heard the noise had jumped into the water too. Molly ran across the bridge toward the pub, she warned them that the dog had leapt in and was struggling to stay afloat.

"I see her Caleb!" shouted Lucius, he had spotted Lillian's arms rise above the water as she tried desperately to stay afloat and alert him to her whereabouts. He made his way to her quickly and wrapped his arm around her tiny waist. With her head tucked in his shoulder he carried her toward the edge. "I have Lillian!" He shouted over to Caleb.

Caleb desperately searched for the dog, he was a small frail thing and the water was so dark and murky. He spun in all directions then thankfully heard Molly shout, "There Caleb, by the fender, I see him! Quick Caleb before he goes under again." The dog tried desperately to get up on to the towpath but with nothing to grip on to he was exhausted.

Molly and Daisy without even acknowledging one another helped Lucius and Lillian out of the water. Both women reached into the water and put an arm under each of Lillian's, Daisy grabbed Lillian's skirts at the waist and yanked her up on to the towpath. Lucius pulled himself out of the water and they all kneeled to the floor to assess Lillian's condition.

Caleb strode fast over to the fender on the front of the boat and tried to grab the little dog. The dog snapped and snarled in fear but Caleb ignored him and grabbed him around the belly. He nipped Caleb a couple of times but mercifully did not break his skin. He slowly calmed down and stopped trying to bite his hands but he panted frantically. Caleb quickly strode to the towpath and placed the dog down safely before he pulled himself up and out of the water. The dog raced directly toward Lillian, he yapped and jumped around her nervously.

Molly had seen people fall in the water on numerous occasions, however Lillian was already so frail, she feared there could be grave consequences on this occasion. She instinctively turned Lillian on to her side and patted firmly on her back. Lillian coughed with force expelling murky water that sprayed from her mouth. She took a loud, deep breath, her eyes opened briefly and scanned her surroundings before they fell shut again. Her trusty pup licked at her face and tried his best to revive her. Daisy looked at Molly in desperation "Please, please help her, she has gone again!".

Molly took Daisy's hand and placed it where hers had been, over Lillian's heart. "You feel her heart beating? She is fine, she is a very frail lady so it may take a while for her to wake properly." Molly placed her hand back on Lillian's heart, "I am sorry, I do not know who you are but thank you for helping us get her out of the water." She looked at Daisy reassuringly who was now fraught with tears.

Daisy stroked Lillian's hair away from her face as she leaned down toward her, "Please wake up, it's me Daisy! Please wake now, we can help you!" She pleaded.

Lucius had run back out of the pub with a blanket to wrap around Lillian and heard Daisy's plea, "You know who this lady is Daisy?" he asked as he wrapped the blanket around her and picked her up as though she were as light as a feather.

Daisy looked at Lillian with deep affection, "I know her Lucius but it is not my place to say more. We will have to wait till she wakens."

Molly ran across the bridge and yelled that she would get dry clothes for Lillian. Caleb had also gone back to the boat to get himself dry.

The moment the pair got inside their cabin Molly exclaimed, "Caleb, that was Daisy! We must hurry back, she knows Lillian, we must be quick!" Caleb stumbled into his trousers in an attempt to hurry and questioned his wife's lack of regard for his bravery. As if reading his mind Molly grabbed his face and gave him a big kiss. "Thank you for saving that little dog, Caleb! You were so brave." Still soaking wet he grabbed her waist. "Caleb, be off with you! You are soaked through in that dirty water!" He chuckled to himself as Molly turned and hid her grin.

Lucius carried Lillian up the stairs and into his room, he placed her into his armchair situated close by the fire. Daisy and the little dog sat on the floor at her side. "Daisy ..." He said with unease, "This lady has been a mystery to us for a long time now, please can you tell me more. I want to help?"

Lillian mumbled and stirred, her head turned restlessly as she suddenly opened her eyes and locked them on Daisy's. In a very faint voice, she pleaded, "Daisy please, you must help me, please don't leave me." Her eyes closed again as she drifted back off.

Daisy's eyes filled again, "Lucius, please do not put me in this position, I cannot say more right now but I promise to speak with her and see what we can tell." She looked at him in anguish. "I will need to stay with her too, she needs someone who knows her, I will go back to the boat with her but I cannot leave her side."

Lucius looked disapprovingly, "You will not go to that boat Daisy, Lillian will stay here until she is well enough to leave. You are welcome to stay here and look after her but I need answers, like I said I just want to help. You will need to find a way to get your brothers approval too. He is not going to be best pleased at you for staying here." Lucius was concerned for Daisy, he had no idea how they knew each other or in fact what Arthur would make of it all.

"I can never thank you enough, do not worry about my brother. I will find a way to get an approval from him. I owe this lady so much and I will not let her down again." She held on tight to Lillian's hand.

"It's not I that need to worry about Arthur, it is you, Daisy. Nora and I could take care of Lillian but if you are determined to take the task then you need to speak with Arthur first. Now where is Mol with these dry clothes, she is so cold!" He worried.

Molly and Caleb ran back, Lucius left to get washed and changed in to dry clothing. The stench of the canal water was too much for them. The two men joined each other downstairs to leave Daisy and Molly to get Lillian in to dry clothes.

Lillian remained asleep for most of the time as the women washed, dried and changed her clothing. Every now and again she mumbled random words, "Rufi." was a name she repeated and when the little dog's ears perked up and his tail wagged, they realised this must be his name. "Aaah, so your name is Rufi!" Molly said as she scuffed the white fur on top of his head. "We will ask Nora for some scraps for you when she is back from the market." She turned her attention to Daisy, "So you are Daisy, Lucius has spoken of you. Caleb and I are friends of his and help here at the pub. Sorry your visit has been such an eventful one!"

Daisy smiled, "Oh no really, I am so happy to see this lady again, though I wish it were under better circumstances. I just hope she will be well soon, she seems to be quite thin and sickly. Surely, she was not under the water for too long?" She felt Lilian's head to see if maybe she had a fever.

Molly nodded in agreement, "Yes, she does seem quite confused but she has been like this for quite some time now. She has never let any of us nearby. How do you know her if you don't mind me enquiring?"

Daisy stood up, looking agitated, "Please accept my apologies, I am not at liberty to say just yet. Hopefully in time I will be able to tell you all more but, in the meantime, I need you all to trust that she is a good woman who needs and deserves our help."

Molly was terribly confused and equally frustrated that she was still no closer to knowing the story behind these women. "Of course, Daisy, you can see that we are here to help in any way we can. Maybe we should fetch a doctor? I am sure Lucius would fetch one for her."

"Absolutely not, please do not call a doctor! Do you think Lucius has gone to find one now? I must go and stop him!" Daisy turned and ran down the stairs, she found Lucius stacking glasses behind the bar with Caleb. She repeated her concern to him and he was compliant with her wishes on the condition that if Lillian gets any worse, they will have no other choice. "I will dash back home now Lucius and get a few of my things if that suits you? I will let Ruth know where I am, Arthur won't be returned from work just yet."

"Of course, Daisy." Lucius concurred, "Do you want someone to come with you to help carry your things?"

"No, I will not need a lot. It's not too far for me to go back and forth but I want to be here when she is lucid again." She caught the look of doubt in their faces, neither of them had ever seen Lillian lucid. "This is not the woman that I know her to be, there is something going on with her and I know for sure that she will be herself again with time." She contested.

She fled through the door, toward the cobble slope where she bumped directly into Nora who was carrying a bundle of vegetables in her arms. "Please do excuse me mam, I am sorry! I am so clumsy, I'm in a such in a rush and didn't see you!" She blustered and squeezed Nora's arm unknowing of who she was. She continued to sprint up the slope feeling guilty that she had not stopped to help but she really needed to get back quickly.

Nora stopped in her tracks and watched this strange woman whom she had seen flee from the pub. Nora was furious, her first thoughts were that Lucius had yet another friend over to stay, of course another ill-mannered woman who had not even stopped to check if she was hurt. Luckily, she had managed to keep hold of the vegetables. She threw open the pub door and saw Lucius and Caleb working behind the counter, she dropped the vegetables to the ground, the brown paper they were wrapped in burst open and caused them to roll out across the floor. "There's the veg, I got up extra early to go and fetch!" She snapped sharply and stormed through the inner door, heading for her room.

Lucius and Caleb looked at each other bewildered by her actions, they shook their heads in disbelief. A large potato tumbled toward them coming to a halt just before Caleb's feet, they both bent down to gather up the scattered vegetables. "I imagine she saw Daisy leaving and made a wrong presumption." Lucius sighed. He was quite clearly in deep thought about Nora's odd behaviour.

"Aaah yes!" Caleb agreed, "Go and speak to her Lucius, I will keep a watch out here, I can come and get you if necessary."

Lucius shook his head, "No Caleb, I know her suspicions of me are substantiated but I am tired of her never seeking answers and just making presumptions." He made his way to the table and brushed his hair back with his fingers. He leaned his chin on his fist and looked totally unhappy with the situation. "You know Caleb, if she were really that concerned with me, she would never have gone to meet Jimmy that day. She knew what his intention may be but she was little interested in discussing any part of it with me. No, she will be eating humble pie soon enough when she finds out who Daisy really is!"

Caleb chuckled, "You are both as stubborn as one another Lucius. You know, I probably shouldn't be telling you this, but Mol said Nora had no intention of accepting an offer of proposal from Jimmy, so you had no need of worry." Caleb knew he should not have shared this information with Lucius but he was tired of the situation too. He just wanted them to get beyond their stubbornness and speak with each other in earnest.

Lucius lifted his head and dropped his arm, "Well that is a surprise!" He beamed. "I thought she would surely have accepted, he was a good man. I have not spoken of it to her since that day in case she was upset but we have been getting along very well." Lucius was brighter now, he had thought Nora would have accepted Jimmy's proposal without much resistance at all.

The men saw Nora re-enter through the side door, she completely ignored their presence and headed toward the stairs. Lucius momentarily thought to warn her of what she was about to find upstairs, when his stubbornness surfaced and he decided to leave her to find out for herself. They heard the mumbled conversation between Molly and Nora that came from the kitchen upstairs, Lucius smiled across to Caleb, "Now she knows who the lady leaving the pub is, let us see what she has to say for herself now."

They heard footsteps coming down the stairs, both pretended to busy themselves and waited to see what Nora would say. "I have come to gather the vegetables, sorry I dropped them, I have butter fingers today!" She said gingerly and added a fake laugh as she waited for their reaction.

"Oh, that is fine Nora, accidents happen, are you going to make a special pie with those?" He winked at Caleb and they both laughed.

Nora knew very well what they were amused at and cheekily threw a small carrot at Lucius. In good humour she jibed back, "Only if you share it with me! You could have told me what I had just come home to?" She smirked at them both. "Our heroes!" She laughed, "I laugh but really well done to both of you, Lillian or little Rufi might not have made it if were not for your help."

"Rufi?" questioned Caleb, then with a look of sudden realisation, "Ah, Rufi is the dog's name?"

Lucius joined in conversation, "So Lillian is talking now, did she have more to say?"

"Apparently not, she mostly mumbles but said the dog's name clearly. She is asking for Daisy, it would seem they must be close. I so desperately want to know the whole story but Mol said Daisy is saying nothing for now." Nora complained.

"Yes, I had the same answer when I asked for more information." Lucius crooked his brow. He was not a particularly inquisitive person, he took each day as it came and each person for who they were but this whole scenario had piqued his curiosity.

Chapter 16 – So What Next?

Lillian had fallen asleep with Rufi curled up next to her on the bed, he hadn't left her side. He had to be coaxed in to leaving the room to alleviate himself and then retreat straight back up the stairs to resume his guarding position. Lillian was still a little fidgety but not so restless as she had been, Molly knew she would be settled enough to leave her to sleep. She closed the bedroom door and joined the others downstairs, who were still waiting for Daisy to return.

The group were quietly chatting together when suddenly Nora banged her hands on the table declaring, "You know, seeing her face up close I am sure I recognise her? Those eyes look somehow familiar!"

"Who? Daisy?" enquired Caleb after she had caused him to almost jump out of his skin!

"No." replied Nora, still in deep thought, she tried her hardest to recall a moment when they may have previously met, "I am talking about Lillian. I know she has been in the basin a while now but none of us have really been close enough to see her properly. Yet seeing her today I feel I have seen her elsewhere, outside of the basin?" It annoyed her greatly that she could not recall where.

"Hmm!" Lucius rubbed at his beard in profound thought. "I must admit her face did look familiar but I just thought it was me."

Nora nodded in agreement, "No Lucius but it will come to me it always does!" She grinned at him. "So, Daisy is returning, what will happen when she gets back?"

Molly interjected just in case there was about to be yet another dispute that no one was supposed to know the reason behind! "She will stay here Nora." She caught Nora's anguished face and continued. "She needs to look after Lillian so she will stay in the room with her."

Nora looked over at Lucius, who had prepared a stoic face ready for the conversation he thought he may be about to have, "Then where will you sleep Lucius?" She asked in a remarkably calm manner.

"I did think about the back yard Nora but then I remembered the resident ghost likes to give us a shove out there!" he joked. "No, I will sleep in the spare room, I have been thinking about turning this place in to a guest house, maybe this will serve as a beginning?" He smirked but he had given it a lot of thought and decided that it would be a great idea! The city boomed with industry and there were always people looking for temporary rooms.

"Yes, it will all be proper if you do that Lucius, the two ladies will be sharing a room and if you mention the Guest House idea to patrons that will put their minds at rest about any impropriety." Molly agreed.

Everyone shared their ideas on how it might be best to make the guest house work, they talked of prices and whether food might be served. The pub had many upstairs rooms but Lucius had never made proper use of them other than storage. Before Molly and Caleb's arrival, he had never had the chance to think about developing the pub any further. He had an ever-changing cycle of helping hands that never stayed long. Most of them moved into the High Street pubs that were maybe a little more interesting with their various rooms to let. It gave people something to gossip about and maybe for some, a certain aspiration. He had begun to come around to the idea and with everyone's encouragement and offers of help, he decided that once all this fuss was over, he would make a plan.

Suddenly, Daisy came bursting back through the door. Her red face shone bright with sweat and she was a little out of breath, she had what appeared to be two very heavy bags that she dropped down on to the floor. "Well, I know I said I did not need a lot but our Ruth was helping me pack and put so much in there! She has sent cakes, bread, and a few scones too, she has done a bit of baking after Arthur had a win at the card table! They are all going to the bath house too!" She stopped and came up for air when she realised that the lady sitting at the table was the one, she had nearly bowled over in the street! "Oooh you must be Nora! I am so sorry about earlier, I imagine that they have filled you in on what happened and you know why I was in such a rush." She dashed forward and grabbed Nora's hand to give a very awkward and overzealous handshake.

Daisy had always been a bit of a chatterbox when she was nervous, ever since she was a child. If she thought she was in trouble she would run in to her parents and spend so long professing her innocence that they would feel like their head spun! Most often they would just send her back outside to give their ears a rest!

"Yes, everything has been explained." replied Nora, mouth still agape with wonder at this whirlwind entrance. "I do hope all went well with your family and they aren't unhappy at your staying here? I am sure they will have their reservations?"

Daisy's face blushed again as she looked across to Lucius, "Well, I erm ... well, I told part truth! I told them that I was going to stay with a friend as she was poorly." She stopped and pretended to look about the room to avoid their gaze. She had known that Arthur would be furious if he knew her real whereabouts and would be there straight away to drag her back home. She could not easily lie to Lucius either, he had been so good to her in their childhood and again now.

Caleb tipped his head at Lucius to indicate that he needed to ask more. "Daisy, please tell me that they know where you are?" Lucius enquired, with raised eyebrows and wide eyes.

"Lucius, I am a grown woman, I have lived away from my family for a long time now. I am sure I can come and go as I please." She declared in an unconvincing tone.

"Daisy, I ask you again, as a concerned friend, did you tell them the truth of where you are? I know your Arthur and I know he would not have agreed without argument." Lucius was impatient, he had accepted Daisy's reluctance to reveal the truth of her friendship with Lillian but Arthur was an old friend that he did not want to fall out of favour with.

"I did not tell the whole truth Lucius, Ruth believes I am with a friend from my job at the button factory. Please excuse my telling an untruth but I must protect Lillian and to tell them where I truly am would mean explaining everything." She looked across at him and could see his disappointment in her. "Lucius, I really do promise that the moment I can share the truth, I will and I will also tell Arthur of your disapproval. Your friends are here to witness this." She appealed.

Caleb could see Lucius was conflicted and tried to be the voice of reason, "The way I see it, is that Daisy is an adult, and I understand she is under the protection of her brother now but it really is her choice to make this decision. She did not have to tell us that she lied to Ruth but she has, that shows we can trust her judgment in this situation and how serious it must be for her to be here." He looked over at Daisy who nodded enthusiastically. "Daisy, you must keep your promise and let Arthur know your true whereabouts at the earliest opportunity, do you agree?" Caleb looked at them, he understood that they were both in a predicament that would require some compromise.

Daisy's eyes filled with tears and Nora instinctively put her arm around her shoulder, "I promise, I will. None of this has come easy to me, I do not like untruths but this is a delicate situation that only Lillian herself can resolve. I know she will just as soon as she gets her wits back about her." She looked around at all of them individually as if sealing her sincerity.

"Fair enough then." Lucius agreed and rose to his feet. He couldn't bear to see her cry, she had always had a nervous disposition and he knew this would not be easy for anyone and more so for her. "Let us take these bags upstairs, so that you can get yourself settled. We can talk again when you have rested and feel a little better." He wasn't happy with this situation but he could see how devoted she was to Lillian, he just hoped that Arthur would be so understanding.

He carried her bags upstairs and took them into the room as Daisy followed behind. "You know, I always feel like I am being watched as I walk up these stairs Lucius. It is quite disturbing." She worried.

"Ah yes Daisy, I know that feeling very well! I never did finish telling you about that did I?! Oh well, a conversation for another day." He smiled reassuringly at her. "Don't you worry, I will not let Arthur down, I will keep a good watch on his little sister. Nothing will happen to you Daisy while I am around. I hope you know that?" He was quite sincere, he had every intention of keeping her safe.

She smiled widely at him, she had few friends as a child but she had always thought of Lucius fondly, although he was her younger, he had felt like another big brother until he moved away. She and Arthur were sad to see him leave and had missed him for a long time afterwards. "Thank you, Lucius, ... for everything, you are a good man and once again just like a brother to me. I know this is a lot to ask of you, please know that I really appreciate what you are doing for us."

He patted her shoulder and left her to make herself at home.

The pub doors were opened and it wasn't long before the patrons started to flow in. Maud and George made themselves comfortable in their usual spot, they chuntered away about how they were going to make their fortune. Old man Jack sat in his favourite spot by the fire, sucking on his pipe, with little Teddy curled up at his feet. The Tradesmen stood around, striking deals and getting far too drunk to take on serious discussion about business. Loud laughter and chatter resounded around the room and Lucius glanced around as if surveying his empire, "Time to expand and develop." he smiled to himself in profound thought.

The next morning the kitchen felt like a different place indeed. Daisy was already awake preparing breakfast for them all. Nora was next to arrive and Daisy greeted her with a pretty smile, she looked much brighter and more awake than Nora felt. "Good morning, Nora, oh and here is Lucius! Good morning, breakfast is almost ready take a seat and I will serve up."

Nora felt a little uncomfortable with this situation, seeing to meals was her job and although a little cumbersome at times for the most part, she enjoyed it. "Daisy, you do not have to do this, it's my job to prepare the food, please take a seat and let me finish this for you." She gently protested.

Lucius sat at the table and had to bite his tongue in a bid to hide the fact that he did not care who put his food on the table but someone please put it there quickly! He knew they were both concerned about being able to pay for board but his concern was his belly and right now it needed to be filled. He drummed his fingers loudly on the table, showing his impatience for what he felt was an unworthy discussion.

"Nora, let us work together? I do not plan to stay for long, so while I am here, will you let me help you with the food preparation? I can save you some chores for a little while. Besides this is a delight compared to the factory." She did not want Nora to think that she was trying to take anything away from her and just wanted to help as much as she could.

Nora smiled happily in agreement. It would give her a welcome break from the tedium of cooking two or sometimes three times a day and it was true, Daisy would not be around for long so she would accept her help and appreciate the rest.

Lucius already had his knife and fork in his hands with fists upright on the table, he allowed for no doubt that he was ready to eat, "Great, that's settled then, shall we eat?" he requested with a deadpan expression.

Daisy placed the plates on the table and put Lillian's, to one side as she was still asleep. She took a seat at the table and Nora noticed a haunted look on her face as they began to eat their food. "Is everything alright Daisy? You look a little pre-occupied with something."

"No, I am sorry." Daisy looked at them both with a little fear in her eyes.

"What is it, Daisy? You have me worrying now too. Please do say, you can speak safely here." Lucius was concerned but continued to place a large piece of bread into his mouth.

"Well Lucius, you and I have already spoken about seeing an odd figure and the feeling of being watched previously." She glanced at Lucius and then to Nora.

"It is alright Daisy, Lucius has already told me about that and I have had an experience of my own here. Please do go on." Nora comforted her.

"Well, last night I was fast asleep on the floor in the room with Lillian when I heard her mumbling and shuffling around in the bed." They listened intently as Daisy continued. "Well, I got up just to check that she was comfortable and well ... she had both her hands outstretched as if holding someone's hands in front of her. She was staring up and mumbling away as if someone were there. Rufi was looking up at the very same spot too." She stopped to give an impression of Lillian.

It was most inappropriate but her dramatic impression of Lillian was so funny to them both that they laughed uncontrollably!

"Do not mock me!" She protested, throwing her arms back down to her side and sitting sharply back in her seat. "You said it was safe to tell you and now you laugh!" She pulled back her chair ready to leave the table.

Lucius gently took her arm and encouraged her back to her seat, "Daisy please, we could not help ourselves. We did not mean to laugh and we both said we have our own experiences so we both believe what you saw. It was just your showing of it." He did an exaggerated version of her impression, throwing his hands in the air with a forlorn look on his face. "There you, see? It is a little funny but not so funny when you were woken by it." He chuckled. "Maybe, I can ready another room for you to sleep in? Give me a day or so and I will sort that out for you."

Daisy chuckled, "You're right, it is funny! Thank you so much Lucius and only if it is not too much trouble. I will help you of course! I really do not think I could cope for much longer in the same room, Lillian seems far more stable now, so she will be fine on her own overnight."

Nora joined in the conversation, "Please come down to me if you find yourself frightened again. You could always bed down on my floor if you need while Lucius prepares another room for you."

With the domestic situation now sorted, Nora and Lucius shared all their experiences of the mysterious man in the shadows with Daisy. She was quite astounded and even more scared than she was before! She told Nora that she would bed down in her room after all, why wait she had expressed, she may as well just sort it out now and she would be of less disturbance later at night. They were both amused by her declaration and Daisy blushed.

Chapter 17 – The Truth

Daisy spent much of her time with Lillian, only leaving her for short periods, mostly at mealtimes and when it was absolutely necessary. Lucius and Nora heard them talk from outside the bedroom door and were really surprised as it sounded like Lillian spoke coherently. Daisy kept everything to herself, she assured them that she was close to revealing the whole story but they must be patient and give Lillian time, despite their persistent prods to learn more, she remained hushed.

Molly and Caleb were away on a day off together and had been inspired by Nora and Jimmy to go off for a walk around the park. Lucius, Nora and Daisy were in a daily routine of taking breakfast together and on this morning, it was no different. As they sat quietly chatting about the warm weather, Daisy interrupted the conversation with a request of Lucius, "Lucius, Lillian would like to speak with you today. She is keen to tell you everything and wanted to know if you could spend some time this morning with her?" She asked.

Nora's mouth fell open with shock and her eyes blinked rapidly as what she just heard sank in, "Lillian will SPEAK with Lucius you say?... She will sit and speak with him...Of course, he can spare some time this morning, I will go and get the pub ready by myself, I have done it dozens of times before!"

Lucius who was equally as shocked as Nora declared, "Why thank you Nora but I think I might be able to answer for myself!" He smirked at her and she returned a look of disdain. "Yes of course I will spare the time, in honesty I cannot wait to hear her story. I will come through with you after breakfast if that suits you. Is it me alone that she wishes to speak with?" He puzzled.

Daisy nodded solemnly, which did not go unnoticed but none of them wanted to delay any further so their observation was not mentioned. Daisy felt conflicted, she wanted the truth out in the open but knew that it was going to have consequences. She had spent the last few days with Lillian who had confided her secrets with her. Daisy had taken her time to try to convince her that the only way out of this was to speak the truth and Lillian had eventually agreed.

With breakfast over and Daisy already with Lillian, Lucius reached the door with a trepidation that was not normally in his nature. He shook his shoulders as if to shake off the feeling and knocked on the door.

"Do come in." He heard from behind the door. As he entered, his relieved expression was clear to see when he saw Lillian sitting upright in the armchair looking nothing like the woman that she had been before. Daisy had dressed her well, styled her grey hair in to a neat bun and put on a little blush and lipstick.

"Mr Turner, please take a seat for I believe that what I have to tell you will come as a huge shock." She smiled affirmatively and gestured toward the bed.

Her voice and her mannerism were that of an upper-class woman and Lucius for some unbeknown reason to him, at once obeyed. Half in surprise and half intrigued, he prepared himself ready to listen.

"Mr Turner, I would like to ask that you allow me to complete my story without interruption. You are going to have many questions but it is imperative that you allow me to finish or I may lose my nerve and not be able to continue. Do you agree to these terms?" It was a question that had sounded more like an instruction.

Lucius grew more nervous at what he was about to hear but nothing was going to stop this conversation, he needed to hear all that she had to say, "I agree, please go ahead." His sharp reply and stiffened manner made him appear impatient but in truth, it was apprehension.

Daisy sat silently on the arm of the chair next to Lillian.

Nora had pushed her ear against the door many times only to discover that she could hear nothing but a mumble and had eventually given up.

Lillian began, "Lucius ... Mr Turner, there is no easy way to tell you this, so I will have to be blunt and get straight to the point." Lucius watched as Daisy put her arm around Lillian's shoulder. He clasped his hands together so tight that his knuckles whitened, he prepared himself ready for news as she went on, "You see Lucius, I am your mother."

At that very moment, he felt his head might explode, he did not know whether to laugh, cry or flee! He heard lies! He heard impossibilities, an absurdity that could not possibly be true! He could not help himself, he jumped up in anger and confusion. "I am happy to see that you are now in good health but clearly your mind is still troubled. I will not listen to these lies, my mother died giving birth to me. You are evidently deluded and I absolutely will not listen!" His hand was on the door handle, ready to leave.

Daisy intervened, "Lucius, please come back and sit down. This is the truth and I know it from more than one source. You need to hear this. Please give her a chance to explain all."

Lillian sat stoic in the chair, she gestured her hand toward the bed. Lucius still stunned with utter confusion, returned gingerly and sat back down.

"I am sorry to bring such shocking news but there is so much more to tell you and I need you to understand that this is exceedingly difficult for me." She appealed.

Lucius furrowed his brow and looked from one to the other in bemusement, "Oh I see, difficult for you?!" He questioned sardonically.

"Please do not think me without heart but I must get through this and then we can have an open discussion." She sipped at her drink, to give pause before she continued, her hand shook and the cup wobbled its way back on to the saucer.

"At the age of sixteen, myself and your father Solomon, fell in love after many years of friendship. He was the Farmers son and I was the daughter of a Lord and Lady who owned a large estate not too far from the farm where you, yourself grew up. My parents were not so strict and I was never restrained from contact with other children living on our land. We had grown up closely together being of similar age. We developed a strong bond as children which grew with us into adult hood. Of course, my parents would never have allowed a romantic relationship between us, so we kept it secret." She took pause again and Daisy squeezed her shoulder.

Lucius sat in silence, as he desperately tried to make sense of it all.

"At the age of eighteen, I found myself pregnant and my parents were understandably furious. After much deliberation they decided to send me off alone to Europe. I was appointed a personal Doctor and met on arrival by a French Housekeeper that spoke only a little English. It had also been agreed by my parents that my baby would be taken from me the moment it was born. Lucius, I want you to know that at every moment, I protested. It was not my decision, I wanted more than anything to keep you. The moment they took you from me, the very moment that you were born I was broken. I was never the same again, it broke my heart." Lillian's words were broken as she struggled to speak but she resumed. "The only thing that I was told was that you were born male and was being taken in by a wealthy European family who was desperate for a child of their own and that you would be exceptionally well looked after. I will add that I only recently had news that you were so close by for all those years and that broke my heart once again. I could have watched you grow, even if it were from a distance, I would have been comforted that you were at least with your father." Her eyes filled with tears and she sobbed into her hands.

Lucius welled up too, he walked toward the window so that they could not see his face with tears streaming down to his beard. He was distraught and his body shook with the sobs he could not control. He couldn't believe what he was hearing, the story filled him with sadness but he could not relate it to himself.

"Shall we take a moment and let the news settle a little before continuing?" Daisy suggested.

"No, I would like to continue." he answered obstinately, still facing the window with his back to them. "I know you said no questions but you cannot expect me to sit and listen to such news without needing answers. I presume my father knew you were with child, did he not try and help you? Did he just allow you to be taken off to Europe against your will?" He barked.

Lillian still in tears, understood why he could not hold back his need for more knowledge, "Your father could not have said or done more than he did. He tried so hard to speak with my father, he offered me marriage but there was no chance that they would allow that. He asked me to run away with him and leave the place forever but I was too afraid. He tried everything he could to rectify the situation but it led him nowhere. I can only assume that an agreement was reached for him to have you or that the European family changed their mind. I am unable to tell you more of that as I was unaware of it but I can assure you that Solomon Turner acted in the most humble and responsible way."

"I would not go so far as to say that either of you acted responsibly, I am here as proof of that!" He countered. "He was not evicted from the farm, he was allowed to stay." He observed, "I would think that is evidence of some form of agreement."

Lillian lowered her glance and continued "My parents were not evil." assured Lillian. "They were for the most part, kind, generous and forgiving but they were in a very privileged position and would not have allowed anything to put that at risk. For you to be placed with your father would have meant a huge amount of trust between them, which despite everything must mean they kept a certain amount of respect for him. I am sure they would have offered him money to disappear which clearly, he did not accept. You have no reason to question your father's integrity in all of this and if things had been different then we would have married."

Although he was still dazed by the news, Lucius felt a little comfort that his father had acted in an honourable manner.

Lillian wiped her face with her handkerchief and placed her hands heftily back into her lap. "So, the years went by and I eventually found the sadness tinged with a little happiness when I met and fell in love with my husband, Lord Ellsworth. Lucius, I am sorry I know this must be so difficult for you. I married him and we moved into the house close to the farm, Ellsworth Manor, so close to you! Still not knowing you were there and not being able to go anywhere near as I could not bear to be around your father without being able to speak to him as I once did. I want you to know there was never a day that my heart did not ache for you."

Lucius once again jumped up off the bed, paced the room a little and sat back down. He struggled deeply but needed to know all. "That explains a lot, the reason I felt like I knew you. It's a long story for another time but we ventured out to Ellsworth and saw your painting. Please continue." His patience was waning, he wanted the conversation finished so that he could get out of the room and be alone to think.

Lillian looked at him bemused but continued, "Many years later, my dedicated doctor began to act strangely when he visited. He repeatedly said that I had a little malady and might need some medication. Of course, I refused, I was perfectly healthy with no reason for medication. I had to keep refusing because he became so persistent about it. One day he came and asked that I give him some money. He was in debt from the card table and owed some undesirable people a lot of money, I am not familiar with these things but I understand they can become serious. It was then that the extortion began, he threatened to tell my husband and ruin my marriage, our good names and the excellent reputation of your father, God rest his soul. He said he would reveal all to the whole of society. I could not allow this to happen so I told him to return a week later to give me a chance to get the money together."

Daisy watched as Lucius began to fidget and his face changed from confusion to anger. She knew he would be angry when he heard this, he despised bullies as a child and this Doctor was a bully in the worst conceivable way.

Lillian sounded a little more resilient as she went on, "It was on this visit that I insisted he would not receive a penny from me until he gave me your whereabouts. After arguing for a while, my persistence and refusal to give in forced him in to telling me. Of course, I became hysterical with this news, I had been lied to all this time and as I said before, I thought you were in Europe when the truth was, I was right beside you. I may have got to know you, even if I could not declare who I was, I could have known you!" She said angrily.

"I was in a dreadful condition and have no idea what it was that he dropped from a tiny bottle into my drink. I remember that my husband came to me in my medicated state after Daisy had spoken to him. I confessed everything to him, right there and then. At first, he marched out of the room in anger, I could hear him pacing back and forth in the room next door. I knew he was struggling with the news but I could not go to him as I found myself unable to move, I was too weak with whatever the Doctor had slipped into my drink. After some time, he returned and was the most, loving kind generous man that I always knew him to be. He said that he had wished that I had confided in him from the beginning and that he had nothing but compassion for my situation. He was going to make sure everything would be settled for you and me to be re-united whatever it took. He was quite an extraordinary man, I should have known that he would have accepted my past." She looked over toward Lucius, he still had his hands clasped together tightly and his head lowered so far that she was unable to see his reaction.

She continued, "I was placed in bed after that and was woken with the terrible news that my wonderful husband had been found drown in the canal, I asked for Daisy and was told that she had gone. I was so distraught that they sent for my doctor, unknowingly, the very same Doctor that was extorting me. My protests were taken as a sign of my dwindling mental health and were ignored. He came every day and due to my being unable to protest, forced that disgusting medicine down my throat, took his payment and left."

Lillian spoke with venom, the months of torture had taken their toll and without the medication, she could finally see through the fog of events that this dreadful man had put her through.

"The staff at the house were becoming increasingly concerned about my health so conveniently he had the very ammunition he needed to have me admitted to the Infirmary. It took me away from everyone I cared for and everyone that cared for me. He still took his money and was living as if nothing had happened. It was not until one day when I found myself particularly clear minded and told him that I no longer cared for his threats and if he did not get me out of there I would go to the police. Of course, I was bluffing, I could not do that to my husband's memory, he was an innocent in all this, I was desperate to get out of there, I insisted he hide me close to you so that I could see you. The infirmary was a cruel, harsh place and what I can only imagine is not that different to a prison with meals provided. I do not remember travelling to the boat and was not privy to the arrangements but I was simply happy to wake up and find that I was out of that horrid place. He still visited me daily and forced that vile medicine on me but it was there that I became most afraid. He presumed that due to my medicated, docile state I would not remember anything he said and the vile man started to treat me like a confessional priest. Telling me of his sick acts of adultery and then the worst thing ever, the callous and cruel murder of my dear husband!"

Daisy and Lucius looked at each other in horror. Lillian had revealed this to Daisy only the day before but it was still fresh on her mind and had profoundly disturbed and frightened her. Lucius was in turmoil, he just could not believe what he heard. It was one shock after another and he felt tremendously sorry for poor Lillian.

Lillian saw their expression and reassured them that she felt well enough to finish and so she persisted, "That night, my husband had gone to find the Doctor. I think Lord Ellsworth had arranged that particular meeting place because he was going to see you too Lucius. He had told the Doctor that he had received more than his due to keep quiet and there would be no more money from us, he warned him that he would go to the police if he continued his pursuit for more. The Doctor said that my husband's biggest mistake was coming to see him and that he should have just gone to the police." Lillian's face changed from anger to despair as she explained further, "As soon as he turned his back, the Doctor told me that he had picked up a large rock and hit him on the back of the head with it. When he fell to the floor, he kicked him in to the canal unconscious, he tossed the rock over the fence and ran away like the coward he is. I have been trying to call out to you all at every opportunity. I could scarcely muster the strength to get out on deck and the medication had left me such little control, I could barely sense reality and struggled to make any sense. The day I saw Daisy leaving the pub, I knew she would instantly recognise me so I tried desperately to get her attention and that's when I fell in the water."

Lucius experienced every emotion he had ever felt throughout his lifetime all at once. He was in turmoil and totally without words. He said the only thing he could muster, "Daisy, you have something to say?"

"Yes Lucius, that same night when the Doctor was threatening to go to Lord Ellsworth, he caught me listening at the door to their conversation. I already had my suspicions about his conduct for quite a while and thought that he was up to no good. The Lady always looked troubled by his visits and I was certain I had seen him moving in the same circles as some of my brothers' acquaintances. The card tables, the houses of disrepute and other ruinous places. You have seen where my brother lives and the places that surround them, I was not certain but I had a feeling I had seen him around there." She briefly paused and walked toward the window.

Her voice shook, "On his arrival that evening, I let him in to the Lady's sitting room, making certain that I had left the door slightly ajar, he must have spotted me through the gap at some point, I don't know how or when but he had seen me. As he left the room, he grabbed me tightly around the throat with his arm thrust hard against my stomach, slamming me against the wall and threatening me. He was so angry, he said that if I did not leave without speaking a word of what I had heard, he would see to it that not only would I be seriously hurt but Lady Ellsworth and my brother too. He said that he knew some nasty people and that if anything were to happen to him, I would regret it. He would hurt my loved ones first and then come for me, he was hissing at me, like an animal! He was evil, like he was possessed, I tried to pull away but he was too strong! I was petrified, had never been so scared in all my life and still am now for fear he may come looking for us." All the emotion that she had felt that evening returned as she recalled that day.

She returned to her seat beside Lillian, "After he left, I went straight in to check on Lady Ellsworth, she was unconscious but breathing steadily. I took the glass out of her hand and placed a blanket over her before going straight to the Lord. I told him that she had been arguing with the Doctor and that she looked in a poorly state. I did not want to agitate the situation or raise suspicion, so I chose not to reveal any of the conversation or threat that I had received. I then went down to Mrs T and it broke my heart to tell her I was leaving. I raced straight to Arthur where I have been hiding ever since. News of Lord Ellsworth's death affected me deeply, I had my suspicions that the Doctor might be involved and that frightened me even more. It was all so sad and I wish I had done more. When I heard my Arthur had seen you, I had to come and find out for myself if you knew anything. I had heard the doctor telling the Lady your name and address and was not sure if you knew anything about your history. If only I had known what was to unfold and the cruel months that followed for you Lady Ellsworth, I would have never left. My attempts to protect the truth have all been in vain. The truth would have been far better out and you would have been safer." Daisy wiped her tears away with her handkerchief.

Lucius was dumbfounded. All this crying, all this news, the emotion, he felt like he was outside his own body observing and hearing a tale that wasn't his. He needed air, he needed to escape. Both women waited for a reaction from him that he was incapable of giving. He finally managed to respond but only to say, "I must apologise, I find myself in need of some air. I may have questions." He lifted one side of his mouth in an attempt to smile, "Though, I am not certain that I am ready for any answers just yet. I am not a man of emotion and I am finding this extremely overwhelming. I will ask you to do something for me before I leave." They nodded in agreement and Lucius continued. "After what I have just heard, I would rather you weren't alone. I know you do not want this story shared but I have good friends here, whom I would trust with my life and I ask that you do so. Daisy, please leave now and fetch them before I go. I want you to tell them all that you have told me and that they do not leave this place until my return. Tell them that it's my request and I promise they will do it without a word ever being shared. Do either of you object?" He croaked.

Lady Ellsworth replied, "Please do what you need to do but come back as soon as you can, I am sure you would be better around friends? If you trust these people then so do I."

"Daisy, please go and fetch Nora, Caleb and Molly, tell them as I have told you to. I will leave from the kitchen. I am not in mind to speak with anyone else yet, I need to leave. Be as quick as you can please!" He forced a smile and left the room. Daisy ran down the stairs in search of the three.

Lucius fumed, he had never felt such fury in his entire life. How could he not have known any of this? Who was this disgusting creature that called himself a doctor? He paced around the kitchen, until he heard the footsteps and the voices of his friends as they came up the stairs. He heard the angst in Nora's voice clearly, "I know you said you will tell everything in the room but please at the very least tell us if all is well with Lucius?"

"Yes." He heard Daisy confirm, "He has had to leave briefly but he will be back soon and you can see him them. You will know everything once we are inside and out of ear shot."

After he heard the door shut, Lucius crept down the stairs and walked out of the pub door.

Chapter 18 – The Aftermath

With everyone else informed, albeit in a less detailed version, the mood was sombre. Each had been left with their own reaction but all had Lucius's welfare at the forefront of their minds. Nora wanted him home and for nothing more than to support and comfort him. Molly, who had known Lucius for quite some time and had seen a softer side to him recently was greatly concerned at how he might react to this shocking news. Caleb felt the urge to run off in search of him but was conflicted as he had also been entrusted to stay with Daisy and Lillian. He knew Lucius would struggle, so it made sense to Caleb that he would need his privacy.

Everyone busied themselves and kept the pub open as usual, Daisy and Lillian remained upstairs as anxious as the rest, they all wanted Lucius to return. The hours passed by and each time the door opened, their hopes of seeing him enter were met with disappointment.

Suddenly the door burst open and Maud marched into the pub looking completed flustered with a crimson face! She yelled over to Caleb, "Oi... your pals at the top of the slope in a right old state!" They all stopped to listen as George shuffled in behind his wife. "He's slumped on the floor, drunk as a skunk he is! Me and my George tried to help him up and he shouted that he didn't need no beggars asking him for money and we should clear off! Insulted we were!" She yelled.

"Yes." concurred George, "Then he threw a load of money at us, like we were asking him for it!" He protested.

"Alright George!" Maud jumped in and thrust her large elbow into his ribs, winding him in the process. "They don't need to know all that, he won't even remember, you fool!"

"Right, well thank you for that." Caleb retorted. "We will go and get him home, I guess he has had a few and will be right as rain soon enough."

Old Jack still with his back turned and pipe hanging precariously from the side of his mouth intervened, "Good luck with that! Let me suggest you take a few with you, I do not fancy yer chances alone Caleb. He might be too far gone to recognise you."

"Your right Jack, thanks for that, I also need to stay inside for the moment, I made a promise to Lucius that I wouldn't leave this evening, we are waiting on a visitor." Replied Caleb perplexed.

Jack nodded toward a group of workmen who were regular patrons and Caleb was pleased with the suggestion.

Caleb approached the group, while Nora and Molly watched on in hope that they would hurry. "Right, you lot!" coaxed Caleb forcefully. "We need your help to go and bring Lucius back home. He's a little worse for wear at the top of the slope so he might give you a bit of hell but you must bring him straight back. All drinks will be free for the rest of tonight and tomorrow night if you succeed. Will you go?" He urged.

"I'm not so sure about that Caleb! I have seen Lucius take out four men in one sweep when they angered him in here one night. I felt sorry for them!" Said one of the younger members of the group, he looked around at the rest of the men who were all nodding agreement in unison.

Harry, who was the eldest of the group, placed his tankard down on to the table and declared, "Look this is Lucius, he has helped every single one of us in one way or another and no I am not looking forward to this but we have no choice. He is one of our own, we can't leave him lying on the floor outside, let's go help him!" They all nodded reluctantly, put down their tankards and replaced their caps from their back pockets. They laughed as they left through the front door, Harry shouted back over his shoulder, "Pray for us!" as they left the pub.

At the top of the slope, they saw Lucius looking rather worse for wear, slumped on the floor. His long legs were stretched out in front of him and his back was against the stone wall, he appeared to be fast asleep with his head nestled on his shoulder. Harry, bent down and tried to rouse him, he tapped his shoulder and spoke quietly, "Lucius, it's me Harry, we need to get you back to the pub."

Lucius's eyes shot wide open, he jolted forward and hollered, "You picked the wrong day to try and mug me pal!" his bent arm reached up and his clenched fist hooked Harry's chin with such a force that it sent him reeling backwards into the group. He slumped directly back against the wall with a satisfied smile and closed his eyes again.

Robert who was younger than the others tried to make his exit but Harry protested, "Get back here! We need everyone! Let me just think for a minute. We need a different approach to grab hold of him." He stroked at his already swollen chin. "He has quite a punch, I don't want another! So, no one leaves!" Lucius began to shuffle a little and they all retreated slightly to ensure they were out of reach.

"Here's what we're going to do!" Harry said enthusiastically. "The biggest of us will grab him under his arms, another two on his legs and I will grab him round the middle, then we pull him up. No one let's go, do you understand me?"

The group arranged themselves in to position, Lucius was a large man so they approached with trepidation. "Right when I say go, grab him and stand him up! Everyone ready?" They all nodded in agreement. "Right go!" He yelled.

Harry was the quickest and just as he reached Lucius's waist, Lucius lifted his leg and kicked out catching poor Harry directly between the legs! Lucius once again laughed and turned his head, shut his eyes, and looked to be asleep again.

Harry writhed on the floor, his hands clutched between his legs, he groaned out in pain! "Why? Why?" He shouted angrily! "Why am I copping all the hits! I told you when I say go, you must grab him! The next time I get hit, I am going to smack each one of you, so grab him properly this time!" He commanded.

Harry managed to regain his breath and composure, he ordered them to get back in to position. This time the group had for some reason, found a renewed concentration and motivation ……! "Right now, go!"

The group moved into swift action, both arms and legs were grabbed tightly as Harry had Lucius firmly round the waist. With earnest effort they managed to raise him from the ground. His drunken, limp body was so heavy and his head flopped around as if it were unattached! Suddenly Lucius lifted his head and his eyes widened, the men almost let go in fear but Harry yelled again, "Keep hold of him, if you know what's good for ya!"

It seemed as though Lucius had a moment of near clarity when he uttered, "Harry, my old friend. What are you doing in the Crown? You should be in my pub! Come on, let's go to the Rest!" With that his head slumped back down to his shoulders and his eyes shut once more.

The men almost slid Lucius back down the slope. His heavy and uncooperative body made him much more difficult to manage. A group had gathered outside the pub to watch as they dragged him inside.

Nora agreed with Caleb's suggested that she let Lucius stay in her apartment and she would go and stay upstairs in his place. As Caleb held the door open to let the men through to the apartment, Maud grabbed his arm. "I know Lucius and I have had our disputes but I have known that young man since he was a kid. I aint never seen him that drunk Caleb, not once! I've seen him merry and on occasion angry but never so drunk! You need to look after him, he's haunted he is, in more ways than one if you get what I'm saying." She looked skyward and across the room, reminding Caleb of the spirit they thought may be present in the pub. "I don't want to know what's up with him, I can't keep my mouth shut when I've had a few the whole pub knows that! I mean no malice when I gossip but I get carried away with myself. He's a kind heart that man, he needs looking after, even if he doesn't say it." She confided.

Caleb was moved by Maud's concern, she was usually so brash and often downright offensive. He returned the kindness, "I will Maud and if it's any comfort, he does speak fondly of you, don't ever tell him I told you so though!" Caleb had spoken the truth, Lucius had a soft spot for Maud and George, despite their cunning ways he had always seen the drive for survival behind their deeds. He knew neither of them could inflict harm on anyone or anything and their humour had entertained the pub on many occasions. Maud had gotten Lucius out of many scrapes when he had sneaked off to the market as a teen and he had never forgotten it.

"Well so long as you don't remind him about the money he gave me, we have a deal!" She cackled as she went back to take her regular seat with George.

"There's the Maud I know!" Caleb chuckled quietly to himself, he asked Molly if she would go upstairs and let Daisy and Lillian know that Lucius had returned. The news was a relief to them both and they knew that tomorrow would bring new questions.

At the close of the evening, Caleb saw to it that all five men took a jug of ale off with them. He was not so sure that it would make its way back to their houses when he saw the slops hitting the floor as they swung them whilst singing their way out the door! Molly and Caleb were to sleep in the room that Lucius had been in and Nora bedded down on the couch for the night. Caleb protested greatly but she insisted that as it was only for one night, she really was not troubled by it. He did not want to leave any of them alone in the house, so he was adamant that wherever he lay his head it would be in the pub. He popped his head in to check on Lucius before he made his way upstairs. He found that he snored so loud that he was certain the walls were vibrating, he shook his head at the state his good friend had got himself in to and left the room.

The next morning Daisy made breakfast for everyone. Eggs for all with bread and butter, washed down with a hot cup of tea. Molly had spent her first night ever, in a proper full-sized bed and protested humorously about leaving it. She had the best night's sleep in such a long while. There had been no scratching or scurrying from the rats that occasionally made their way inside the cabin. She had been able to stretch out in all directions and still had room to roll! As she stepped down on to the floor, she instantly felt the absence of the gentle rocking motion that she had known all of her life. She paced around the room, taking large steps to demonstrate to Caleb how much space there was around the bed, a fact that seemed to hold her interest far more greatly than it did Caleb's. "Moll, as delightful as it is watching you prance about this room, we really must get on." She made one last twirl around the room before both went downstairs. Molly went directly to see to Cobbles and Caleb to get the pub ready.

Caleb knocked Nora's apartment door loudly to ensure he would wake Lucius. "Come in for a moment Caleb." Lucius croaked from behind the door. Lucius looked as grey as the skies on a dark winter's day. He sat on the edge of the bed, bent forward as if he had forgotten how to stand. Caleb laughed loudly and Lucius smirked back at him. "Please tell me what damage I have done before I walk out the door? I cannot face anyone until I know exactly what happened. I remember right up to leaving the Crown and from there, just momentary glimpses of people staring down at me." He leaned his head back down and cupped his forehead with both hands.

Caleb chuckled, "Well Lucius, I think you owe poor Harry a new pair of trousers because his were torn the second time you knocked him to the floor!" He watched as Lucius sunk his head deeper in to his hands as the memories started to return. "Lucius they were all fine, they understood that this was not something that you would normally do and besides, I promised them free drinks this evening in order of apology." Lucius looked sideways at him in shock. "Don't look at me like that Lucius, it was the least I could do after the trauma you gave them!" They both laughed and shared the rest of last evenings stories.

Daisy and Nora were seated at the table talking over their concerns about Lucius when they heard his gruff cough as he came up the stairs.

Nora kept her eyes down as he entered the room, Daisy greeted him far too raucously, "Good morning, Lucius! I hope you're not feeling too sick today. I have prepared you some porridge to ease your stomach just in case." Nora chuckled to herself and waited eagerly for his reaction.

Lucius's face resembled that of a child who had just had their toy taken from them," Excuse me Daisy, you have prepared what?" He winced and hoped that he had misheard her.

Nora jumped up to get the bowl, "Porridge oats Lucius, Daisy has been very thoughtful of your condition last night and added a little salt for flavour." She turned her head to hide her laughter.

Lucius visibly wretched as he put his clenched fist to his mouth to prevent vomiting.

"Here you go!" She declared in an exaggerated happy tone as she pushed the bowl right under his nose.

Lucius took one look at what he considered to be slimy, lumpy slop in front of him and ran toward the window, which he flung open and sucked in the air deeply!

Both women laughed hysterically as he hung his head out the window, he cursed his friends at The Crown for encouraging him to take so much drink!

"Here Lucius." Daisy said, once she had managed to stem the giggling. "I saved you some eggs as well just in case." She placed the plate on the table and they watched him walk back as if he had been seriously injured.

Daisy and Nora spoke amongst themselves as Lucius struggled to eat. Each mouthful of food, seemed to take an age to chew, he had to pause in between bites to take in some air. He was not sure what ailed him most, his head or his stomach so his free arm switched between the two.

"Thank you, Daisy," he mumbled as he swallowed the last mouthful. "Would you mind leaving Nora and I to speak for a while please? I will come through and speak to you shortly." He wiped his mouth with the back of his hand. Nora looked on and felt nervous at what might be ahead.

"Nora, would you come and sit with me please?" Lucius politely requested.

Nora took the seat opposite Lucius and wiped down at her skirts, a habit she had formed when she was feeling anxious.

"Nora, I have spoken a little already with Caleb this morning when he came to check on me but I wanted to explain to you first." He used his most charming smile for Nora on this occasion because he always caught a softening in her face when he did. Nora sat quietly and waited for more. "You heard my news and I assume they explained all?"

Nora nodded in confirmation, "Yes Lucius and I am so sorry that you have received such a shock. Of course, I know that's why you were in such a state last night. I cannot imagine how news like that might make you feel." She could see the sorrow behind his eyes and just wanted to hug him.

"Yes, it has been a shock but what is done is done and cannot be undone." he replied softly, "When I left here last night, I went to get some air and an idea came to me while I was walking aimlessly. I realised that I might get information about that doctor if I went into the Crown. You know I have friends in there and thought a few drinks might get them talking freely." His hand went up to his head again as the throbbing pain continued.

"Did they tell you anything Lucius, what did you ask?" She queried and pushed his drink toward him to encourage him to sip.

He took a large gulp and replied, "I thought they might know of this Doctor and his whereabouts. There can't be many doctors that have such dodgy dealings around here but you can bet that if there are, then they would know."

"So, did they? Did they know him?" She impatiently enquired.

"Well, I ensured to keep my conversation very vague, the last thing I wanted was to be in their pockets for any favours. You know what those men are like Nora and I won't be owing them any favours, not for anything. Anyway, I turned the conversation to card tables and how wasteful I thought it was and they mentioned a doctor who had been turned away from the classy tables and had been forced to take up a seat with them." Nora's eyes widened with intrigue and Lucius went on. "They said that he had not been seen around for a while and he owed quite a few nasty people some money. They think he has gone in to hiding. So, you see his threats of getting his vicious friends to deal with Daisy were idle. He has no friends as far as I could understand, just enemies and lots of them!"

"It must be him! But oh dear, how on earth can we find him now if he's in hiding?!" Nora replied.

"Oh, I already have a plan for that Nora, he visits regular to Lillian remember, he must be returning in her absence to try and locate her? I just wanted to know more about the man and what we are dealing with and how best to conduct myself in this situation. I fear no man Nora but I cannot be in all places at all times and those ladies in there could be in danger if I cannot protect them." He suddenly looked up at her in angst. "That's not all though, there is more I want to confide in you." He reached his hand over and took Nora's hand in his.

She really wanted to put her arms around him to comfort him but she held back. She had no idea of what he was about to say, so decided to wrap her fingers in his instead. "Please go-ahead Lucius, you can tell me anything you know that."

"On a previous visit to the Crown before I had all this news, I saw another old friend in here, well I say friend but not really." He stopped for a few seconds and searched for the right words, he squeezed her hand. "Clara was in there Nora." He felt her hand withdraw from his as her face changed from intrigue to sadness in one moment. He held her hand a little firmer. "I did not tell you before because we were caught up in this other business but I found out that she is married."

Nora tore her hand away and leant as far back in the chair as she could, creating more distance between them. "Really Lucius! A married woman!" She yelled. "I know you have a long history but this is far too much, even for you!"

He stood up and slowly walked around the table and took the seat next to her, he pulled both her hands in to his, "Please let me finish and then you can do whatever you will but I need you to hear me. She was in The Crown again last night and I was so angry about everything, seeing her there was the last thing I needed in that moment. The marriage was a complete surprise to me, I had absolutely no idea of it, I promise you I didn't. I am disgusted and ashamed, I would never have been involved if I had known! You know me well enough now to know that!" He appealed.

"So, what if I believe that then, what now do you have to say? You could not help yourself and went back home with her again? Please continue before I get up and leave!" Her face was red and her hands trembled.

"I manged to get a moment alone with her. I told her how shocked and disgusted I was and that I never want to see her again. She apologised and seemed sincerely sorry. I don't know what has caused her to behave that way and I never will, she will not be a part of our lives anymore Nora." He looked at her with deep sincerity and searched her face in hope to find confirmation that she had believed him. "You are going to see a change in me Nora, I am going to show you the man that I really am and not the one that I have been hiding behind all these years. I am asking you to let me show you that?" He looked at her in serious anticipation, he was being completely genuine with her. He had heard the consequences of denying true love although it would seem forbidden love for his parents. He had compared that to Molly and Caleb, who despite everything and everyone being against them had remained together, here they were, a couple with the most minimal of belongings in life and yet the happiest people he had ever met.

Nora was stuck for words, she had not expected this. She had waited to hear this for so long now and yet was not ready for it! "I think you should go and speak with Lillian and Daisy now, they must be getting anxious." Was all she had been able to muster.

Lucius furrowed his brow in confusion, he had hoped for more than that. He had built himself up to be more honest with her and speak from the heart and she had barely reacted, he felt disheartened.

"I also think that you could let me come in with you, to be your support and to make sure you don't run off and get involved in pub brawls again!" She gave him a sassy grin.

He was so pleased to hear this, it was confirmation that she understood and believed what he had told her. "I would be grateful for that Nora, I cannot think of anyone else I would want at my side more than you." He smiled at her, he examined her face and saw the real concern she showed for him and recognised that he could share so much more.

"I'm sorry Lucius" Nora declared, "You have so many difficulties to manage and I really do not wish to add to them, you must be in such confusion."

Lucius looked pensive, "I have no idea what to think of all this, I find myself grieving a mother that I never actually had and was too young to grieve when I supposedly lost her. He crooked his brow, "I am grieving a woman that never existed?" He chuckled nervously

"Now I do have a mother, who I have known as two different people, a crazy old lady called Lillian and an elegant, respectable Lady Ellsworth." He laughed loudly now. "I don't even know what to call her?!" He walked toward the window and took a deep breath.

Nora stood beside him and shared his gaze from the window, "You do not have to find all the answers right now, it has been a huge shock but I think you must remember how hard it would have been for them both. Especially for Lillian who had to face going off to Europe alone at such an early age with child, she must have been terrified and bereft afterwards too. They had little to no choice of any decisions being made for them but between them, they still ensured you had the best life possible and I think it is important for you to remember that." She placed her hand on his shoulder.

"Of course, you are right." he conceded. "I am shocked at the news but most of my anger is directed at this Doctor. He must be found! It seems my parents did the best they could with the input they were allowed. I have a good life and my father was the best man I knew, I suppose I never thought of him as being anything other than perfect. None of us are though, are we? We can only try to reach for perfection." He turned and smiled at her.

She grinned and leaned forward to peck his cheek softly.

The peck was a small gesture but a huge symbol for them both. It was an unspoken signal of hope and a renewed truce between them that they both planned to build on.

The pair walked through into the room where Lillian and Daisy sat looking out of the window. Lillian smiled at them both and declared, "I see you are looking a little under the weather Lucius, I hope you are not too sickly today?"

"Yes, I am not feeling quite myself and it was all my own doing!" He confirmed, "Nora will be joining us, I have just couple of questions to ask."

Daisy gave Nora a knowing smile, she had secretly hoped that these two would sort themselves out and it appeared they were a little closer to that.

"Very well." Lillian grinned, "Then maybe it would be best for you to ask anything more you need to know?"

Lucius felt quite exposed, as if all eyes were upon him now and he suddenly wished he was invisible. He composed himself, "Did my grandmother know, any of this?" It was a question that had been on his mind ever since he had been told.

"I am sorry, I do not know that. I was not informed myself and the Doctor did not go into a lot of detail. I do know that your grandmother would never have judged your father harshly had she known. She would have been greatly disappointed and would not have hidden her feelings from him but she would have forgiven him. Sol ... Solomon always took great care of her and showed her profound respect." Lillian affirmed.

"Yes, my grandmother was a wonderful lady, salt of the earth!" He squeezed his hands together and looked down, he recalled the affection he had from her as a child. "Does anyone know, other than this Doctor? I do not know why I am asking, what does it matter really?" He realised how futile his question was the moment he asked it.

Nora squeezed his hand, which was noticed by all! "It's understandable that you want to know Lucius, you probably feel like you are the only one that did not know, that should have known." She said affectionately.

"Yes of course and you have every right to ask any question you wish. I can only tell you those that I am privy to having knowledge of this and that would be my parents who are now deceased, Mrs Tranter my housekeeper, who was my family housekeeper at that that time and Doctor Morgan who attended me in Europe and has tortured me ever since. You shall not be a secret anymore, it has caused us so much pain and I am terribly sorry for all of us." She was solemn but had made up her mind that she would not live this life of lies any longer.

Lucius was surprised to hear this, "That must be your decision. It will affect your life far more than it would mine and I certainly do not ask for you to do that. I would like to know of this Doctor Morgan, I am certain you said he visited you often at the boat. He would know by now that you are not there. He must be looking for you, do you have any clue as to where I might find him?"

"I am not sure Lucius." she said regretfully, "I would not think it prudent of you to go hunting for this man, it might end badly and then we would have more trauma to deal with." She looked at him warmly as she continued, "He visited me regularly each evening and now I have my wits about me and Daisy as witness, I will fetch for the Police as soon as my strength is restored well enough to tell them the tale." She searched his face for confirmation that he would leave it to the Police.

"There, Lucius, you see no need for you to go getting yourself in any strife now is there?" Nora spoke as if in instruction, rather than request.

Daisy knew Lucius well enough to know that although calm on the exterior, he was not a man to wait around for the Police. She looked at him in angst and hoped sincerely that he would listen to their reason.

"We will see." Lucius replied unconvincingly, "I am just thinking that maybe I could catch him and take him to the station myself." He smirked over at Lillian. "Let us concentrate on getting you well, I am sure you are eager to get back to your life. In the meantime, I must get back to my pub, Mol and Caleb must be tired of my leaving them." He stood up to leave, with his hand on the door.

"Indeed Lucius, we all have many things to look forward to." Lillian grinned at Nora as she spoke, making her blush. "I am here, should you want to know more and thank you for taking such diligent care of Daisy and I, we are both very grateful to all of you."

"One more thing before I go down to work, Daisy may have told you already that we have both seen a shadow like figure of a gentleman roaming this place ... I don't really know how to explain whether it be imaginary or something else but not a physical person? I'm sorry I don't know what you must think but could it be your deceased husband?" He grimaced at what he had just said, to his surprise Lillian beamed.

"Oh, you have no need to explain more!" She asserted. "I thought that the withdrawal of the drugs was causing me to hallucinate. He was here with me often when I was in and out of sleep. I could see him as clear as I see you all now and felt that he was holding my hands as I slept. I could hear him bidding me to open my eyes. Daisy told me about the experiences that you have all had and I am convinced that he is here. I believe he was trying to get us together and encouraging me to get well again." She spoke with conviction, there was no hesitation in her conveyance.

Lucius paused and smiled before he left the room. As he headed down the stairs, he heard such a commotion that he ran toward the pub lounge. He thought to himself that if one more thing may happen, he might run for the hills and become a hermit. He heard Caleb shouting and what sounded like Arthur cursing and repeatedly calling out for Daisy. Daisy and Nora ran down the stairs behind him.

Arthurs huge frame loomed over Caleb making him look small and vulnerable. Despite the vast difference in size Caleb remained stoic and refused to back away from the entrance to the steps that led to the living quarters. "You are not going up there." Caleb snapped defiantly. "I will call Lucius to come and speak with you but you must calm down and lower your voice if you care anything at all for your sister." Thankfully there were only a couple of patrons in the pub, however that meant Caleb dealing with the situation on his own until Lucius appeared.

Lucius at once placed himself between Caleb and Arthur, "Arthur, you need to settle down and let us speak about this calmly. Daisy is here and I will gladly fetch her for you but not while you are in such a rage."

Arthur was furious, his clenched fists hung by his side, "You will fetch her here right now! How dare you bring her here to this place, I told you I would not allow it! She lied to us, I had to hear it from gossip on the street. Bring her now Lucius or I may lose my temper!" He seethed.

Lucius felt so bad for Arthur, he completely understood why he was so angry but he was not going to be threatened like this in his own pub. "Arthur, we both know the outcome of you losing your temper and I have no desire to hurt you. Let us explain, it is not what I imagine you are thinking. Let us sit down and talk about this before we have regrets." He did not want to fight with Arthur, he knew that Arthur would be the loser in this match and did not want to cause him any more pain.

"Regrets!" He bellowed, "Regrets, there is no regret in defending my sister's honour!" He was so disappointed in both of them. He had been on an errand to fetch supplies from the market for Ruth, when he had stopped to chat with Richard his friend who lived close by. Richard had mentioned rather casually of seeing Daisy working in the Boatman's Rest. Arthur had been blinded by rage and left his friend mid conversation to confront Lucius and Daisy.

Daisy burst through the door, "Arthur, you need to listen, this is completely my own doing and absolutely no choice of Lucius! I will not speak to you in here. Please come outside and speak with me privately!" Daisy stormed outside in the hope that Arthur would follow and the argument with the two men would stop.

Arthur and Lucius continued to argue indoors, Daisy had reached the arch where the cobbled slope split in to two. She was just about to turn back because she could still hear the commotion from inside, when she felt someone grab her from behind. A hand was placed firmly over her mouth and she could hear the rasping breath from her assailant as she was dragged toward the tunnel entrance. Her heart pounded so fast as she struggled to escape, she tried to pull herself away from whoever it was that had such a tight grip but their strength outmatched hers. She shook her head violently trying to remove the hand from her mouth, her arms were held so tightly against her body she could not move them. She felt terribly nauseous and close to fainting as she could not catch a breath. She could still hear the shouts from inside the pub, so knew that Arthur was still inside and she feared she might die.

"How lucky am I to bump into you out here and not have to go into that dreadful place!" Daisy knew this voice, it was Doctor Morgan and she at once knew that she was right to fear for her life, her legs felt ready to collapse! "It's you isn't it!" he rasped, the scent of stale alcohol emanating from his foul breath. "I know that you've been hiding her somewhere! Where is she? You will tell me now or you will join that stupid husband of

112

hers." He hissed through his breath at her as he shoved her toward the water and threatened to throw her in. "I can't risk having her roaming around, where is she?" He shoved her closer to the water.

Inside the pub, Lucius and Arthur had come to their senses and realised that Daisy had gone outside. "I think you've scared your sister enough Arthur, she's run off!!" Lucius warned as he marched outside with Arthur in tow.

As they stepped outside, they immediately saw Daisy grappling to free herself from a strange man who was hovering her precariously over the water! The scene sent them both into a fury!

"My God!" Lucius yelled as he raced toward them. Arthur followed close behind him. "Oi! Let go of her!" he shouted as he grabbed the Doctor by the scruff of his neck and threw him to the floor, pinning him to the ground. Daisy ran straight to Arthur and threw her arms around him, trying to catch her breath in between sobs. "One of you run for a Policeman, you will find one at the top of the street!" He ordered to the crowd who had run to join them outside.

Arthur raged at the Doctor, whilst still trying to comfort his sister," What were you doing man?! How dare you lay your hands on my sister!" He wanted to go and punch him but Daisy clung so tight he would not leave her.

Lucius had to use every essence of will power not to beat this man, he had wanted to track him down and hurt him since the moment he had heard of the cruel treatment he had inflicted on two defenceless women. He knew he had to show restraint if he wanted to see him come to justice. He did not rate his chances of being judged at the courts against an upstanding doctor. It wasn't long before they heard the Police whistle and two officers ran down the slope toward them. Daisy had been led to the seating area where Molly and Nora attempted to console her.

"Officer!" Doctor Morgan yelled before anyone had chance to speak. "I am Doctor Morgan, these men have assaulted me, while I was trying to attend my patient." He looked sideways at Lucius and sneered smugly.

Lucius raised a clenched fist in anger but heard the appeal from Arthur, "Lucius, NO!! He is not worth it, he is not going to get away with this!" Although conflicted, he lowered his fist but increased his grip on the Doctor, pinning him harder to the ground.

"Come here you!" Shouted the elder of the two officers to Lucius. "Assaulting a doctor trying to do his work, I think you and your friend will be coming with us!" Lucius was not about to let go of Doctor Morgan, he did not move, even as the officer grabbed at his arm, he was steadfast and frozen. The second officer took hold of Arthur's arm who looked down at him with a contemptuous frown, the officer looked tiny next to him and he knew this would not be easy.

Lucius looked up directly into the officer's eyes and in quiet defiance asserted, "He's lying and you will have to kill me before I let this murderer go."

The crowd shouted at the officers, "He's no Doctor! He was attacking that young lady!"

"That man is a murderer and he was just about to throw me in the cut. Please do not believe him, he is a liar of the worst kind!" Daisy pleaded with them.

Molly and Nora were both hanging on to Caleb along with two other men trying to restrain him, as he desperately tried to get to the policeman who had hold of Lucius's arm.

Doctor Morgan, who had managed to sit up yelled, "I am a doctor, see, there is my bag over there on the floor, they were trying to steel my medication ..." Suddenly mid-sentence he fell silent. He looked up into the distance and saw the shadowy figure of a man that he recognised as Lord Ellsworth, the man he had callously hit with a rock and heartlessly kicked into the canal. He felt his heart might stop at the sight of him, he was frozen with fear! The figure of the man, he had plunged to his death stood there before him, glaring directly into his face with his finger pointed right at him. Swiftly, the figure hurtled toward him, water dripping from his body, his angry grey face like nothing he had seen before and the Doctor became paralysed with fear. The figure stopped right beside him on the floor and bellowed louder than anything he had ever heard before, right inside his head, encompassing all his senses. "Tell the truth or I will never leave you in peace!" The Lords soaking wet, grey figure kneeled before him on the floor and scowled directly at him with eyes as dark as the night sky. He realised that the past had come back to haunt him, in every sense of the word.

Lady Ellsworth had heard all the commotion and made her way down the stairs, she arrived outside in time to hear the Doctors accusation. The crowd parted to let her through, whispers of her possible identity rippled amongst them.

"Officers, I am Lady Ellsworth." She declared as loudly as she could muster above the noise of the crowd. Everyone was silenced and turned toward her. "This man is Doctor in name only, he murdered my husband and has been threatening myself and this young lady here." She pointed to Daisy. "Please take him away and send someone to speak to me, I will tell you everything you need to know."

"Lady Ellsworth!" exclaimed the elder of the two, he knew the Lady very well. To say he was shocked to see her in this part of the world, was an understatement he was so confused! "You are safe Ma'am?" He immediately enquired. "Do you want us to take this man and send an Officer here to you, or can we call for you to be escorted safely home?"

"No thank you Officer, I will take the call here and you can be proud that you have caught the monster that murdered his Lordship and has been holding me against my will. Now please release these innocent men, who helped to capture that evil creature and take him away from here. I cannot bear to look at him any longer!" She turned and walked back inside and straight back up to her room, she was in no state to stay any longer.

The Officers placed cuffs on the Doctor and after giving Arthur and Lucius an unnecessary warning to stay out of trouble, they took the doctor to the station. The crowd slowly filtered back into the pub and were ablaze with gossip, each shared their own version of the story. Maud in her usual brash manner marched straight over to Lucius, with her hands on her hips and chided, "Oi, what's a Lady doing, shacked up here? What was that murder business about?"

Lucius looked at Maud, shook his head and laughed, "The only business you have to now about Maud, is your own, now go and mind it and let me get on!"

She scoffed and chuntered off to earwig at other conversations in the hope she may glean some juicy information.

The Chief constable arrived with a second officer to speak with Lillian and Daisy, their evidence was taken and the officers informed them that Doctor Morgan had surprisingly given a full confession. Once again Lillian refused the offer of an escort back to her home. The Officers also explained that there would be no further threat to either of them, despite the Doctors warning.

Daisy sat with Arthur and finally explained the whole story from beginning to end. He was bitterly disappointed that she had not come to him with her troubles when they arose. "Daisy, haven't I always looked out for you? There is nothing that you cannot tell me! Surely you know that. Ruth too! You must promise that you will never keep anything secret from me again".

She tried to reassure him that it was not the trust between them but the fear within herself that had her silent. "I promise to never keep anything from you again and assure you that as much as you have always protected me, I have often done the same for you. You may not see it that way, but I did not want to see you in serious trouble for protecting me, Arthur. You would be no help to any of us from prison." She gave him a hug. "I will leave the pub as soon as I know what Lady Ellsworth's plans are, meanwhile, I will pay a visit to Ruth and Hettie, I have missed them dearly!"

The group all gathered in the pub after the customers had left for the night. Daisy joined them and let Lucius know that Lillian was asleep and would like to speak with him in the morning. "I am so relieved that he has made a full confession". Daisy concluded. "It was very odd, how his demeanour suddenly changed and he fell silent. It seems he had a moment of guilt or fright, I could not tell what it was that caused it. I felt certain that he was going to allow you both to take the blame had the Lady not interrupted."

"Yes, he was oddly silenced." Concurred Lucius. "I am just grateful that you are all safe now, I don't think he will be feeling the same with the enemies that he has made." He observed.

"Maybe the guilt had suddenly got the better of him and made him want to confess." Caleb suggested.

They were relieved by his confession and happy that Doctor Morgan was no longer a threat. None of them could understand his sudden silence, one moment he was shouting his lies and the next he sat like a petrified puppy on the floor. He showed no resistance to his arrest and looked quite grateful when he was dragged off by the officers.

Chapter 19 Home

The next morning Lucius felt happier than he had in a long time. He had eaten his breakfast and was seated downstairs with Caleb. "Nora, was telling me how well Molly enjoyed her stay, do you think you might one day leave the boat life Caleb?" He questioned.

Caleb thought for a moment before he replied, "I think Mol will always need to be part of the boating life. She loves travelling the canal and crafting but I do think that she would like to live on land. We've become accustomed to living in a very small space but I know she would like more. Maybe one day we will find that. Like you Lucius, I grew up on a farm with all that space so it was a tremendous change for me when I moved on to the boat, I do not know how large families manage. I think Mol spending a night in a large bedroom that needed no dismantling of the bed was like a holiday for her." He grinned at the memory, "Her smile was a picture! She was prancing around like it was Christmas morning waking in that room." He chortled.

"You will both be most welcome to come and stay here any night when I have sorted those rooms." Lucius chirped happily. "I have decided to pursue the guest house idea and will request the help of you and Mol if you think that is something you would like to do. I know that Lillian has sent a messenger to the Manor, so I am certain she will be off soon too."

"Yes, we would happily help you with your new venture Lucius and a night or two of being able to stretch my legs to their full length in bed would be welcomed of course." He chuckled and went on, "Will you stay in touch with Lillian ... Lady Ellsworth ... your mother?!" His eyes widened at the renewed realisation that Lucius was the son of a Lady and landowner.

Lucius chuckled too, "Yes, it's strange isn't it! We know her as three different people really. I am never quite certain of how to address her now, I generally avoid using a name at all. Mother just doesn't feel right and she has not invited it but maybe that will come later. I will probably leave any further contact with her, it will greatly affect her life being known as a woman having a son out of wedlock and him being a pub owner too! It won't be easy for her and I am happy either way. It would be nice to get to know her better but might not be the best idea." He looked up in thought. "I now have a mother, feels strange to think of! I should go up and see her, she asked to see me this morning. I think it will be to say goodbye. I won't be long, Sorry to leave you in charge again."

"Lucius, you know I am happy being in charge! There is nothing I enjoy more." He was speaking the truth, he loved managing the pub. He enjoyed every part of it but mostly chatting with the customers. He and Molly were naturally sociable people and all the patrons loved them.

Lucius headed up the stairs and went into Lillian. She was seated in the armchair, now looking years younger than she had in the days previous. Her thick grey hair was tied up in an elegant bun at the back of her head, courtesy of Daisy's fine hand. Her face was no longer sallow but now brighter and plumped into fullness when she smiled. She would look quite glamorous were it not for the ill-fitting dress that she had been loaned from Molly.

"Please take a seat Lucius, Daisy could you leave us please." She smiled at Daisy as she left the room. She looked over at Lucius happily. "I shall be returning to my home later today, I must prevent the Manor from being closed or sold which I imagine could be happening in the near future if I do not make an appearance soon." Rufi fidgeted in her lap and she stroked his back to settle him.

"Yes, I thought that you might be." Lucius responded quietly.

"I am aware that I have no right to ask anything of you. After all, you have been most generous in your reaction to me and you would have been more than just in your right to ignore me from the beginning." She broached.

Lucius grimaced when he heard this and Lillian noticed.

"It is true Lucius, you owe me no loyalty and yet you have helped me more than anyone could ever have asked for. I would very much like us to know each other better and would like to start with thanking you and your friends for all your help." She looked at him questioningly. "I would like to send a carriage next week, for you all to come and dine with me at the Manor. Maybe afterwards, we could go for a walk alone around the garden and we can start to know each other a little. What do you say?"

"I would say, yes of course that sounds like a grand invite! I am sure the others will be happy to come too. You know already that we have visited the manor before. I now know why the face in the picture looked so familiar, we have the same eyes and nose." He paused briefly and recollected his reaction to the painting he had seen when on his visit to the manor.

"Yes, we do Lucius, though you have your father's hair colour and the rest of your features come from him." She paused as she remembered Solomon, the tender moments that they had shared had never been lost to her. "Dear Solomon." She smiled fondly. "I am grateful you will be joining me again soon."

"I think Nora would not be so happy with me if I were to refuse." The pair chuckled.

"You like Nora very much Lucius and she is in love with you too. I think that is quite clear to anyone." She grinned affectionately.

Lucius felt his face blush, "Yes, I am yet to prove myself to her." He said bashfully and fidgeted awkwardly at the thought of it. He rolled the box that held his grandmothers ring inside his pocket, he had taken to carrying it with him permanently.

"I am sure that is not beyond your control. I do not think it is proving yourself that is needed but more being yourself that will win her heart. You are a good man Lucius and she will soon see that if you just be yourself around her. Remember she has stayed with you regardless of all this dreadful business going on. Surely you can see that she is worth keeping?" She affirmed, she looked up toward the clock. "In the meantime, if you would be so kind as to gather your friends to the pub for a small surprise on the hour, I would be grateful."

Lucius widened his eyes with curiosity, "Indeed I will, what surprise is in store?"

"Where would the surprise be in telling you what is to come?" She smirked.

"Very well." He said happily and rose from the seat. "Let Daisy know when you would like an escort downstairs and I will return for you." He was a little sadder than he had anticipated that she was leaving so soon, he liked her frankness and found himself wanting to know her better.

"Lucius, before you leave, I hope that you will not mind me enquiring but … how was your father? Was he well and happy?" She asked tentatively.

He was unsure of why but it pleased him that she enquired after his father. He had been the most important person in his life and felt forever grateful for the life he had given him.

"He was a very healthy man, strangely there always seemed to be a little sadness behind his eyes but Grandma said that was because my mother died." He noticed Lillian's unease. "He really was a happy man and the sadness was sweeping, it never stayed with him for long. We worked hard but he made everything so much fun, it never felt like we were working! He was a good father to me and a great son to Grandma, everyone who knew him respected him for the fair man that he was. I think of him all the time and feel like he still guides me because I often ask myself what he would do if he were in my situation. I miss him." He smiled affectionately.

"Thank you, Lucius, I appreciate you telling me this. I knew he would be a good father, of course I never dreamt it would be for our son but I am so glad he was. It seems that you both had a good life and I am grateful for that, you had your lovely Grandma too, such a lovely, funny lady!" She said cheerfully. "I recall her stories, full of fun and adventure." She beamed.

Lucius nodded, he loved his Grandma's stories and maybe one day he could share them with a child of his own. He squeezed Lillian's hand before leaving the room.

Nora, Molly and Caleb were already downstairs, the pub doors were not open yet. Lucius told them about the news from Lillian and they were thrilled to be going to the Manor for dinner! Lucius glanced up at the clock on the wall opposite the fireplace, just as the hand had hit the hour. There was a rattle from the door as someone tried to open it, followed by a loud knock. The group looked at each other in turn, "Are you expecting a delivery today?" enquired Caleb of Lucius.

"No." Lucius replied with a frown as he headed toward the door.

He had barely unlocked it, when the door burst open and in walked Albert and Mrs Tranter! "We received word this morning to come here for 11 am Mr Turner!" Albert yelled, as he shook Lucius's hand with great enthusiasm! Everyone rose from their feet and greeted both like they were long lost relatives. Molly introduced Caleb to them.

Mrs Tranter unpinned her straw hat which sat neatly above her bun adorned with tiny flowers in a multitude of colours that helped to light up her already bright face. She looked exactly as they remembered her minus the apron, with the little pockets. She looked straight over at Lucius, "You have your mothers' eyes and nose!" She gave him a huge hug, gripping him tight and he could sense the genuine affection she felt toward him. It was just like the hugs that he had received from his grandmother, they had always made him feel safe and loved, it made him feel quite emotional.

Albert wandered around, it was his first time in a pub and he was intrigued by it all, he asked Caleb how the pumps worked and what the optics were and anything else he could find to question. Caleb enjoyed showing him around and allowed him to pour the drinks for everyone. They sat together at the table where they all told them of the story that had unfolded after their visit to the manor.

"Well, I never!" Declared Mrs T. "I never did like that Doctor did I Albert?" She nodded over to him, her glasses balanced precariously on the end of her nose. "I am so excited to see Lady Ellsworth, I cannot tell you how excited I am! That poor woman, will be spoilt rotten when she gets back with us, won't she Albert?" Albert once again tried to reply but soon closed his mouth again without being able to speak a word, which was a regular occurrence for him during conversation with Mrs T.

"The coach will be back to collect us all at one, I think Daisy will join us too. Coming back to us, she is! It will be so much busier at the house with everyone back again." Albert was happy, he had received little company for the last few weeks, the thought of things getting back to normal cheered him up from the moment Mrs T had read him the message. She had run around yelling with joy, the instant she had opened the envelope.

As if she had heard her name, Daisy entered the room, she rushed to Mrs T and before she could get up, Daisy had thrown her arms around her in a tight embrace. Both had tears in their eyes, the affection could be felt all around the room. "Daisy!" yelled Mrs T, "Let me look at you! You have gotten taller I am sure and you need some feeding up! Look at you, wasting away you are. It's very well, that you are coming home my dear so we can take safe care of you." She twirled Daisy around to inspect her thoroughly.

Daisy turned and gave Albert a hug, his face was crimson and he tried his best to peel himself away from her. "Good to see you, Daisy." He said gingerly as he retreated.

"Well, I will have to pinch myself, I can't believe this is happening, all back together again!" Mrs T raised her arms high in the air, as if giving a sermon in church. Her plump cheeks almost closed her eyes with a smile so big.

Daisy turned to Lucius, "Can you please escort Mrs Ellsworth down now Lucius, she wanted to see everyone before she leaves and there's not long now before the coach returns."

Lucius rose from the table and Albert enquired, "Shall I come and help you with the bags?"

Daisy intervened, "Oh sorry, I forgot to add, she asked that Caleb come and help too, you rest here Albert and finish your drink. You will have enough to do when we get back home." Albert was happy to comply!

Lucius and Caleb headed for the stairs, the rest stayed and chatted amongst themselves.

Lucius tapped on the door, "Do come in." He heard Lillian call. She was seated ready in the chair, with Rufi on her lap. She looked up at Caleb, "Could you take Rufi downstairs for me please, he may have been abandoned once but I shall not let that happen again. He shall be coming back to the Manor with me, won't you Rufi!" She squeaked at him and scuffed the back of his head, he nestled down into her lap. Caleb reached down to pick him up, the dog indicated a minor refusal as he snapped and snarled lazily at him. He had to remove his hand from danger twice more before Rufi decided to give in and allow him to take hold of him.

With Caleb now gone, Lady Ellsworth rose to her feet with an elegance and regained agility that had escaped her in the past few weeks. She held her head high with a steady and strong stature. Lucius watched her and instantly noticed the difference, he was pleased to see that the woman he once thought was tortured by madness was a strong, self-determined lady who was back to her old self.

"Are you ready Lady Ellsworth?" He beamed as he held out his arm for her to take.

"As ready as I shall ever be Mr Turner." She chuckled. She stopped for a moment and looked around the room. "You know, I have enjoyed being here! I do hope that one day, you may call me Mother, Lucius?" She looked at him and waited for his reaction.

"Yes, so do I." was all he could reply for the moment. He felt her arm tense but her face remained focused and determined. "Are you feeling anxious about your return?" He enquired.

"I must say Lucius, I am a little. So much has happened since my departure and I will have a lot of official business to deal with on my return but I shall be happy once all is settled." She squeezed his arm. "Of course, I will be returning home without my dear husband but I dare say, I will be taking him in spirit." She looked behind her back up the stairs and smiled. "No one ever truly leaves us Lucius. Every bit of influence and energy they have had on our lives, we carry with us, the part of them that intertwined with us, we get to keep forever." Lucius was silent and Lady Ellsworth worried that he might think she was quite mad ... again! In truth he thought about what she had said and it made sense to him.

"You know, I think you are quite right!" He put his hand over the top of hers and they continued down the stairs. "Please do take the spirit of your husband back with you though!" They both laughed as they entered the room where everyone was gathered.

Mrs Tranter could barely contain herself, the tears flowed down her face and rolled over her plump cheeks. Lady Ellsworth held her arms out to her and the two women embraced! Albert waited patiently behind, then the Lady took his hand in between both hers and held it tight with a welcome smile on her face.

"I knew you would be back, didn't I say that, Albert!" in her usual manner of not waiting for his reply, Mrs Tranter continued. "Look at you, my Lady! You need feeding up, we will get you fed the moment we are back! Plenty of rest as well, our Daisy will see to it that you put your feet up." She fussed.

Lady Ellsworth smiled happily as she listened to Mrs Tranter and Daisy chunter on about how well she was to be taken care of. She turned to Nora and Molly, "Now you will both be attending for dinner next week and Caleb of course?" Both ladies confirmed that they were extremely excited to see the manor again. "Excellent! It will allow me to say a proper thank you to you all but in the meantime, when the coachman arrives, he will have parcels for you all."

"Please Lady Ellsworth." Molly said with hands clasped, "There is no need to thank us, we did what was right and we are all just grateful that you are out of harm's way."

"I will have it no other way, I will never be able to thank you enough, so please accept my gifts and let me entertain you at the manor. After all, I am alone now, you will be keeping me company." She gave their hands a squeeze and moved toward Lucius.

"The coachman will be here shortly, I took the liberty of sending Daisy to buy gifts for you all, the coachman will have them on his return. I hope you will accept." She had seen that Lucius was a proud man, who might not accept gifts readily but this was important to her. "It is done with the best of intention and to show my sincere gratitude, it will help with your visit next week too."

"I am not in the habit of expecting anything for doing nothing more than being a decent human being, but as you have already gone to the trouble I will accept. Please do not think you have to do this though, there really is no need for a thank you!" He said reluctantly, he really wished she would stop thanking him.

"Not all human beings are decent Lucius, as we have seen for ourselves. Let us celebrate those that are with our gratitude and our time." She advised.

The coachman arrived precisely at one pm, much to the coachman's surprise, Lucius and Caleb went and helped him unload the parcelled gifts and carried them to the pub.

"I was only here for a brief time but I will miss this place and I look forward to seeing you all next week." She turned toward Lucius. "We can talk more then."

Daisy was happy to be returning, she would never have left had it not been for Doctor Brown. "I have sent message to Arthur to tell him that I am returning to the Manor. I will pay him a visit him on my day off." She informed Lucius.

There were hugs and farewells and Albert swallowed his drink down fast before he raced behind them toward the coach and shouted, "I will be back soon, great pub Lucius, great pub!" Mrs T shook her head and hoped that she wouldn't be nursing his hang over as well as everything else she would have to do today.

Lucius felt quite sad as he watched them leave, he found that he already looked forward to a visit with her again next week. He opened the door for the customers who complained as they entered, that he was late opening. Even with the noise of the patrons the pub felt suddenly quieter. Lucius realised that it wasn't just the pub that caused the quietness, it was his life in general. They had all been so busy trying to find out why a ghost like figure had suddenly appeared at the pub, which had then led them to Daisy, then Lady Ellsworth and then the Doctor. The past few weeks had been like something they would only read about and now the mystery was solved.

"Shall we open our gifts?" suggested Molly when she noticed Lucius looking a little lost.

"Yes!" Nora agreed enthusiastically. "I cannot believe she brought us gifts and I am so excited to see what they are!"

The four went up into the kitchen and unwrapped the parcels carefully, being mindful to fold and keep the paper for future use.

Nora gasped as she lifted up the fine cloth in front of her. The purple gown was made of the finest silk, with pearl buttons down the breast and intricate flowers detailed in a lighter shade of purple and black. The neck and cuffs were finished in lace of the finest quality. "It's beautiful!" Shouted Nora. "I have no idea when I shall get to wear it again after dinner next week but it is absolutely beautiful!"

Molly held her gown against her and twirled around to show it off. Molly's was dark blue, also made of the finest silk with a lighter blue underskirt that showed through a parting at the front. The puffy sleeves were gathered at the wrist with ruffles. "My goodness!" She chuckled. "Imagine you and I sitting on deck in these Nora, what would we look like! This is magnificent, I cannot wait to wear it!"

Both men had the smartest suits, made with beautiful fabric in dark grey. There were crisp white shirts and dark grey ties to match. With pestering from Nora and Molly, they reluctantly held them up against them. Despite their fake disinterest they were both extremely impressed.

"Oh look" said Molly, holding up an envelope, there is a note here too, Lucius read it out to everyone.

'My dearest friends,

Please accept these garments by way of my gratitude for all that you have done for me. Daisy spoke with me about your visit to the manor and your feeling overwhelmed by the grandiosity and felt a little out of place. I took the liberty of tasking Daisy, who is quite the seamstress herself, with gaining an estimate of your clothing size and sent her on a visit to my tailor. I thought these items may help you to feel more comfortable when on your next visit. My Tailor's card is enclosed if you should need any alteration, which I will of course take care of.

Please know that you do not have to choose to wear them, it is your company I crave and you will be welcome regardless. The gifts are yours to keep and to use whenever you so wish.

I look forward to seeing you a week hence.

With great affection,

Lady Ellsworth'

Molly took the letter and folded it back into the envelope carefully and handed it to Lucius, "You should take this, keep it safe." She smiled. "Your mother is a kind woman, she shows compassion in everything she does, maybe that's where you get it from."

Lucius scoffed but placed the letter gently into his pocket.

Chapter 20 Return to Ellsworth

The week seemed to drag on as they counted the days to their dinner date at Ellsworth. They had all received official invites, which had arrived as small rich white cards with scrolled, gold leaf handwriting. Each were presented beautifully in their own envelope stamped with the family crest to seal them.

Molly jumped for joy when Lucius gave her the invite. She had never seen such a pretty thing with her name on and she vowed to keep it forever. Caleb watched his wife as she had repeatedly removed it from her pocket to view it, smiling broadly to herself as she replaced it.

Everyone had treated themselves to the wash house before they got ready in their fine new clothes. They dressed at the rooms in the pub, Nora and Molly had both tied their hair in rags the night before and their ringlets hung perfect below their braided buns.

Nora was stunned when she saw Lucius in his fine suit, he stood tall and although his face showed his awkwardness, she found it difficult to take her eyes off him. The jacket framed his muscly torso to perfection, she had never wanted to kiss him more.

"Lucius, I have never seen you in anything other than your work clothes, what a fine gentleman you make!" She said bashfully and swiftly added "As do you Caleb!".

Molly nodded in agreement, she was equally thrilled with Caleb's suit and she threw her arms around his neck, giving him a kiss. They all looked fabulous in their finery and were delighted when the coach man arrived to collect them.

"Right, enough of this." Lucius announced. "Let's not keep this good man waiting." He ushered them all toward the door. A small group of locals had gathered to take a look at the coach, curious to see who would have the pleasure of travelling in such style. When they caught sight of Lucius climbing in, they were shocked and shouted out to ask him where he was going. "I might tell you next time you call in to the pub." He teased.

The four sat snugly in the coach, the clip clop of the horse's hooves and the gentle sway of their carriage quietened them all. As they watched through the window the scenery changed from the hustle and bustle of the dirty city streets to the quiet calm of the countryside. Their spirits lifted as the sun sent flickering light across their faces as it passed through the trees. Lucius stuck his head outside the window when he recognised a remarkably familiar spot. He looked across at what now appeared to be a tiny cottage with land stretching far out all around. On feeling the wind catch his hair, his mind was cast back. He saw the vision of his grandma, watching from the cottage door, as he and his father walked hand in hand toward the cottage after finishing a hard day's work. Nora noticed him smile to himself and guessed that was his childhood home.

"Was that your home Lucius?" Nora enquired, they all turned their gaze toward the cottage.

"Yes, it was, it looked so big as a child yet so tiny now!" He smiled affectionately. "We're nearly there." he informed them. It was almost as if they were getting ready for an army inspection as they began to pull and brush down at their clothes. The sound of the horse's hooves revealed that they were on the gravel of the courtyard entering the main gates that led to the building.

"Woah, woah there!" they heard the coach driver yell just before they came to a smooth halt.

Lucius leapt from the carriage like a whippet being released from behind his stall gate! The coachman gave him a look of disdain as he lowered the steps and offered the ladies a hand. Albert, being the footman had come out to greet the coach and attempted to stifle the laughter at the scene he had just witnessed. Lucius, not being a man who had particular interest in etiquette strode at once to Albert and shook his hand vigorously, the Butler who stood on the opposing side of the door remained straight faced with a tiny glow of outrage which forced his nostrils to flare! "Good to see you again Albert!" Lucius declared, he tipped his head toward the Butler and rolled his eyes.

The Butler prized the party away from Albert and escorted them through the grand hallway into the Drawing Room at the back of the house which overlooked the garden. Lillian (who looked barely recognisable) stood up from the sofa to greet them with the happiest of expressions. "Lady Ellsworth!" exclaimed Lucius, "You look remarkable, I am happy to see you looking so well!".

"As do you all." Replied Lillian, she was genuinely delighted to see them and had craved the sight of her son in her home since the day she had met him again.

With the greeting over and pleasantries exchanged, the bell rang to signify that dinner was ready. The Butler returned and escorted each to their seats.

The dining room was a sight to be seen! A huge silver chandelier hung from the ceiling with tiny crystal droplets that radiated light around the room. The table was adorned with a pure white tablecloth, there was so much cutlery that they were confused just looking at it. The silver candlesticks stood tall strategically along the length of the table. The walls were adorned with artwork and likenesses of various family members from times past.

Lillian sat at the head of the table with Lucius to her right and Nora next to him. Caleb and Molly were seated together to her left. Conversation flowed so easily with this group of people who had come from vastly different backgrounds to their host. It seemed Mrs Tranter had been feeding everyone very well, "Please do not worry if you are not able to finish all the food that will be coming our way, Mrs Tranter seems to believe she is feeding the whole village with every meal she serves me!" Lillian chuckled.

"Well, she did promise you were going to be well fed!" Laughed Nora.

"Daisy is incredibly happy and is proving to be an excellent hand maid." Lillian said proudly. "Of course, you saw Albert on your entrance, he is so pleasant, I was worried we were going to lose him to your pub Lucius!" She teased.

The food was like nothing they had ever tasted before and they watched Lillian closely as she picked up items of cutlery to make sure they chose the right ones. The courses seemed to go on forever and they wondered if it would ever end. Onion soup to start, followed by potatoes, lamb, vegetables, and gravy! The homemade apple pie to finish was simply divine!

"Lucius," Lillian, placed her napkin on the table in front of her. "May we have a private talk? We could go for a walk around the grounds whilst the others take refreshment in the drawing room."

Lucius looked across to the others who gave nods of reassurance, "Yes, it's a beautiful day and I'm looking forward to seeing those grounds." He gestured toward the lawns outside the window.

Lucius offered Lillian his arm as they walked slowly by the fresh flowering daffodils, they stopped to admire the tall willow trees that stood bowed in the middle of the lawn.

Pansies, marigolds and sweet peas were scattered around giving the whole garden a bright cheer and a reminder of warmer weather on its way.

"Lucius, I know that we have only just found each other and we have a lot to learn, I want to get to know you well and you, I." She smiled up at him. She steered him toward a bench close by. Lucius sat next to her and listened intently. "Please take a look around you, the building, the grounds, all this land is mine and is nothing if I have nobody to share it with." She paused, she could sense his apprehension. "Lucius, you are my son and this is yours too but I would very much like you to share this with me, while I am still here."

Lucius stood up and paced as he always did when he felt awkward. "Lady Ellsworth, I could not possibly ..."

Lillian stopped him with a hand on his arm and bid him to return to the seat. "Lucius, you are not the first, I have shared this conversation with who did not see that there may be a problem. I have investigated this thoroughly and if knowing this may help persuade you, then you should know that my dear husband left provision for you and quite legally too, he was never a man to do as other's do. He sent papers at once on discovery to his solicitor, he was a fair and unselfish man who I wish I had confided in many, many years ago. I believe if he had not met such a cruel death, he would have explained that this was his way of showing forgiveness for me and his acceptance of you." She conveyed sincerely.

Lucius in deep thought, had expected Lillian to want contact but assumed that, given his station, it would be bare minimum and in secret. "I don't know what to say." he looked perplexed. "I have The Boatman's Rest and all the things that go with that ... Nora, Molly, Caleb, and a community of people who depend on me for reprieve and escape from what are sometimes, gruelling days."

Lillian squeezed his hand, "Lucius, I understand these things and I do not want to impose my own wishes on you, but please do consider what I have to say. I have spent this last week thinking of little else and seeking advice for my hopes. I am certain Molly and Caleb would be set for life if you were to allow them to take The Boatman's Rest. I would be happy to make that happen after all that they have done for me and if you agreed of course. I know your plans for making it a guest house and I would do that for them. Arthur and Ruth, I am certain would help with that too, Daisy told me of their living conditions and with Arthur's pride it would be a practical way of helping them to move on. I hope you understand that I see a great service in helping all those that helped me and you would be allowing me to achieve that, if only you would let me do this." She looked at him with candour, she had thought of nothing else since she had returned home. She wanted to help the people that were important to her son.

Lucius was a proud man but by no means was he stupid or selfish. When he heard how his friends would also benefit it gave this whole exchange a completely different aspect. The thought of being able to give such a huge gift to the people he loved most in his life filled his mind with hope.

Lillian watched as his expression changed from anxiety to deep reflection. "All of this will be yours regardless of the choice you make now Lucius and I will make provision for your friends in any way you wish. My hope is that you will choose to share it with me first. Of course, you will need to discuss this with Nora, I am sure she would be happy here too, would she not?" She looked deep into his eyes, she knew he was in love with her.

"I am not sure, what you are suggesting Lady Ellsworth?" His face reddened and he began fidgeting as if ready to get up from his seat again.

"Lucius, I am old enough and wise enough to see what is happening so clearly right in front of me. You are both very much in love with each other and equally as stubborn as to not admit it." She grinned. "I thought after our last conversation on this subject that you may have already asked a very important question of her." She pushed.

Lucius smirked, it suddenly seemed so petty to continue to deny his feelings.

Lillian went on, "She is an intelligent, beautiful, kind natured woman Lucius and you would do well to hurry and make your intentions known before she is taken by another." She grinned at him and questioned, "You would do well, from listening to your mother, wouldn't you agree?"

"Yes Mother!" He laughed!

Little did he know the joy that he brought to her heart when he spoke those two words, that she could feel the tears of happiness burning her eyes.

"I would be so happy to live in such a magnificent home with these stunning grounds and know that I am giving my friends an incredible fresh start at the same time. I will still need time to think, I hope you understand that. I warn you though, I am not practiced in this way of life and there are many things that I do not care for." As he spoke, his decision became clearer to him. "We would both have to compromise and take time to adjust. I will be found taking a seat in the kitchen with Mrs Tranter or sharing a beer in the pub with Albert. Or teasing our Daisy when she does something silly! You may not want me at the dinner table with your friends, or I may not want to join with them. You see, it would not be easy but if we can get beyond that, then I will talk with my friends and decide?" He came up for air, after his long speech!

"Lucius, I think you have judged me as you think yourself are judged. I take tea with Mrs Tranter, she is my confidant! I tease Daisy as she does sometimes me. You would love my friends as I love yours! I do draw a line at taking a beer with Albert though." She chuckled. "You see my parents …. your grandparents were not like most others in our fortunate position. They were generous, kind, and compassionate with a good understanding of how they fit into supporting society and community. Their empathetic nature did not extend to my marrying a farmer but I have long forgiven them for that. So, you see, we are not who you might imagine and whilst my first love was lost to me, yours need not be." she said softly.

She reached up and gave him a tight hug, "Now, shall I return to the house and send Nora out? Beautiful day and beautiful surroundings for a special question, wouldn't you agree?!" She grinned.

"Yes Mother!" He laughed!

Lucius began to pace and felt in his pocket for the third time to make sure that the ring was still there. He was glad he kept it with him always, he thought it would be best as he knew he would have to do it spontaneously. He looked around him and made his way to stand just before the willow tree, he had always loved them. He could never have imagined being able to do this in such a beautiful spot as this. He turned back toward the house and saw Nora racing across the court toward him, he felt the butterflies soar in his stomach and his mouth was so dry. He caught sight of Molly, Caleb and his mother watching them from the lattice window of the drawing room.

"Lucius, what on earth has happened" Nora enquired anxiously. "Lady Ellsworth said that you had something to tell me in private, she looked very worried!" She panted, out of breath from her short run.

He took both her hands in his, "Nora," he began.

"Lucius, what is it, you're scaring me now!" She exclaimed. She was preparing herself, convinced that he was about to tell her that he was leaving everything behind and making his life at the manor.

He reached into his pocket and bent down on one knee.

Nora had both hands across her mouth and felt her eyes fill with tears.

"Nora you are the craziest, yet most beautiful and kind woman I have ever met. I have loved you for a long time and you would make me so happy if you would agree to spend the rest of your life with me. Nora Baker, will you marry me?" He looked up at her, internally praying for her to say yes.

Nora could barely speak, her head nodded in agreement so aggressively, he thought it may fall off! "Yes, you stubborn man, yes, of course I will marry you!"

He placed the ring on her finger and they kissed for so long that the three in the drawing room were at their side when they finally parted lips!

The party went downstairs to break the news to Mrs T, Daisy and Albert who were all unsurprised but absolutely delighted with the news!

The celebrations back at the Boatman's Rest could be heard far across the canal.

Chapter 21 New Beginnings

It was the day of Solomons fifth Birthday, dressed in his best clothes, he had opened his presents and raced down the stairs, where Mrs Tranter, Albert and Lucy were all waiting to see him. He remembered that Mrs T had promised to sneak him some cake and he was so excited! He had ensured Daisy and Nanny were well out the way as he stepped down the stairs into the kitchen. His parents knew he was going downstairs but would not have been happy if they knew he was eating cake at this hour!

"Happy Birthday!" All three of them declared in unison as he entered. His little face beamed with happiness as Albert helped him to climb up on to the stool. "Are you having a good day?" Albert enquired.

"Yes." nodded Solomon, his eyes fixed rigidly on the Victoria Sponge cake placed right in the middle of the table.

"I see you're ready for some of my special cake young man." Mrs T chirped, then mumbled under her breath, "I see Albert is too ..." She chuckled to herself and cut each a piece of cake, placing them on to four small plates. "Now mind you don't go getting any on those lovely clothes you have on Solomon or your mother will scald us both!" She warned.

"Thank you, Mrs T, you are very kind." he smiled up at her as he took his first bite. The strawberry jam and cream oozed from the side of the cake and he licked it quick before it fell. The sugary sweetness was perfect and he ate every mouthful without so much as having dropped a crumb. Just as Mrs T congratulated him on managing to keep his clothes clean, he felt the sticky jam on his chin beginning to irritate him. He pulled up his arm and before Lucy was able to stop him, he wiped it straight across his mouth, bright red strawberry jam was smeared all down his sleeve. Mrs T gasped and ran to the sink, where she wet a towel and wiped profusely at the sleeve, praying for the stain to be gone. He giggled up at her and she couldn't help but join him in laughter, he had an infectious giggle and his little face would melt the hardest of hearts.

"Mrs T." He stopped to enquire as Albert helped him back down from the stool. "Why do you have two chins and we only have one?" Albert and Lucy looked at each other aghast not knowing what to do or say but tried their best to suppress their laughter.

Mrs T shook with laughter, she had never heard such a thing before. "Out of the mouths of babes!" She bellowed. Albert and Lucy felt safe to join in with the hilarity. "I use my lower chin to store extra dinner for later, you know in case I get hungry." Everyone laughed again and Solomon looked to be in deep thought.

"Then I shall have one too Mrs T and I will use it to store cake for later!" He yelled as he cheekily took a large bite from Alberts cake and headed back out the door upstairs to meet his father. "Thank you, Albie!" He shouted from the doorway. He left them all in great spirits, his comments gave them a chuckle as they went about their day.

He met with his father by the door, "Solomon, we must leave for our walk now, I don't think we will need a coat this morning. It looks like a hot sunny day! We won't have long before we must leave in the coach." He looked down at his little boy staring up at him, "Sol, why does your cheek look swollen?" Solomon ignored him and shook his head in denial. Lucius paused to watch him, his cheek definitely looked swollen. "Are you puffing it out?" He touched his cheek softly.

Solomon immediately began to chew, "No Papa." He replied, his words were a little muffled, with his mouth full. "I'm trying to get another chin like Mrs T has. She said she uses it for storing dinner for later. I want mine for cake, look Papa." He opened his mouth to show his father the contents. His father could not see as his eyes were almost closed with raucous laughter!

"Well, you are still here, so I guess Mrs T took your comment well!" He quipped.

"What do you mean Papa?" Solomon asked.

"Never mind Sol, we will have a chat during our walk about good manners." He took his hand and they headed outside.

After a short wander, stopping to name the trees and the flowers, they walked hand in hand back towards the mansion. Nora stood at the door and watched them as they made their way back toward her. She loved to watch them together, they had such a wonderful bond. Solomon adored his father and of course the feeling was mutual. However, she was still a little irritated, "Lucius! Have you been walking him in his best clothes, you know we are taking him visiting today!" She scolded.

"Mummy, we have seen so many flowers!" declared little Solomon with excitement. "Can we go now, will Hettie be there, let us go!" he enthused. Nora scooped him up in her arms and kissed his cheek.

"Nanny said he has not stopped asking when he is going to see the water and his aunties and uncles, didn't she Sol?" Lucius grinned at his little boys excited face.

"Shall we get Grandma Lilli? Let's gooo!" pleaded Solomon enthusiastically and pointed toward the gates.

"Grandma, will be here soon Solomon, come and get in the carriage, she won't be long." Lucius lifted his little boy into the carriage and put an arm around his shoulder, Nora joined them both. Albert held the door for Lady Ellsworth and helped her into the carriage.

"Hurray!" Solomon shouted as his Grandma took the seat opposite.

"I had to hand Rufi over to his walker Sol. You know what he is like when we go out." She smiled sweetly at him.

Solomon loved his travels in the carriage, he was off to see some of his favourite people in the world. His Aunties Molly and Ruth and his uncle's Caleb and Arthur as well as his best friend Hettie.

This was just one of their regular visits to The Boatman's Rest, they all met at least once a week and for the most part they took it in turns to visit each other's homes. Although Lucius enjoyed spoiling his friends at the manor, he still felt at home at the pub and loved to spend time with all the regulars who were always overjoyed to see them.

Nora and Lucius had embraced their new position in society, they had quickly become the fair and just landowners that his father had always shown such admiration for. With Lillian's guiding hand they had settled well into Manor life. The birth of their first child had been a joyous occasion for everyone. Lillian had never had the opportunity to be a mother to her son but she embraced being the doting grandmother and loved her first grandchild with all her heart. Young Solomon had been aptly named after his grandfather Turner and was already quite a little character, adored by them all.

Molly and Caleb were now proud owners of a newly refurbished, Boatman's Rest and had enormous success with their room rentals. Arthur and Ruth, with little Hettie had gratefully accepted the offer to move in and help. With Lillian's generosity, the pub had become a popular venue that was sought out by many. The bedrooms had been redecorated and furnished, as was the kitchen and sitting room. Both rooms downstairs had been freshly painted and new furniture installed that was far more suited to a fine hotel than a canal side pub. Still, it drew more people and for those that had been patrons for years, it gave them a much-improved place to rest.

The room that had once been refuge for Nora had now become a small store that Ruth took care of. She sold her home baked goods and Molly's craft ware to bring in further income to their ever-growing pot. Hettie had become quite the helper, she kept record of the money and displayed the items artistically on the shelves. Molly had taught her to paint in the traditional way and she had proven to be quite a natural.

The boat was now available to rent at a reduced rate for any boatman that was able to get work for it. Cobbles, retired by his adoring owners had quickly become accustomed to being spoilt, he was taken on long walks and rested in the nearby field.

Everyone was happy, even Maud managed not to argue as often with George, probably because Lucius had made certain that his regulars received special provision. They were never to be without food or refreshment, whatever their circumstance.

None of them could ever have imagined the immense changes that had occurred in their lives. As happy as they were before, this new way of life had taken away the burden of ever having to worry about not having work, or where their next meal might come from.

On their arrival, Solomon raced across to Caleb who lifted him up on to his shoulders the moment they entered through the doors. "Go that way Uncle Caleb!" he yelled, as he pulled on his neckerchief to get him to do as he bid, Hettie ran in front of them and pretended to be chased.

Jack and his son Tommy were to take care of the pub for the day. It had become a regular routine on Sundays since the refurbishment. The rest of the group had congregated at the table, where the food had been laid out ready to celebrate Solomons Birthday. Mrs Tranter had prepared and sent it to the pub with Daisy to be ready for their arrival. "Solomon! Come and take your seat next to Grandma." Lillian requested. Solomon happily took the seat next to her.

Lillian looked around the table and knew that she had all she wanted. She would never stop missing her beloved husband but she had her son, daughter-in-law, and her little grandson to fill her life with purpose and happiness. Molly, Caleb, Arthur, Ruth and young Hettie had all become extended family members and she could not imagine her life without them.

The group ate, drank and talked together until late evening, they enjoyed each other's company as they always did. Lucius paused to look at the boat as they left, "Looking as sturdy as ever!" Caleb nodded in agreement and pride at Lucius's observation.

"Until next week." Nora said, hugging Molly.

"Until next week." Molly agreed.

Printed in Great Britain
by Amazon